The Strike

The Strike

• by ISABEL ALVAREZ de TOLEDO
Duchess of Medina-Sidonia
• *translated from the Spanish*
by William Rose

Grove Press, Inc., New York

863
AL 8s
88736
May 1974

First Printing
Originally published in Spanish as
   La Huelga *by Coleccion Ebro,*
   Paris, France. Copyright © 1967 by
   Editions de la Librairie du Globe.
Manufactured in the United States
   of America

Contents

The Strike

The original Spanish word "syndicato" has been translated as "union" in this book. However, the word refers to the government-controlled labor organizations imposed by the Franco regime after the Civil War, and should not be confused with traditional trade unions.—Translator's note

One

Juan got out of bed trying not to wake Fernando up. It was early for those who were going to school. He walked toward the door on tiptoe. The dampness of the earth floor bothered him. He opened the door and saw that the weather had changed, as he had thought. The flagstones in the little patio were dry and no moisture was oozing out of the broken-down wall. The adobe that had fallen out of the wall during the winter was still there, turning yellow between large splotches of lime.

He looked for his clothes in the drawer where he usually left them.

"Mama! Mama!"

Salvadora struggled to open her eyes.

"I can't find my clothes!"

"Look for them!"

"Luisillo must have them."

"What are you bothering me for?"

The woman turned her back on him. Juan went over to the little boy who was sleeping on a pile of rags.

"Hey! Give me my clothes."

The child was waiting for him. He had heard the conversation but didn't intervene because he was warm in the coarse-woven cotton jacket and mended pants. He wriggled out of them and surrendered them to Juan without a protest.

"What a whack I'm going to give you if you take them again!"

Juan dressed quickly. As he left he picked up his straw hat and a hoe.

Puddles of dirt and garbage were shining in the street. It would take many rainless months before dust would take the place of the mud. He crossed the ditch. The planks that served as a bridge swayed. He held out his arm to keep his balance.

Two ditches emptied into this hole, which got larger every year. First it was just a stagnant pool, then part of the street. Now it reached the houses. A little boat that some child had made out of cork was floating on the dirty water among the empty tin cans and bottles.

At first people had protested to the mayor. Paco, Juan's stepfather, had gone to City Hall on many occasions to say that it was a source of disease, but they didn't listen to him. The only thing people ever got were polite words. Just words. In time the smell became part of the life of the neighborhood. It was no longer any different from the usual smells. The residents put four planks over the sinkhole and renamed the place "The Louse."

Paca's stout figure appeared in a second floor window.
"Look out below!"

Her garbage joined the rest flowing down the stream.
"Be careful the cops don't see you."

The woman shrugged her shoulders.
"They're still in the bar. Besides, they won't have to go far to collect it."

Juan waved. Other men were walking up the street toward the plaza. They were wearing hats, hemp-soled *alpargatas,* and black sashes wrapped around their waists.

"Good morning."

Sleepy boys were serving the first drinks in the bars. Juan entered Largo's bar.

"A coffee, and put it on my bill."

The bartender looked for Juan's tab, in the form of numbers chalked up on the wooden wine casks.

"You owe more than twenty *duros* already."

Juan smiled.

"The weather's changed."

"It was still cloudy this morning."

"But they have to let us start working in the fields soon."

"You think so?"

"Everything is way behind."

"You said it! There are people who are so far behind they couldn't find their asses with a lantern."

The men laughed. Juan was apprehensive. Largo cut off people's credit when they least expected it, and there was no way to live without credit.

"Don't worry, I'll pay my bill. I always have before."

The bartender went to the shiny metal coffee machine. He addressed himself to everyone present as he raised one of the levers.

"Don't get into a sweat! We always trust people here. No one can say Largo doesn't give credit! The only ones who don't get it are a few who forgot to come back when their pockets were full."

The men came up to the counter.

"A coffee."

"A drink."

Those who had exhausted their credit sat down at empty tables. They waited there like the rest, killing time with interminable conversations that crossed back and forth across the room.

"This time last year we were already at work."

"It didn't rain like it has this year."

"I remember coming in more than once soaked to the bone!"

"And what good was the sulphate? No good at all."

"That's going a little too far. It's true that it was

washed away, but there was no mildew, and it was on the way for sure."

"We're losing time and we're also losing wages. They're tighter with money this year. They don't want to pay out money unless they really can squeeze you for it. It's harder to work in wet earth."

Chunga reached under his broad hat to scratch his bald spot. They all fell silent. He wanted to talk, and they respected old men. The old-timers had lost all hope of getting work. They went to the plaza from force of habit, but the only thing they had to do there was give advice.

"In my day you went to work, rain or no rain, when the time came. And the work lasted as long as there was something to do. This is what you've got by making all those demands!"

Mochuelo protested. "What do you want us to do? A sheep that doesn't bleat . . . Everybody knows they don't raise our wages just because they feel like it."

"Before, you could live nicely on the ten *reales* they paid us. There was even enough left over for a ticket on the shady side at the bullfights. What good is it for you to get ten *duros* if you're as hungry as a snail on a mirror even so?"

"That's true, but it's because of the prices. We just ask for enough to get by on, but when we get what we ask for it's not even enough to buy food with."

"And the mechanization plan? That's certainly done a lot!"

"And it'll do a lot more! In the beginning machines were hard to get and cost a lot. Now they can buy as many as they like, and they pay for themselves in a year with the wages they save. All you have to do is look at farming. They can get along with two workers and a tractor now, when before they needed a hundred men."

"And just look at the vineyards. All the work that used to last a month can be done in three days with half the manpower."

Negro walked over.

"Today makes four months and sixteen days that I've been out of work."

"You're lucky. There are people who have been on vacation for half a year."

Juan looked at the clock on the wall. It was eight-thirty. If the foremen were going to come, they would already have arrived.

"But there are plenty of cars, parties, and big houses. There never were this many in this town."

"And they wouldn't give anything to their own mothers!"

"Yes they would. Four blankets at Christmas and a plate of food when they feel like it. They don't want us to starve to death while they still need us."

Chunga got ready to tell one of his stories. Any time was the right time for a story. The younger men knew them all by heart.

"When I was a boy there was also unemployment, although there was no comparison with the way it is now. The bosses—we called them masters—used to warn us three or four days in advance: 'Whoever wants to can look for something else, because we're finishing up here.' We knew better than anybody else how much there was left to do, but we didn't bother looking for another job. It was better to stay home. There was always something to eat where we had been working. I was at Torrecilla, which belonged to Don Claudio Albornoz. The last day we always had a party and then we went to town. All we had to do was go by the office in the house where the Credit Bank was located. Don Claudio talked to us from behind his desk, where he had a bottle and two glasses for drinks for us. We went in one by one. 'How are things, Chunga?' he used to ask me. 'I'm doing all right,' I answered, holding my hat in my hand, like we used to do. 'Have a drink.' I sat down facing him and talked for a while about one thing and another. Just five minutes, because he didn't have much time. He would look at the clock and I'd get up. 'How much do you need?' 'Whatever you say.' I always made out. He wrote the amount down in a little book and when the harvest season arrived we paid him back."

"How?"

"He raised our wages and took back the amount of the raise. Of course not all of them behaved that way. He was really a good man. And he was good until he died, ruined by that bastard César."

"Don't you mean Don César?"

"Don César? You'd call anybody 'Don.' Well, that's right, it was César's fault. He went to work for him as a boy, carrying water. The fact is that he was just a pain in the neck, but Don Claudio was fond of him because he was the son of a maid of his who had been with him a long time. He wanted to educate him, but a fat lot of good it did. He was so dumb he could never learn anything. After a couple of years he just barely knew how to do figures. They put him in the office and it wasn't long before he won the trust of the master, who was already sick. Don Claudio's health got worse and he had to go to Madrid with his son, who was a student. He didn't come back very often. César sold his lands behind his back, registering them in the name of his wife or his brothers and sisters. I don't know what all he did, but when Don Claudio protested, he said that it was his own fault for doing things the old way. Things changed fast and the new masters wouldn't hear of giving away a penny in the winter. The truth is that César didn't pay us even half of what he put down in the ledgers, but we kept our mouths shut in order not to lose our jobs, hoping that Don Claudio's son would return soon."

"Did he?"

"Yes, after the master died. The only property he had left was 'La Dehesilla.' I went to see him at home. 'Don Claudio,' I said to him, 'César stole everything he could from your father.' He smiled the same way his father used to and replied, 'I know that, but I can't do anything about it.' César was already very powerful. Don Claudio sold what he had left and went away to work. I think he's somewhere in the Americas. I'd really like to see him again."

The men had listened with interest. Andalusians like old stories. They were nostalgic about those days that they had barely known but nonetheless considered better than the present.

"Well, that's nice, but it doesn't help us any. Nowadays they won't even give you the time of day."

"You're right, boy, not even the time of day! And do you know why? Because that way they give themselves class. The old-timers were called 'Don' even though they had holes in their shoes, like Don Luis Bermúdez, who couldn't even afford to buy tobacco and yet we all respected him. Today if they don't have a car and a big house to show off, they're nothing."

"But that isn't what we're talking about. We want what they owe us, not charity!"

"Who's talking about charity?" Chunga answered in a tone of wounded pride. "What happened then was a question of friendship among people who understood each other and helped each other without having to talk about rights or unions. Money didn't matter much, and if a person had some he didn't put it in the bank. He spent what he needed to live on and gave the rest to those who didn't have a regular income. They did

8·

what was right, and that way we all got along. But today's bosses ought to be in jail. I could tell you exactly how they've made their money, because I've watched them do it. They put things that belonged to other people in their names and threw ignorant farmers off their lands, because nobody had their land registered legally, especially if it had been in the family for generations. Then they invested the money they got that way. I'm telling you the truth—the best of them is a thief."

"If it was so easy to make money, why didn't you end up with any?"

Negro wanted to pick a fight with the old man. He didn't like his ideas and the others were listening to him.

"Because you have to be like them to do it. I'm not, and that's the way it always is: the worse they are, the richer they get."

"So here we are without a cent and there they are, scratching their full bellies. And whose fault is it? Ours! We're like slaves who let themselves be led around by a few guards, without realizing that if we get together we can kick them out before they know what's happening. This business of keeping our mouths shut while some share the hunger and others the money is no way for real men to act."

The others moved away from Negro. Somebody might hear him and there would be trouble. It's hard to answer the questions they ask in the barracks. Your tongue gets stuck and the only thing you're able to say is, "Yes, sir." Then come the beatings and the arrests without your knowing any of the whys and wherefores.

Private Pérez of the Civil Guard walked into the tavern.

"Good morning."

Nobody answered. Negro was left standing in the

middle of the room, with his legs spread apart. He was alone.

"Give me a drink, kid."

The boy served it with trembling hands. Pérez commented on the weather. The conversations started up again. Juan left. It was sunny outside. The men walked down the narrow streets with their heads low and their hats pulled down over their brows.

Two

San Antón Street went up toward the toll station. Casimiro was basking in the sun, with his visored cap pulled down over his eyes. A cart loaded with wheat was rolling into town.

"Hey, you have to pay."

The driver came over to him.

"How much?"

"Two *duros*."

Casimiro went into his little booth to write out the receipt. The driver searched in his pockets. He found several crumpled banknotes and some coins, and counted them carefully.

"Sixty *reales*."

The driver handed forty to Casimiro and put the receipt into a grimy notebook.

"Good day."

The driver ran downhill behind his mule, which had gone its own way ahead of him.

Casimiro noticed Juan.

"Man, I'm glad to see you!"

"I still haven't found a job."

"You ought to look for one like mine. No worries. We don't make much, but we get our eight *duros* whether it rains or not."

Juan agreed.

"Of course, it's hard to get in and you need an education . . . I think they're going to retire Basilio. I'll

let you know. Prepare yourself for it and I'll recom-
mend you. You're sure to get the job because the mayor
listens to me."

"But I can hardly read."

"That doesn't make any difference. The main thing
is to know how to write receipts, and you can memorize
that. With two words and a number, you're all set . . .
Of course there are the names, but they write them in
themselves. Everybody knows how to sign his own
name."

Juan shrugged his shoulders. He couldn't see himself
as a bureaucrat.

"Can I leave my hoe here? I don't want to go home
or walk around with this thing on my shoulder."

Casimiro pointed toward the little toll booth.

"Leave it in there."

Casimiro was sweating. He put his hand in his pocket
to take out his handkerchief and felt the ten *pesetas*.

"Juan!"

"What is it?"

"Take this."

"What's that for?"

"For you to have a drink . . . You can pay me back
later."

Juan thanked him.

"It's not important. It'll be your turn another time."

The crumpled bills felt good in his pocket. He walked
down Ganado Hill. Brakes screeched.

"Stupid!"

He stepped onto the sidewalk without looking at the
driver. He was just another face. Men were talking in
the doorways of the taverns. From time to time they
went in to have another drink.

"Hello!"

Paco came up alongside Juan. They went on in the
same direction.

"Do you want a drink?"

"No, it's too early."

"You're right."

Paco was just coming from his house. He didn't like to get up early when there was no reason to. He was well acquainted with the foremen and knew beforehand when the work would start.

"Chunga is a fool."

"Why?"

"He says things are bad because we demand our rights."

"Don't pay any attention to him. He's old."

"But the others listen to him."

"The others listen to anybody. They don't have anything else to do."

Juan was insistent.

"We have to strike."

Paco stopped dead in his tracks.

"Again? We're going to end up in a mess."

"One way or another, it doesn't make any difference. In a hundred years we'll all be bald."

"The longer it takes, the better."

"What do we have to lose?"

"I don't know . . . that depends."

"But suppose we can get something? Don't you think it's worthwhile? Remember what it was like when we were earning six *duros*."

"They raised our wages four *duros,* and everything else forty."

"We've got to make them even off wages and prices. If we insist, they'll have to do it."

"Don't hold your breath waiting. We breed too many parasites in this country."

"You don't lose anything by trying."

"Trying what? Another war? We had enough with the last one."

"I don't know . . . I don't remember."

"I do. I was fifteen years old."

"Your father was a Red."

"That's not true! My father had nothing to do with politics."

"He told me so himself, when I went to work in the wine cellar."

"That's a lie!"

"Remember that I'm as much a man as you are and I know what I'm saying."

"Your father is the one who was a Red!"

"I don't deny it."

"Of course not, after they killed him."

"They didn't kill yours. Pure luck."

"What do you mean, luck! Mine was a Falangist."

Juan didn't want to fight.

"All right, don't get mad."

"A person's got to listen to more crap . . ."

When they passed by the church they crossed over to the other side of the street. As far as saints were concerned, the farther away the better.

Father Demetrio was strolling in front of the church door waiting for the two girls from Catholic Action to finish arranging the parish show window. Like any other business, the church displayed its limited and, if the truth be known, not very attractive wares: a copy of the Sunday newsletter with the traditional religious drawing on the masthead—price fifty *céntimos;* two saints' lives in paperback; the announcement of religious ceremonies in blue letters outlined in red ink; another sign with an engraving of the Virgin of Hope inviting the faithful to attend classes in religion that, to quote the governor himself, "were having such a good effect on the youth"; and three signs containing the moral classifications of the movies that had so upset the priest: "Very dangerous", "For adults, but with reservations" . . .

Don Demetrio knew that the people of Sanlúcar

would go to the movies, that they would thereby sin, and that the sin would offend God and the bishop. His Eminence had called him several times, ordering him to put a stop to the immorality of the movies which contaminated the parish. Steeling himself, he went to the manager's office to deliver the bishop's august message. They kept him waiting for more than an hour in the deserted waiting room. There he sat looking at the movie posters which revealed the unsuspected charms of a number of female film stars. Garistán appeared just in time to keep the priest's morals from suffering a severe blow. "What do you want?" "The films that you're bringing to this town are dangerous for the morals of the people and are a constant source of scandal!" "So what, if people like them? I'm a businessman. I show what brings me money. If they ask for edifying films, don't worry, I'll put them on. But for now they prefer pretty legs and things that make them forget the bad times. It's up to you to convince them." "Señor Garistán! That's tempting the devil!" "What do I care? If God had meant me to be a saint, I'd be in a hermit's cell and I wouldn't have a chain of movie houses. It's either one extreme or the other for me. I'm not like you, a big nothing." Father Demetrio recalled that his answer was a model of eloquence, beginning with the first lines of a sermon that he had prepared especially for the occasion and that was so successful during the twelve o'clock mass on Sunday. He would have gone on if it hadn't been for that ill-mannered interruption: "I realize you don't have much to do and that you keep yourself amused by bothering me, but I do have things to do. Good afternoon!" Garistán walked out, leaving Don Demetrio trembling, his priestly dignity shattered.

This was why he hated to go anywhere near the movie house, but it was evident, in view of the signs the girls were putting up, that His Most Reverend Eminence would make him repeat his first visit.

"Father, where should I put the signs?"

"Wherever you want to."

"Some place where they're in plain sight?"

Don Demetrio shrugged his shoulders. Why bother? The masses filled the movie houses, the masses were made up of workers, and the workers didn't come near the church except during Holy Week and the Rocío. And that was not because they were religious occasions, but merely because they were popular ones.

Don Demetrio greeted Juan, who, being concerned with how to spend the day with two *duros,* didn't respond. Don Demetrio scratched the top of his head to conceal his annoyance. His former altar boy irritated him. Juan had begun to perform that function when he was barely seven years old. Tall, with an angelic face, he made a good impression on the altar steps. He was a quiet child who didn't play with the censer. But he didn't show up one day soon after his fourteenth birthday. That day there was a funeral—for Don Tobías, no less. The priest was late, waiting for Juan. The next day he sent for him, but he didn't show up. For two weeks Juan was nowhere to be seen. Finally they found him. "What happened to you?" "I went to work in the fields." "But that's not for you! You're meant for better things than swinging a hoe—don't you want to go to the seminary? I promise you that you have a good career cut out for you." The boy adopted the respectfully distant attitude that Andalusians take when they are scornful of something: his head lowered, his eyes gazing into space, and his body swaying with a barely perceptible, rhythmic motion from side to side. "All right, good enough! I can see you're not interested in the priesthood. But what would you say if I named you sexton? What about it? Good pay, tips, easy work . . ."

Juan didn't blink an eye. Don Demetrio lost his head. A hard slap made the boy sway a bit more, but produced no other effect. "That's enough! You can leave!" "Do you want anything else?" asked the boy, observing the traditional rules of good behavior. "Go away!" Juan said goodbye courteously before leaving.

He walked faster.
"Why such a hurry?"
"No reason. I just don't want to see that priest. He's always looking for me."

Workers occupied the center of Cabildo Plaza. These men wearing their *alpargatas* had begun to frequent the rich neighborhood only recently. They didn't go into the bars. Bars were for gentlemen. Nor did they drink there. They established their presence. Nothing more.

On Sundays the "well-to-do" sat at tables at Martinez's place so that they and their families could watch television together. Two worlds confronted each other while seeming to be unaware of each other's presence. For the workers, the others were café "seatwarmers"; and for the seatwarmers the workers were "manpower" that only had value when it was needed.

Business was the topic of discussion at the tables. The price of must, the sale of a farm, or an effective suspension of payments took up the time of those who had nothing else to do. The aisles were full of people offering real estate deals.

"Are you interested in Don Luis' house? It's for sale."
"Well . . ."
"It's in a good location and Don Luis is a little hard up. You can get it cheap."

"Potatoes have gone up again."

"My wife had to pay eleven *pesetas* for half a kilo of chickpeas. And that's just about one for each of us!"

"Did you know that Petra Méndez is going to have a baby?"

"Whose? Because her husband . . ."

The women were knitting in the Valenciana and discussing the latest gossip. Much time was spent talking about dresses that had been made for them in the past and were presently being made for them. In a place where few things happen, the dressmaker is someone worthy of attention.

Those who were going to the beauty parlor walked by quickly. When they came out they approached the group to receive the women's extravagant compliments.

Don César puffed hard on his cigarette.

"A strike? Don't be ridiculous! If there's anyone who's not working it's because he doesn't feel like it. Every day the emigration officials ask for people to go to work in Germany or France."

The clock on City Hall presided over the plaza. Three flags—the Falangist, the Spanish, and the Traditionalist—flew from the balcony on holidays. They were out today, but nobody knew why.

Juan and Paco approached the others.

"What's new?"

"Nothing . . . They're afraid it's going to rain, and since they have to pay us now for the morning if we begin to work . . ."

Chuli felt in his pockets.

"Do you have a cigarette?"

Juan smiled. A cigarette!

"What they need is a good attack of mildew."

They spoke loudly so that they could be heard at other tables.

"What good would that do? Do you think it would make them any poorer?"

The clock struck two. Don León came out of City Hall.

"The dirty bastard!"

Don León got into his car, checked the position of the gearshift, and started the motor.

"He's got millions."

"He's as full of shit as he is of money."

Juan walked away from the others. When he reached the theater he stepped into the street to see the movie posters. The Indians had the stagecoach surrounded. A cowboy was galloping away with an arrow stuck in his shoulder. Sophia Loren was offering him a kiss.

Don León honked his horn without slowing down. Juan jumped out of the way. He walked on toward the beach. It was getting hotter. He felt like jumping into the water, but he had never learned to swim, and he recalled that you always feel hungrier after swimming.

He sat down on a bench near the bandstand. They didn't play music there now as they used to when he was a child. On the other hand, they had put up fluorescent lanterns and garden shrubs. The mayor didn't like the old mulberry trees.

Well-dressed children were playing beside their nursemaids. A little farther on the other children were throwing stones. They were going toward the river and trying not to walk in the middle of the promenade. The middle was for rich people and adults only. Juan followed the children. He rolled up his pants to wade in the water. In the distance the dock divided the bathing beach from the work zone. It was built before the war, when Sanlúcar was the San Sebastián of Andalusia, for

the boats that brought vacationers from Seville. But it
ceased to be fashionable and the company decided to
discontinue the line. The dock was abandoned and the
sand had gradually piled up against it without anyone
bothering to clear it away. Now it only served as a
refuge for oysters and as a springboard for the children of Bajo Guía, who were jumping into the water
from the bare beams and engaging in all sorts of per-
ilous acrobatics.

Juan went under the cement pilings.

It was the noisiest time of day. Boats were arriving.
They came up to the beach with the rhythmic sound of
their motors and the splash of anchors plunging into
the water. The smaller boats moved by silently, coming
alongside "their" fishing boats to remove the cargo.
The sailors jumped into the water near the shore to
unload the boxes. It's nice in the summer because you're
not cold when you have to go into the water up to your
waist.

A burro galloped by, his hoofs splashing in the water.
"Ice cream!" Sailors shouted incomprehensible orders
toward the boats at the other end of the port. In the
bars the fishermen were having their first drink on
land for several days.

The official auctioneer approached a catch of fish.
Buyers and curious onlookers gathered around him.

"Fifty . . . forty-five . . ."

In Bajo Guía they talked in *duros*.

"I bid forty-five!"

The watchman in his cap and grey jacket noted the
figure in his book. The ship owner and outfitter did the
same. A sailor moved his lips, repeating the amount to
himself. He didn't know how to write so he had to
memorize the amount in order to defend his interests
and his mates' when the time came to settle their accounts.

Two Civil Guards smoked and looked absentmindedly at the people. They were talking about transfers and length of service.

"For Bernabé!" shouted the auctioneer.

And he continued selling the fish, box by box.

Children, bare from the waist up, played on the skeletons of boats half sunk in the sand, and kept an eye on the watchmen. The watchmen knew that at the slightest opportunity a small hand would slip into a box in search of a meal.

Juan went over to the ice cream wagon.

"Give me one for two *reales*."

The vendor lifted the shiny metal top and took out a minute amount of yellowish cream which tasted of artificial custard flavoring.

Two nuns approached Don Matías, the chandler.

"Alms for the orphans."

Don Matías picked up a handful of fish and threw them into a basket carried by two little girls in uniform. They thanked him obediently in unison, looking shyly at the ground as they had been taught to do.

"God will repay you, Don Matías."

Pirri was carrying a basket on his arm.

"What are you doing here?"

"Trying to find work."

"But you work in the fields."

"So what? In these times you have to go where they give you something to eat."

"Doesn't it make you feel bad?"

"It sure does. But it makes me feel worse to go home without a *céntimo* in my pocket."

"Same here."

"There's always work on the water."

"That depends on who asks for it . . ."

"I think they're looking for someone on 'El Duende'."

"Could you get me on?"

"I don't know . . ."

They looked for the owner of the boat. The opening was filled.

Pirri continued on toward the shipyards. Carpenters were making and repairing boats there, using their great-grandfathers' work methods. The wooden skeletons, in varying stages of construction, stood out against the sky.

The fishermen, hidden behind the shells of the half-finished boats, were engaged in their own little auction. Pirri emptied the lunch basket. Fish with no commercial value fell on the sand.

"Fifty, forty, thirty . . ."

They were talking in *reales,* not *duros.*

"I bid thirty!" A woman picked up the little pile of fish.

"Are you hungry?"

Juan shrugged his shoulders.

"Come on."

Three

Pirri lived in El Novales. His inheritance from his father was a garden and a fear of water. He received the legacy on a summer afternoon. An afternoon when there was a rough sea. Three days later the body was washed up on the beach. "He made a meal for the shrimps," a woman said. It was Pirri Senior's funeral oration.

Paca brought two tomatoes and bread dipped in olive oil. Juan thanked her.

"There's always something for a friend."

"When you have it."

Paca continued peeling potatoes for their supper.

Pirri took out a bag of loose tobacco.

"Do you want some?"

They smoked, sitting on the porch. Early cicadas were buzzing in the sand and frogs were croaking in the pond. Juan pointed to the truck garden.

"How is it coming along?"

"It's a lake! If the weather doesn't get better, we're going to have to plant anchovies. It seems to me that the best thing to do would be to sell it."

Paca raised her head.

"I suppose they're going to give you enough money to buy the Iraola farm."

"At least I'll get enough to buy a place where the water doesn't come up to my chest. With the way prices are going up they pay more for land."

"And you have to spend more too. You're not going to sell anything! You know very well that without the garden you'll be eating horseshit more than once!"

"Be quiet, woman! You don't know anything about business."

"Look at Juan. Knocking his head against a wall looking for work, and all for nothing."

"But I didn't have anything to begin with."

"I know what he'll have left if he sells out. Or do you think I don't know him by now? He'd leave it all behind in the tavern soon enough."

Juan raised his head to look at the moon. Paca went back to work.

"There's talk of a strike . . . rumors . . ."

Pirri said nothing.

"I think that it's high time to rebel, don't you?"

Paca stood up.

"I don't want to hear you say those things in my house! Don't you think we've had enough? They put my father and my brother up against the cemetery wall and shot them both. An old man sixty years old and a boy of fifteen. And for what? For complaining to Don Julio that we didn't even have potato peelings to cook in the pot. We're going to have bad times and we're going to have to tighten our belts, but at least we're still alive!"

"She's right. You'd be better off forgetting all that and taking what you can get. Anyone who wants to work manages to get along without starving to death. If you don't think so, then just look at me."

There was the sound of loud splashes as the frogs jumped into the water. A flock of ducks flew over toward the river. On the porch, silence.

"If it keeps up like this you'll have work tomorrow."

Juan nodded.

"Of course I'm going to ship out anyway, just in case."

"I hope they get a mildew warning and we really have to pitch in."

Pirri touched wood to dispel the evil omen. He had some vineyards in the Carrascal. Ten or twelve thousand *duros* if all went well. Before the cooperative was formed he would have agreed with Juan. The vintners fixed the price of grapes with a tight fist. "Take it or leave it . . ." And you had to take it, because the harvest declined once the right moment went by. You barely netted a thousand *duros,* the same amount you would have earned as a day laborer. And that was so only if you hadn't had to mortgage the land in order to continue working it.

"Remember that you were once in the same situation we're in. You ought to think about others."

Pirri shrugged his shoulders. Let others take care of themselves.

Juan realized that his friend had changed, become more callous, and he didn't know why.

"Hello."

Juanillo appeared, eating bread with olive oil. He sat down on the porch, paying no attention to the adults. That afternoon it was his turn to be a bull-fighter. He, Juan Navazo, making his debut in the ring at Las Ventas. The bullring—like Sanlúcar's, but much bigger—was full. There wasn't one empty seat in the stands. The bugle sounded and a treacherous black bull as big as a cathedral charged out into the ring. Juanillo spread his cape open. "Olé!" One pass, two, another and another, until he was tired of playing with the beast. He acknowledged the cheers with his hat in his hand. The spectators threw their hats into the ring.

When he had been carried around the ring for the second time on the shoulders of the enthusiastic fans he got up and walked off, taking the path to town.

"Where are you going?"

"For a walk."

"You'd better not go to the movies."

"Why not?"

"Listen to him! Because I don't feel like getting up to knock your head off."

The boy shook his head and ran off. He rounded the corner of the sawmill and headed straight for the movies.

He stopped near the ticket window and began to beg from passersby.

"A *peseta,* for the love of God."

In a little while he had the two and a half *pesetas* he needed, and handed them to the ticket seller with a lordly gesture. Then he ran inside and gave the ticket to the man at the door.

They went up San Juan Street.

"Two glasses."

They went from bar to bar until they reached the toll station. Calero was there.

"We're going on strike!"

Juan smiled.

"You want more money still?"

"Right. We have to get eighty *pesetas.*"

"You're aiming awfully high, friend," said Pirri. He had never believed in "The Revolutionary," which is what Calero had been called since the war.

"You have to aim high if you want to get anywhere."

"Like the barracks, for example."

"No, because we're all going out."

"Who told you so?"

"I'm telling you so and that's enough!"

"And who are you? Look at this guy with his airs!"

"I'm the one who got you out of trouble more than once in the union—you should know me by now."

"Well, the union's legal and the strike isn't."

"Count on me," Juan broke in. He said it more to irritate Pirri than to support Calero.

"Thanks."

"Well, don't count on me," Pirri snapped. He was brave enough when it came to dealing with his equals, but he didn't want to have any trouble with the bosses.

Negro approached the group.

"Remember that whoever goes to work has to answer to us."

Pirri drew himself up.

"Threats and all, right? We'll see how big you talk when you run into the Civil Guards."

"We're not afraid of the Civil Guards or of God himself! And I'm going to lay you out in a minute."

Pirri leaped at Negro and fists flew. Calero and Juan separated them.

"Come on, don't cause trouble."

The owner of the bar didn't like disturbances. He had already leaped over the counter and was about to call the police.

"You're all going to end up in jail."

Calero left him a *duro*. The owner kept the *peseta* left over.

"It's my tip," he said.

Juan took the long way home to keep from going by Largo's place.

Fernando was reading near a single fly-specked bulb. The new teacher had given him an encyclopedia. He wanted to memorize it because they didn't teach any of the things in it in school. Luisillo was playing with an empty can. Juana was watching a pot full of a thick broth that smelled like a mixture of dishwater and stew. Juan saw a shiny can of American cheese in a corner of the room.

"Who brought it?"

"Mama. The nuns were distributing food today."

"Is this all they gave her?"

Juana pointed toward the pot.

"A kilo of potatoes."

"Were there many vouchers?"

"They say there were about fifty. And more than a hundred women stood in line for nothing."

"You know I don't like her to do those things. You should have gone."

"They don't permit it. It has to be the one whose name is on the voucher."

Juan lay down on the bed. Fernando took advantage of the opportunity to ask questions.

"What we see in the sky at night are called planets, aren't they?"

Juan fixed his eyes on the ceiling. He had never heard that word before.

"Yes . . . and stars."

"But there are also planets."

"I guess so."

"Don't you know? They don't give off their own light."

Juan lost patience.

"Leave the books alone and spend your time learning to use a hoe. At your age you ought to be working!"

"I'm going to school."

"You're lucky, you little gentleman."

Fernando went back to his book. It was safer than continuing the discussion. Luisillo scraped the tin can he was playing with, making a nerve-shattering noise. Juan was in a bad mood. Without thinking he turned and hit the child so hard that he fell to the floor. Luisillo began crying loudly. His cries reached the street where the black woman was listening.

"They're killing him!"

She ran off looking for Salvadora, who was waiting

for her husband at the door of the tavern, as she did every night.

"Something very bad has happened to your Luisillo."

Salvadora jumped up from the curb, alarming the whole street with a piercing scream. She ran toward her house, crying and stumbling over the uneven cobblestones. Several women followed her, concealing their morbid curiosity with anguished gestures. Meanwhile, the women of the neighborhood burst into the room. Luisillo was passed from one to the other, still crying at the top of his lungs.

Juan tried to hide. Fortunately, only his brothers knew what had really happened. They wouldn't say anything as it wasn't to their advantage to let the truth be known.

Salvadora pushed her way through the crowd, snatching her son out of the arms of the woman who was comforting him at that moment. Luisillo stopped crying. Several voices murmured, "He's dying." Some of the women made the sign of the cross.

Juan took advantage of the moment to escape. In the street he passed his stepfather Paco, who was running home in a state of near hysteria. They had told him about Luisillo while he was having his tenth drink.

"To the hospital," Paco shouted, picking up poor Luisillo. He ran with him to the old hospital building as fast as he had run home.

"An injury! An injury!"

Sister María was making the beds in the second ward. She looked out. The group was crowding into the patio and alarming the patients with their cries. She ran down the stairs to restore order.

"Leave immediately! You can't shout in here!"

They didn't hear her. A woman went up to the nun.

"He's in very critical condition, Sister, very critical."

"Call the doctor!"

"What doctor?"

"Any doctor . . . whichever one is on duty . . . this is the hospital . . . make out the paper and bring him in."

Paco approached, showing her the child.

"He's here."

"All right . . . Take him to the first-aid station."

"Where is it?"

The nun rang the bell to call the porter, who was inexplicably away from his post at that moment. She walked out of the patio to save time.

"Come with me."

They all followed her.

"Will you all please go away?"

Nobody left. They all bunched together at the entrance to the small adjoining pavilion, pretentiously called the "first-aid station."

"Very well, we won't go in and I'll call the police if necessary."

"But the mother is here."

"Where?"

Three women stepped forward.

"I'm his mother," Salvadora said.

"You two are not needed."

"We're his aunts."

"You're not needed in the slightest."

The women were offended. A murmur of indignation ran through the crowd. At that moment the porter arrived with Pepe, the intern.

"What's the matter, Sister?"

"The same thing as always—there's a whole crowd with the patient!"

Pepe shouted and threatened. He managed to disperse them fairly quickly.

"Give me the child."

Paco regarded him suspiciously.

"I'd like to stay with him."

"That's not allowed!"

"All right, at least let his mother stay—in case he cries."

"That's enough out of you. I said no!"

Pepe took the child and went inside with the porter and Sister María, who wanted to accompany them, even though it was not required of her.

Luisillo began to cry again.

"Come on, now, it isn't that bad."

Sister María closed the door from the inside.

"Such a commotion!"

Pepe examined the wound.

"This is nothing."

The scratch was cured with a little alcohol and mercurochrome.

"Here's your son. He'll have a bump on his head tomorrow and in four or five days there won't be a trace of the cut."

The parents took him, a bit let down. Luisillo wanted to walk home, but Paco wouldn't let him.

Juan was hungry and worried. Bothered by a very bad conscience, he decided to return to "the scene of the crime," as they say in the movies. The house was empty. Only Fernando was still there, calmly reading.

"What happened?"

"They took him away."

"Dead?"

"No, just dazed. People like to make a big fuss."

"And Juana?"

"She went with them."

"Why didn't you go?"

"I wasn't interested. Besides, I'm more comfortable here."

"Do they know anything?"

"No, but you can bet Luisillo will tell them about it."

"I'll break his neck if he says anything!"

"That would just make it worse. You can hit me but not him."

Juan considered punching him, but it was too much for one night. He was deeply pensive when the procession returned. People were dropping in for more than an hour. Even Aunt Amalia came in from the countryside where she had been told that her nephew was breathing his last. She went by the hospital but nobody had been able to tell her anything there.

Each person told the story in his own way. Finally, after much discussion, they settled on the version which had him being hit "by a speeding car." The men thought they should file a complaint, but Paco shrugged his shoulders. He didn't want any more problems. The next day the whole town knew who had run Luisillo down.

The judge didn't bother to investigate the incident. What for? He had lived in the town for too many years. However, to soothe his conscience he instructed the hospital to submit a more detailed report. According to the child's statement, "he had fallen down while playing."

Toward dawn Juan went over to Luisillo.

"What did you say?"

He spoke in a very low voice in order not to wake up the others.

"Nothing . . . just that I fell down."

Juan patted his little brother affectionately.

"You won't hit me again, will you?"

"No, of course not."

"I didn't take your pants today."

Juan returned to his bed and promised himself that he would buy Luisillo a toy with the first wages he was paid.

Four

He had no sooner reached the plaza than Don León's foreman hired him to work at Alijarillo. Fifty men walked down the path to the farm. They couldn't go into the lowlands, since they were a sea of mud. But the whitish earth of the hill was all right for working. The group sang and greeted friends who were going to work in other fields. The dead season had ended. Even in the way they wore their hats it was obvious that this wasn't a day just like any other.

"You, take the sulphate!"

Juan dropped his hoe. He mixed the powder with water in a large tin drum. He had to be careful to protect his hands and above all his eyes. Many workers were blinded by the poisonous mixture. He stirred the green liquid with a stick, taking care not to splash it. They then poured it into the copper containers they carried on their backs. The men pulled a cord and directed the stream of chemicals toward the plants, trying not to miss any of the grapevines. As the hours wore on the container became heavier and heavier and the heat more unbearable. Juan's shoulders and back ached. He wasn't used to the hard work after the long period of inactivity. The rows became longer. Time dragged.

The first cigarette. The men sat down. Fifteen minutes to breathe. Calero came over to Juan.

"We're not coming tomorrow."

"Is everybody sticking together?"

"Yes."

"Are you sure?"

"Absolutely."

The foreman gave the signal to go back to work. Again the grapevines and the green liquid.

After work they came down the hill leaving trails in the fields.

"I've heard we're not working tomorrow."

"I have too."

"It's bad for the vines."

For Chato the vines were the main thing. He knew that one hour of mildew would destroy half a field, that there would be no harvest, and that the vines he himself had planted would be lost. He remembered the year of the phylloxera. The American disease, as they called it, because it came from there. It had killed all the shoots his father had planted. He didn't want the same thing to happen to his plants. A man dies and the plant remains, as much ours as though it were a son.

"Things are worse for us," Negro answered. He didn't feel the slightest sentimentality for things that belonged to the bosses.

"When there's work, we decide not to work; and when there's no work, we might as well drop dead."

"We have to earn more."

"A little is better than nothing at all."

"They've told me that nobody is going to work."

"I don't know . . . I have seven kids."

"Strikes are all right for single men."

The word and the protests went from group to group and from tavern to tavern. There were arguments, fights, threats. That night everyone went home convinced that it would be a failure.

And it was.

The men went to the plaza, as they would on any other day. Juan went out with his crew toward Don León's farm. As he passed the Amarguillo well, he felt Calero's eyes on him. Calero was leaning against a wall watching the "cowards" go by. The rebels, standing at the corners or sitting by the side of the road smoking, silently reproached him. He was ashamed of the tools he was carrying and felt like a slave.

There was little talk when they took a break for cigarettes. That afternoon the money burned in their pockets. They tried to invite the others to have a drink when they got back to town.

"We don't want anything bought with that kind of money."

Calero talked to the men, trying to convince them.

"We're acting like fools. We won't get anywhere this way."

The bosses shrugged their shoulders.

"They won't be able to get together. With a few more or less we'll get the work done as it's always done. They're the ones who'll lose."

A number of them who had political ambitions went to the plaza to see how the men felt.

"Would you like a drink?"

"No, thanks."

And the worker would move away.

"They're asking for eighty *pesetas*. Eighty blows is what we ought to give them! They'll all be back at work tomorrow or the next day. There's no danger."

The Civil Guards avoided the bars. Why take the chance of something disagreeable happening when there was no need?

The following day Juan returned to Alijarillo. His

stepfather also went to work in the fields, but before leaving he called Juan a coward.

"You young men are the ones who can't do anything."

Several young workers were waiting for them on the way out of town.

"Stop being foolish. Let's get the eighty *pesetas!*"

Some stayed with them instead of going to the fields. Juan went on.

It was eleven o'clock when the men from Casilla came down.

"All right, boys, no more work."

Those who were working there felt a great weight removed. They left their equipment on the ground without listening to the foreman. They jumped over the fence and went through the fields spreading the word. The vineyards were emptied. The first foremen arrived in Sanlúcar at two o'clock.

The men spread out in the various bars. "You shouldn't form groups, talk in loud voices, or fight," Calero had warned them.

Carlos, the old pruner, had been looking for him.

"You're happy now, aren't you? But who's going to feed my children?"

Calero winked at him.

"Come along."

They entered a store.

"Where's the boss?"

The boy had been taught to obey. He raced out into the street and to the owner's house.

"Don Manolo, they're looking for you at the store."

Don Manolo got up in a bad humor. He didn't like his nap to be interrupted.

"Who's looking for me?"

"Calero."

Don Manolo lay down again.

"Tell him to fuck off."

"He says that if you don't go, you'll regret it."

Don Manolo had heard rumors about what was going to happen. The storekeepers always know everything. Don Manolo was not cut out to be a hero. He
had had an irrational fear of revolution ever since he
had made some money. His father told him before he
died: "When you don't have any money, you have to
be a Red. But now, my son, become a Falangist."

He joined the Falange in the forties.

Of course, if times were changing . . . He went
down the stairs buttoning his pants.

"What's going on?"

"You're going to sell people what they need on
credit as long as the strike lasts. If you don't, remember
that a worker will never come into this store again. Not
even to pay what he owes."

"I agree."

"You'd better."

Calero made the rounds of the stores and taverns.
The owners all gave in. Those customers who bought
two *reales* of bacon and a hundred grams of chickpeas
kept their businesses going. They paid whatever they
were asked to, and they never forgot to settle their accounts. They were slow but sure. Naturally it was to the
storekeeper's advantage to extend credit now.

The question of living from day to day was solved.

"And now, boys, let's tighten our belts!"

The authorities met in Don León's house. He was the
richest, and therefore the most respected. Doña Carmen
had coffee prepared and some bottles brought out. Don
Gaspar produced a typewriter and some sheets of paper.
His son would do the typing. No one was to know
what was discussed there that night.

All the chairs in the house were taken to the living
room, even those from the kitchen. Don Antonio was
nervously preparing speeches to the workers in his head.

Peláez smiled, sure of himself. Don César discreetly spit into the receptacle that had been set out for that purpose.

Don León spoke first, launching a direct attack on Don Mariano.

"These are the ideas they get in the labor unions. Workers shouldn't get ideas!"

Don César, his mustache bristling, got right to the heart of the matter. "This can all be settled with the Civil Guards. It's a crime to go on strike."

This frightened Don Luis. How wise would it be to bring the Guards into this situation? It would cause an uproar.

"But this isn't a strike."

"If it isn't then, it resembles one too much for comfort."

Don Mariano was afraid—of the workers, of his friends, and of the authorities in the capital.

"I think it would be better to reach an agreement with them."

"I won't pay one *céntimo* more," asserted Don León. "The minimum wage was set at thirty-six *pesetas* and we're paying close to fifty. I don't think a handful of peons have the authority to change the law. Nor do you."

Don Mariano lowered his head. The others looked at the mayor. Don Luis tried not to draw attention to himself. His business affairs didn't depend on agriculture and he wanted no complications. He tried to make his response as ambiguous as possible.

"As mayor, I can't order any action to be taken against these men. As a friend, I'd like them to commit some crime, to violate some law, because in that case I could arrest them. But as long as they continue to act peacefully, I can't do anything unless our good friend, the post commander, finds some way to legally intervene."

A call was immediately placed to the captain, but he

wasn't at the barracks. Don Luis thought that he was avoiding the issue, but he didn't say so aloud. Two policemen were sent to look for him.

"Bring the judge and the notary here too. That is, if they choose to come. . . . Legal authorities are very important in these matters."

The captain appeared and knew exactly what was happening.

"This is all the doing of a man called Calero."

"What can be done about it?"

The captain was basically not a bad person but he was concerned about his future in the corps. If Calero's hide could help him, so much the worse for Calero.

"We can catch him and give him a beating that will be a lesson to the rest."

"On what charge?"

"As an agitator."

"Is there any proof?" asked the judge, who tried to abide by the law if possible.

"He was a Red during the war. He escaped by the skin of his teeth as he was being taken to the cemetery."

Don Alberto sighed with relief. It was possible to eliminate the key figure without overstepping the bounds.

Shortly thereafter, a pair of Civil Guards arrested Calero in the plaza. "The Revolutionary" proudly took his place between the Guards and said goodbye to his friends.

"Do what you know you should do."

That remark brought him a sharp thrust from a rifle butt in his ribs, a small sample of what he was to receive later.

"What if it isn't enough to make an example of Calero?"

"We'll see."

The town's leading citizens said goodbye to each other.

"I'll see you at the club tomorrow at the usual time."

Doña Carmen had been bored by the meeting. She was also concerned with how much it had cost. It began with a few small bottles and ended with whole crates of wine and lots of appetizers being consumed, which would cost Don León a pretty penny.

The men dispersed. The news spread through the town—spread by everybody and nobody.

"Bastards!"

In the bars there were voices filled with fear and helpless rage, rage that had been stored up for years. Glasses dropped "accidentally" and bottles slipped out of bartenders' hands.

"They're going to beat the shit out of him."

"And out of us, too, unless we keep our nerve."

Negro was there, his cap pulled down to his eyes, grey eyes that he fixed on his friends. They were the eyes of a farm laborer, used to sunlight and distance. He was not afraid but he had the taste of blood in his mouth. It was blood that came from a point in the distant past. He had seen it as a child—the blood of three bodies which were found on the street early one morning. People killed for no reason by nobody in particular. After he had walked away he ran into three boys just a little older than himself. They had innocent eyes, pistols in their belts, and the blue shirts of the Falange. "This one makes five for me." And the young man caressed the butt of his weapon, counting the little notches in it.

"You certainly are men! You're a bunch of fairies who have to raise cocks to see what it's like to fight."

His friends hung their heads and tried not to listen. Negro continued talking, loud, not at all afraid that others would hear him. He had had enough.

"What will they say about us afterward? The same thing that we say ourselves, that we're good for nothing, not even for standing up for our own children. Didn't they say the same thing about the ones who won the war against the Moors? We aren't men any more. Can't you see that?"

Antonio stepped forward. He was just twenty years old, but he knew that he wasn't acting the way he should.

"I'll do whatever you say."

The others followed Antonio, some with enthusiasm, others indifferently. Many of them just went along with the whole thing so as not to be different.

"Tomorrow we're going into the fields. And at ten o'clock we stop working."

"Why are we going to do that?"

It was Lechuzo who asked the question. He was inwardly cursing this spontaneous agitator who was tearing him away from his work and destroying his peace of mind.

"Because I say so and because we have to stick together."

Lechuzo moved away. The rest silently agreed.

That night the word of what was to happen the next day spread from house to house, through the bars and the streets. Juan was in Largo's bar when Negro came in. He went straight up to the boy.

"You were one of the first to say yes to Calero and one of the last to stop work. Do you want to come with us?"

"What for?"

"To lay out the first one who tries to enter the vineyard."

"But you told us to work till ten o'clock."

"That way we'll know tomorrow night the ones we have to lay out."

"That's dangerous."

"Dangerous or not, do you want to take care of things, or do you want to be taken care of?"

Juan was suddenly afraid of the Guards, afraid and ashamed. He drank one glass of wine and then another.

"I saw Negro."

Paco nodded.

"I did too."

Salvadora didn't like that. Disturbing rumors had been circulating among the women concerning a strike and jail.

"What did he tell you two?" she asked.

"We were just talking. Nothing important."

"It didn't have anything to do with that strike, I suppose."

"No, nothing."

Paco winked at Juan, congratulating him for having kept his mouth shut.

The workers gathered in the plaza at seven o'clock. Very few had their work baskets with them. Negro, flanked by Juan and Pelao, went up to one who had his basket.

"Leave that at home."

"I don't feel like it."

"You heard what I said."

"If you keep it up, I'll call the Civil Guard."

"Go on, if you dare."

A pair of Civil Guards appeared, coming up Santa Brígida Street. Negro and his friends moved away, arguing in loud voices about the last soccer game. The Guards leaned against a wall. The younger Guard ostentatiously checked his rifle, moving the bolt back and forth. They stayed there for two hours. The workers filed past them, following the foreman or head of the work gang who had called them.

"It's all straightened out, captain. They all left together."

The captain smiled, stroking his thick, almost white mustache.

"That's good."

He had them call City Hall. Don Luis was not there yet. Perhaps he would arrive about eleven o'clock. The captain personally called Don Luis at home. A bad-humored nasal voice answered the phone.

"This is the post commander."

"What's going on?"

"Something important, sir."

"I assume that it is. For you to be bothering me at this hour in the morning it must be important."

"The men have gone to work."

Don Luis' little eyes gleamed. He hung up the phone without saying goodbye and hastened to call all the omnipotent gentlemen who determined whether or not he would continue to occupy his chair at City Hall. An important chair that assured him enormous social, and economic, benefits.

At eleven o'clock it seemed like any other day in Sanlúcar. The gentlemen were having their first drinks in the casino or the bars around the plaza, salesmen were buying and selling, the town idiot was shouting out a bit of fictitious news in order to sell his newspapers and get tips, and men were talking about machines that would take the place of manpower and of an unchanging future based on the continuation of order and peace.

A group of men reached the center of the plaza and then were joined by another, and then another. They were in work clothes. The gypsy stopped shining the brown shoes that Don Anselmo had placed in front of him, and watched how they slowly filled the space between the houses. He knew something was happening, said nothing, and began shining the shoes again.

López, the waiter, came up to the bar.

"Two coffees, four half bottles for Don César, two plates of shrimp and one of sardines."

Carmela served him.

"Is something happening?"

"I suppose so."

The woman pointed at the tables.

"Do they know about it?"

López shrugged his shoulders. His job was waiting on tables.

Don César was getting impatient. Manuel, his secretary, did his best to calm him down.

"It must be just a few holdouts."

Don César shook his head. He was in no mood for jokes. Manuel said nothing further.

There was the sound of a horse's hoofs on the street going up Ganado Hill. It broke into a gallop as it turned the corner of Victoria Plaza.

The foreman was happy as he rode into town. It was high time the boys did something right. For the record he had asked them to stay on the job, but he also let them know that they were doing a good thing. And he had taken his time getting to town. Of course he was one of the first to arrive, since his field was just outside of town, but that wasn't his fault. He went to the boss's house, even though he knew perfectly well that he was at the casino. He knocked at the door insistently. The maid came running down the stairs.

"Keep your shirt on. We're not going to break our necks here."

The maid was a plump girl with pretty eyes and a

stupid face. She had always been the foreman's weakness. He was married to a bony, hardworking woman who was over thirty and looked fifty. He saw the girl many afternoons behind the garden wall when her boyfriend was away. The foreman thought that he might be able to spend a little time chatting with her, but this wasn't the right day for conversation.

"The mistress is worse than ever. I don't know what's eating her. So say what you've got to say fast."

"I'm looking for Don José."

"Listen to him. As though you didn't know that by now he's downing his first drink."

"How should I know that?"

"You ought to. You've been around this house a lot longer than the cans in the pantry."

"All right, can you call him?"

"Look for him yourself. Or did somebody cut off your legs?"

The maid slammed the little peephole in the door. The foreman led his horse to the wall of the wine cellar and tied him to an iron ring that was there for that purpose. Then he walked toward the casino, refreshing himself in the bars that he found along the way.

When he found Don José he touched the brim of his hat.

"What's happening?"

"The men have walked off the job."

People came over from the other tables. What had happened? Was it just on his place or on the others also?

"Well, I'll tell you what I saw. They came when they were supposed to and sat down. No matter how much I urged them they refused to do anything. Some had brought their tools along with them, others didn't even want to look at a hoe. I got hoarse from talking to them, Don José, I swear it by my children!"

"Stop swearing and tell me the rest."

"That's it. About ten o'clock they all got up and left without saying one blessed thing."

Don León was biting his nails.

"Do you know if they left Alijarillo?"

The foreman looked as though he didn't understand a word.

"Answer the gentleman!" Don José ordered.

"Look, sir, I don't know anything about it, but I did notice when I came down the road that a lot of men were walking toward town. I don't know if they were coming from your place, though. I don't know who went to work there this year."

"If it happened at ten o'clock, why did it take you so long to get here?"

"I spread the sulphate myself, in order not to lose what was in the sprayers."

It was a lie, but it made no difference. There was no danger that Don José would go into the fields as long as things were not normal. He was afraid, because during the war someone had beaten him up.

"Let's go."

Don José and the others disappeared. The foreman decided that they were going to meet in some back room. He calmly rolled a cigarette. His boots echoed in the plaza. Some of the workers greeted him and he replied cautiously. They gave him his horse back at the wine cellar.

"Don José said that you should go back to the fields and go on working."

The foreman nodded, spitting on the ground as he did so. Afterward he went toward the red-light district. Now that he was in Sanlúcar he wanted to spend a while at China's—there were always girls there.

The groups of "vigilantes" hid by the sides of the

roads among the pears and the magueys. They were waiting for the scabs.

Juan was sweating as he crouched by Negro's side. The thought that his stepfather was at the Callejón de la Reyerta comforted him, but not enough so that he could get rid of the stupid trembling that he "happened to feel" in his knees.

"Here comes one."

Lechuzo came trotting down the road with his basket under his arm. He looked back from time to time, stopping at the curves in the road. He tried to scurry past the group.

Negro jumped on him.

"Let's go."

Juan and Pelao struck at Lechuzo. The man rolled on the ground for ten minutes trying to free himself from Negro's hold. Negro held his hand over Lechuzo's mouth so that he couldn't shout.

"He's had enough."

They rubbed his body with prickly pear leaves before letting him go.

"We're going to kill him," Pelao said. He knew that a crime was a serious matter and that the Civil Guard would investigate.

"Keep it up. Let him find out that we're worse than the Guards."

Negro finally picked Lechuzo up.

"Remember that if you say anything the others will take care of you for good."

Lechuzo was crying.

"Shut up!"

"Don't worry, I'll do whatever you say." He left, limping as he went back down the road.

"That one won't work for a week. Not even in bed!"

That night cries of pain could be heard all over town. The Guards listened from their post.

"Should we investigate?"

Pérez shrugged his shoulders.

"What for? They won't give us a raise for it and we might get something we're not looking for."

Núñez put out his cigarette and cocked his rifle, just in case.

The investigation began at dawn. They went from house to house, interrogating the victims.

"What did you find out?" the captain asked them afterward.

"Well, captain, I don't know. They all say the same thing, that they ran into a very tall man dressed in white, a stranger."

The Civil Guards didn't look for the phantom, but instead prepared a full report on the mysterious stranger, mentioning the other times he had appeared, and sent it to their superiors.

"At any rate, when things calm down we'll find the person responsible . . . as always."

Five

There was a meeting at the club. Flies. The smell of old cigar butts and wine. The gentlemen were talking about minor matters. "Something will happen out there, and the men will go back to work."

Don César turned toward the door. It was the waiter with a load of glasses and bottles. Don Mariano lit his pipe. There was just a little tobacco left. Don Luis went to the window, cautiously lifting a corner of the curtain. He didn't want them to see him. The judge closed his Bible and Don Gaspar ordered another bottle. The conversations died down and the murmurs from the street filled the room.

"There are a lot of them," said Don Luis.

"What good are the Guards?" asked Don León impatiently.

"In this case, the people aren't committing any crime."

"But they're there!"

Don José had seen more of war than the others. He had been in Ronda when it broke out and he had been frightened. Now he felt the same fear he had felt then.

Don Luis went back to his seat.

"This can't continue," said Don César. He was right. Everyone looked at Don Luis.

"Yes, you! That's why you're mayor. Go out and tell them something. Tell them anything, but make them go away."

Don Luis turned pale. When he had asked for the position he had told the governor very clearly that he was not interested in a political career. It was just that he needed some extra income to supplement his meager retirement pay. It was for this reason that he only gave speeches when he was ordered to by his superiors, and only then to a submissive audience that applauded whenever he paused, without bothering to listen to what he was saying. This mob was something different! The slightest slip, one thought poorly expressed—he knew deep inside that he had never been a good speaker —would be enough to bring that mess of people down on him, without giving the Civil Guard, and much less the poor municipal police, time to protect him.

"Come on, go out there!"

He felt trapped. No, he didn't want to be a hero.

"Don't you see that they're going to kill me?"

"That's your problem. You shouldn't have taken the job as mayor."

Don Mariano removed his pipe from his mouth.

"I know the people of my town. They're good until they decide not to be, and then you have to be careful. This is no time to provoke a riot. It's better to wait a while. We'll have time later to pick them off one by one and then it'll be their turn to be afraid. They're brave when they're all together in a group like that, but when each one is in his house with a Guard in front, they shrink right down to size."

"But it's a question of the grapes, of our money! We can't wait. So . . . "

Don Mariano shrank back without getting out of the chair.

"Don't get angry. That's the last thing we should do. Let's see what can be done. That's why we got together, damn it."

Silence in the room again allowed the murmur from

the crowd in the street to reach them. The judge got up to speak.

"I suppose that you're waiting for my opinion. I am sorry to inform you that for the moment we can't use the forces of law and order. There have been no crimes and no fights. An alarming state of affairs, in my opinion, because even the usual quarrels have not occurred. The workers are not bound by any contract, and the Guards and the foremen have a perfect right to refuse to spread the sulphate, since that's not their job."

"What's the matter? Are you another radical?"

The judge smiled.

"Let me finish. This situation can turn ugly in a number of ways . . ."

But the grape growers were in no mood to listen. A change in the weather and it would be the end! The harvest would be completely ruined.

"What good are your labor unions? Now they have a chance to do something. Tell those people that you listen to when they protest that they have to go to work!"

"I agree. Tomorrow I'll call their representatives together and I'll try to work out a solution with them."

Don César finished his drink in one gulp.

"Labor unions! Don't be stupid. Since when have they ever solved anything? We're all friends here, so let's not fool ourselves. We know only too well how we appoint the rabble's representatives. They're under our thumbs! Nobody listens to them, not even the stones. And the two or three that slip by us are out there in the street with the others. That's no solution. If we face the facts, it's the worst solution."

"What then? A police charge? We can't do that either. We can arrest a half dozen tonight, but no more. Tomorrow nothing will have changed."

"Maybe tomorrow they'll go to the jail to protest. Then the police can attack."

Don Luis was frightened.

"You're all insane! Then the foreign newspapermen will find out and I'll be called on the carpet by Madrid."

At that moment Don Antonio came in. He was elegantly dressed and smiling, as usual. The fact that he had just crossed the plaza through the mass of workers without receiving a scratch conferred a certain prestige on him.

"Do you have a plan?"

No one answered.

"All right then, I have the solution."

Some of them stood up to hear the speech better, because they were sure he was going to make a speech. Antonio dreamed of a brilliant political career with the Monarchists. He had still not begun his "campaign," but he was carefully laying the groundwork by making as many friends as possible.

"Neither an attack by the police nor a meeting of the labor unions is practical. Much less an improvised speech, since the workers, when they feel their strength, can be expected to say exactly what they think, whether it's true or not. That would harm our prestige and the prestige of the various legally constituted bodies. In principle, we ought to avoid the old parliamentarian methods, as well as gestures that would indicate that we are a country which lacks freedom."

"We already know what we mustn't do. We're interested in what we can do."

Antonio flashed his teeth in a paternal smile. He had acquired the habit from dealing with workers and couldn't keep himself from doing it when he was addressing his peers.

"Be patient. Now, as I was saying, both force and reason are out of the question, partly because we won't convince anybody. We ought to respect the workers and we will respect them, but the vineyards need men to

work them, and they need them now! The logical thing
to do is to look for men somewhere else."

The gentlemen nodded their approval. That curly-
haired boy, just out of the university, really had something.

"If you need money . . ."

"No, for heaven's sake, I have a stake in this too."

The word of the strike had spread quickly. From
Sanlúcar to Chiclana men listened to Don Antonio's
proposals while looking at the ground, as though he
were not with them.

"We can't, sir. There's work here. Sanlúcar is very
far away."

"We'd go if it were somewhere else. But Sanlúcar
isn't a good place."

Antonio went to Medina Sidonia to look for Manijero. He was in the Central Bar, as usual.

"Don Antonio! I'm glad to see you."

Manijero greeted him without getting up. He knew
that Antonio was not coming to see him because he
wanted to, but because he had to. His fat legs dangled
in the air without quite touching the floor.

Don Antonio sat down.

"I need two thousand men."

Manijero threw away the stub of one cigarette and
lit another without answering.

"Two thousand—what for?"

"The vineyards."

"I heard that you were having trouble there."

That remark annoyed Don Antonio. He didn't like
people to make fun of him. In Medina they knew perfectly well what was happening.

"Yes, and that's the reason I'm here."

"I didn't like last year's settlement . . ."

Don Antonio recalled how this strange individual,
who had resuscitated the slave trade, had demanded,

on the day when final payment was to be made, two thousand *pesetas* extra "in order to buy candy for the children." Don Antonio hadn't wanted to give the extra money to him because things had gone badly. He hadn't made as much as he had expected to on the sale of chickpeas, and the government hadn't been willing to raise the price of wheat. They had finally reached an agreement, but their relations had been strained beyond the point of Manijero's going to look for mountain people for the bosses when they were in a jam.

"All right. We'll make better terms this time."

"Before we begin to talk business, I'd prefer to settle past accounts."

Don Antonio took fifteen hundred *pesetas* out of his wallet.

"Is that enough?"

"I have more coming."

"This is all I have."

Manijero hesitated for a moment. Then he took the money and called the waiter.

"A bottle. Don Antonio is paying."

Then his tone changed.

"I can't get more than five hundred."

"What are you talking about? You're not going to leave me holding the bag."

"This is harvest time everywhere. I have orders that I have to fill. Old customers . . ."

"Let's see if you can't get a few more. It'll increase your market. You know that you're not very highly regarded in Sanlúcar."

Manijero didn't pick up on the last remark.

"I can only get you those in six or seven days, because it's impossible right now."

"I came to take them back with me."

"Well, it can't be done."

Manijero stared at a girl who was walking by. The conversation was obviously at an end.

"How much do you want for them?"

"Sixty apiece, and ten for me."

"You'd think they were machines!"

"You won't find even one for less than fifty."

"But with food, tobacco, and wine they cost us eighty or more."

"That's fine, Don Antonio. It's apparent that you don't need them very badly."

Manijero stood up. Don Antonio caught his arm.

"Can't we even talk about it any more?"

"I have a lot to do."

Don Antonio made some rapid calculations in his head. At fifty they came to sixty with the ten for expenses added in, which was almost the amount they were asking for wages in Sanlúcar. It was a bad deal. The landowners would be upset, but he couldn't return with empty hands . . .

"Come on, sit down. We can't work things out if we don't talk."

Manijero sat down ill-humoredly.

"All right. I don't want to offend you."

"I'll give you fifty, everything included."

Manijero appeared hesitant.

"Well, since it's you, I'll settle for fifty-five . . . and the gift."

Don Antonio decided not to push it any further.

"Agreed. Are they worth five thousand?"

"Yes they are."

"The only condition is that they have to come with me."

Manijero smiled.

"We'll round up a few."

He walked up the street toward Ayuntamiento Plaza with his hands in his belt and the dead cigarette dangling out of his mouth. Don Antonio amused himself by drinking another bottle and making remarks to the women who walked by. He did the same thing every afternoon in the casino at Sanlúcar, but of course he couldn't say anything to the women there, because it wouldn't look good.

Manijero called to a boy who was sitting, waiting, under the arches.

"What can I do for you, Don Juan?"

"Find two hundred men for me right now, and three hundred more for tomorrow."

"I'll have to go to the villages. I can only find about seventy here."

"Bring them."

"How much should I offer them?"

"Thirty *pesetas*."

"They're not going to want to work for that, with the rising prices."

"Nothing's rising here!"

The boy disappeared down an alley. Don Juan entered a bar.

"A beer—fast!"

He turned toward the men in the room with his glass in his hand. Good men from the mountains, with nothing to do but rub their empty bellies.

"Is there anyone who wants to go to Sanlúcar?"

Almost every hand in the room was raised.

"We do."

"All right, let's go."

"But how much are they paying?"

"Whatever it is, it doesn't matter. I'll tell you when the job is done. You're going to get meals, wine, and tobacco. What more can a man ask for in these times?"

"But my children . . ."

"There'll be something for the children. I haven't ever let you down, have I?"

Don Antonio was smothering in the third-class car. It stank of sweat and bad tobacco. He could have made the trip in first class or in his automobile, but he didn't want to leave the workers alone. It wouldn't be the first time that they got lost in the stations.

Manijero had done very well. They were young, strong, and obedient men who asked no questions and made no comments.

"So that's the way it is. Don't talk to anyone and mind your own business, because the people in Sanlúcar just want to get rid of you so that they can take your jobs."

"Yes, sir."

He repeated it to them several times. These things bore repeating so that they wouldn't be forgotten.

They changed trains at Jerez. The men followed Don Antonio with their little bundles of clothing under their arms. A blanket was a most important item, because the boss never provided one. Don Antonio strutted along in his fashionable grey suit, a little ashamed to be seen in such grubby company.

"Are they for the grape harvest, Don Antonio?"

He smiled at the conductor.

"Yes, my boy, we have no choice except to look for them elsewhere."

"Because of the strike, right?"

"That's correct. If they'd go to work, these things wouldn't happen."

The foremen were waiting at the stops.

"I need fifty."

"Well, you'll have to be satisfied with ten. The rest won't be here until tomorrow."

The men were ordered off the train a few at a time. Some of the foremen got on to make a personal choice. Don Antonio kept twenty of the strongest for himself.

"Get off, kid."

"I want to go with my brother."

"I told you to get off. This is your stop."

The youngster obeyed.

Juan was leaning on a wall and watching Matías' store to see if he was carrying out the agreement he made with Calero. Before leaving home Juan had warned his mother: "Don't get much at the store. We'll have to pay for it later."

He passed the time counting up his debts. It would take him a month to pay them off, and that wasn't taking the strike into account. Pirri came up. He had switched once and for all from the coarse-woven cotton jacket of the laborers to the blue shirt of the fishermen.

"What's new?"

"Nothing."

"I've heard you're all on strike."

"Somebody made that up."

"Do you take me for a fool?"

"I'm not working because my back hurts."

"And the others?"

"How should I know?"

Pirri smiled.

"What do you intend to do when it stops hurting?"

"Work, if I can find any."

"For eighty *pesetas*?"

"For whatever they pay. Besides, what do you care?"

Pirri invited him to have a drink. They entered a tavern. A glass of wine always hits the spot. Negro came over to them. He looked as though he were in a bad mood and he was paler than usual. He took Juan by the arm without greeting Pirri.

"Come along."

Almost all the strike leaders were in the patio of Manolo el Pelao's place. They were those natural leaders who always appear when they are needed.

"They've screwed us."

"How?"

"They're working in all the fields. Men from the mountains."

They hadn't counted on that. The mountaineers frequently came to work on the farms, but never in the vineyards. If the others, the indecisive ones, found out about it they'd go back to work. Once again the bosses were winning.

"The hell with that. We'll deal with them the way we did the scabs."

"There are a lot of them, and they'll bring more."

"We have to go to the mountains."

They chose lots among the best speakers. Negro, Pelao, Paco, Antonio . . . Pelao and Antonio won. Each of them looked in his pockets. There wasn't enough money for the tickets.

"We'll go on bicycles."

"That's no good. It's a long way and there's no time to lose."

"We'll have to ask for the money."

"We're workers, not beggars."

"What difference does it make? Haven't we begged for food many a time? Well, now we have to beg so we can work."

The women undertook to raise the money. They went from door to door with their children in their arms, asking the rich for money "for the love of God."

"Señorita, my child is very ill."

"All your husband has to do is work."

"But if he works they'll beat him up."

"Who?"

"A very tall man in white who's been seen around."

"Have you seen him?"

"I think I saw him one night, but I didn't get a close look. I was afraid and ran away."

Most of them offered work, while others, to get rid of them, gave them a *peseta* or ten *céntimos*. That night they met in Antonio's house. There were so many people that there wasn't room for them inside, so they filled the patio. Negro counted the money.

"Two hundred and five. More than we need."

Antonio and Pelao left on the first train. Several workers accompanied them as far as the toll booth.

"Good luck."

The authorities took no notice of the two travelers.

"They must be going to work. Don Antonio didn't have a bad idea at that."

Civil Guard Pérez smiled.

"I'll have to spread the word. I've seen them with the strike leaders very often."

Six Negro went out into the fields. Contact had to be established with the outsiders. The straw hats moved slowly among the grapevines. The mountain people were not used to the equipment for spraying sulphate. From time to time a hoe flashed in the sun. Negro jumped over the fence.

"Good morning."

The mountaineer didn't answer.

"So how do you feel? Are you eating my children's bread?"

Silence.

"You mountain pigs! You're all a bunch of mother-fuckers!"

The mountaineer dropped his hoe on the ground. Negro skillfully sidestepped the punch the mar aimed at him.

"That's what I wanted! To find out that you're men like everyone else and not pack mules. It's just that you live away from things and never find out about anything. They brought you here because we want more wages for everybody. For us and for you too, because if they raise them in Sanlúcar, they'll have to raise them up there where you come from."

The mountaineer didn't understand a word.

"And to tell me that you had to call me a mother-fucker?"

"But I didn't mean it. I said it so that you'd listen to me, because there you were, working like a machine and not listening to a thing."

Negro talked all morning. The foremen threw him out of the fields, but he just circled around and climbed the fence somewhere else.

"Negro, you're going to get us into a lot of trouble. Don't you see that we're under orders to tell the Civil Guard if someone comes around saying things like that? You know I don't want to do anything to hurt you."

"Call the Guards."

"No, I swear to God I won't do it. I'd rather get into trouble myself."

The mountain people listened to him. Then they went back to work. Most of them didn't understand him and those who did pretended they didn't.

The first one to throw down his hoe was a man from Arcos.

"He's right. I'm not going to stay here."

And he jumped over the fence.

It was growing dark when Negro walked across the plaza between two Civil Guards. The corporal came over to beat him. Private Pérez tried to stop him.

"You can't do that here in the street."

"You shut up. I know these people. It's always good to set them an example."

Negro didn't protest, and took the blows standing firmly on his feet. The blows didn't hurt, but the humiliation did. He walked on toward the barracks with his head high.

Juan was biting his fists.

"That they should beat you is only to be expected," he said to himself, "but it's disgraceful that they should do it in front of everyone."

The commander took the news to the gentlemen's club.

"We caught another and we're after a third."

He was disconcerted by the cold reception he received.

"Do you know the mountaineers are leaving the fields too?"

"Bring more of them."

"What for? Do you think we're just giving away those trips?"

The captain cleared his throat angrily. He was used to giving orders, not being criticized.

"We already know that there are agitators among them. If you can prove that this is a political movement, we can prosecute them," he said.

"And how is that proved?"

"By finding Communists mixed up in it. That's your business."

"No, it's yours. That's what you're paid for."

"Sometimes it's hard."

"That makes no difference. If there aren't any, then invent some."

The captain thought to himself that that was very easy to say and difficult to do.

"No attention should be drawn to what's happening here. If they were to find out about it in Madrid, they might even raise the wages. You never know what the bigwigs will do."

Don César could stand no more. Millions in profits were at stake in this strike.

"We could carry out a small-scale repression on the sly."

This disturbed the mayor.

"You can't be sure. There are always people who talk and there would be an uproar at the first sign of blood."

Don Antonio Vázquez returned to Medina Sidonia.

The others stayed where they were in the casino, talking about the strike. Outside, workers walked down the street with their hands in their pockets and their hats pulled down over their eyes. They were two worlds only waiting for a sign from history in order to destroy each other.

Don Antonio called from Arcos.

"I went everywhere and couldn't find anyone who wants to come. Apparently two individuals who can't be identified arrived here to convince them that they're all being sold like slaves."

The strike ended its first week. The stores were beginning to ration goods. The people no longer got whatever they asked for, but only up to a certain limit set arbitrarily on their credit by the shopkeepers.

"I can't buy goods without money. The shop is almost empty."

"The wholesalers won't give anybody a break. They've already questioned two of my drafts."

Antonio and the others knew that was not true. That morning they had seen two trucks unload at Manolo's place, another at Matías', and several casks arrive at Largo's. They also saw the shopkeepers enter City Hall to attend a meeting the mayor had called with them. They were in his office for two hours. Manolé and Juanelo were waiting in the plaza for them to come out. They didn't look very happy when they finally appeared.

They cornered Largo on the stairs.

"What were you talking about?"

"It's none of your business."

"Are we friends or aren't we?"

Largo climbed on up to the landing, followed by the two workers. There, under the shadow of the tree peeking over the wall in the Garden of the Prince, he explained the meeting he had been to as best as he could.

". . . we had no choice, we had to give in on something. He wanted us not to extend any more credit and he threatened to close our shops. Some of the others were ready to give in, but Manolo and I refused. We agreed to continue rationing."

"And those who have more children, the ones who need more?"

"I don't know, I don't know. Things are going very badly."

Largo climbed the remaining stairs two at a time. Then he ran down Monte de Piedad Street toward Plaza Alta, where he was sure to find people. It wasn't the way to his house but he was afraid and wanted to put some distance between him and the others.

Manolé and Juanelo let him go.

"Let's look for the others."

The churches stopped distributing American cheese and milk. Small signs, generally placed inside the churches, announced that Caritas would only aid those who could prove that the head of the family was working. It was only natural. The priests' vineyards were also being hurt by the strike.

Soup kitchens, associations, and houses where "Christian charity" was usually distributed closed their doors, some because of self-interest, others because giving charity at such times was frowned upon.

The strikers went to the beach with their families. The men, in water up to their necks, scraped the submerged rocks with makeshift rakes, taking care not to step in the wrong place. It was just a matter of inches. The water was six, ten, and even twenty-five feet deep in places and agricultural workers don't know how to swim. The women and children walked along the shore, bending over to pick up the little shells that the tide left there. Piles of oysters were black against the white sand.

The men made their way back to the beach with their baskets on their heads, maintaining a precarious balance on the stone sea wall covered with sharp shells. The buyer waited on the shore. It was a good time for him. The law of supply and demand lowered the prices he had to pay. It was the right time to store up goods.

The women didn't understand the strike. Their hands, covered with small cuts, hurt them. The children, their feet wrapped in rags, complained of hunger more than anything else.

At night the pot was filled with water without olive oil, and only a few potatoes and poor quality fish. They had to make do with that, a few tomatoes and just one loaf of bread for the whole family.

The children asked for more. The men—and anyone over fourteen is considered a man in Sanlúcar—swore that they had too much to eat. The women protested.

"They'll win. They've always won. The only thing that we'll get out of this is a piece of lead from the Civil Guard."

"Nothing's happened so far."

"Negro and Calero are in jail. Do you call that nothing?"

"They're living off the state."

"You don't call that living, getting beaten all the time and eating worse food than we have here."

"What do you know about it?"

"I know what everybody knows."

"You'd think you'd spent your life in jail."

"I've never been in jail and I never intend to be. How shameful!"

"That depends on why they put you there. Our men are heroes."

"You'd do anything for people to point at you and say how great you are. But in a short time all people will say is that you were in jail and they won't even mention *why* you were there. That reflects on a man's honor."

"Be quiet. You don't understand."

"I understand that it's better to be a whore than a worker's wife."

"You wouldn't do it. You have children."

"If this keeps up, you'll see. It isn't the children's fault and I don't want them to starve."

"But we give them food, don't we?"

"Look at what you call food."

The gentlemen listened to the newscast. They had developed the habit during the war. Afterwards it was fashionable to know what was happening. They barely knew where Korea was, nor why that war had started. Nor did they understand the danger it involved for them, living far away as they did in Spain. However, they did want the Americans to win, because the United States was a guarantee of the survival of their world.

After the news they heard the weather report. The conversations in the club stopped. The notary got out of his chair to turn the volume up.

"A storm front located above the Azores is approaching the peninsula. It will affect the Atlantic coast, especially the zone of the Straits of Gibraltar."

The barometer on the wall was the object of great attention. It had dropped noticeably. Rain and sun meant mildew.

Don Antonio left the room. Don Gaspar heaved his huge bulk out of the armchair with great difficulty.

They were worried.

Chirlo looked at the sky.

It was evident that the weather was changing.
They didn't need barometers or radios.

Don León Alvarez paced around the room with long
strides. It was all foolishness. It was quite plain that
the authorities were useless. It made no difference
whether one appealed to the governor or to Franco
himself. It was a rotten regime that was handing the
country over to the rabble, openly betraying those who
had supported it during the war.

"The mailed fist! Don't they beat people up? Then
we should beat them up. It cost us a lot of lives to defend what rightfully belongs to us. We're not going to
turn soft now when it's just a matter of a few blows
more or less."

"Just look at the facts. We, the founders of the
Falange, solid citizens, are the most abused."

"I was with Mora," Don Gaspar recalled. "I was one
of those who saved Andalusia, and they want to ruin
me because I risked my neck for them."

"Well, how about me? I was a high official in the
Falange and for years I had the responsibility of defending the rearguard. And as a reward I was given a
job in the labor unions and another in the Savings
Fund, and between the two I didn't even earn enough
to buy food."

Aurelio Peláez yawned. He wasn't interested in the
past. He remembered the war years as one long night-
mare that ended on the day Don Mariano's friends took
away his father. His indignation didn't last long. He
was a practical man who preferred to carve out a fortune that his father, a simple mule driver, would never
even have dreamed of acquiring.

"That's enough reminiscing. We all know that half
of the people here only smelled powder during the executions. Your war ended against the cemetery wall. It

was a very interesting mopping-up operation, I don't deny it, but it wasn't very dangerous."

"That's called dotting the i's and crossing the t's."

Don Antonio was amused by Peláez's statements, but not Don Mariano, who felt that he was being personally attacked.

"I'm going to denounce you."

"It's not '39 any longer."

"We'll see about that."

"We better see how the little matter of the vineyards is resolved. That's more important, don't you think so?"

"And I insist on what I said before. The mailed fist!"

Don León, called "Black Whip" by the workers, was known for being pigheaded.

"We can't, it would put us in a bad light. And besides, they have more physical strength."

"We can hire some strongarm men."

"No, friend. I think we ought to pay what they're asking. Among other reasons, because strongarm men are very expensive."

Peláez was afraid. He had gone too far, but it was too late now. The words, "we ought to pay," were out. Four dangerous words. There was a prolonged silence. They took each other's measure. Aurelio didn't lower his head. Without realizing it, he adopted a defiant attitude. However, the fear was there inside of him and it kept growing. He was the son of a Red.

"I can't."

"I can't either."

"Well, don't expect us to."

"On the one hand, it's quite clear that neither the Civil Guard nor the mayor can help us. And let's not even talk about our friend Mariano. The harvest will bring in a little cash. If we do some figuring, it's obvious that we can afford to pay eighty, and even two hundred! But it's hard to swallow, I agree."

Don César realized that Peláez could jeopardize them all.

"You're not going to be the first to give in . . ."

"Yes, I am. Tomorrow they'll work in my fields for the wages they're asking for."

Don Mariano emptied his pipe.

"This is what happens when the son of a mule driver sits down with us."

"That's what I am and I'm proud of it! I don't hide it the way you do. You've forgotten the smell of ground pepper and storerooms."

Don León was right next to Peláez. He felt like hitting him. He did. Peláez wasn't expecting the blow and fell to the floor. Someone kicked him, then another followed suit. It was Don Antonio who pulled him away.

"If you people want to behave like this, then go out into the street. But not in my house."

Peláez struggled to his feet.

"Good day, 'gentlemen.' "

Don Gaspar stopped him.

"I know that you didn't mean what you said. You won't really pay what they're asking, will you?"

"I'll do whatever I have to do. On my land, I'm the master."

"You're not getting out of here."

Peláez pushed him out of the way with no difficulty. Don Gaspar was not a strong man.

"Well, one less."

"Two less."

Rocío, the only woman landowner in the region, had also left.

"It doesn't matter. Between the two of them they don't employ more than two hundred of the bastards."

They discussed the possibility of waiting for them in

the street and beating them up, plans for mechanically fumigating their vines, with the possible loss of the crop. They agreed to stick together to prevent a lock-out.

Don César and Don Antonio decided to leave for Madrid.

"It's better to talk to them personally so outsiders don't find out. We have to give them a clear idea of our situation in order to convince them that they should help us."

They caught the last plane out of Seville.

Antonio and Pelao returned from the mountains on the last train.

Seven

Perico ran into Juan's house. Jumping over a mattress, he reached the table where the men were arguing without worrying about those who were trying to sleep.

"My brother's going to work tomorrow!"

Antonio was deserting them. Juan raised the boy off the floor by his lapels, ripping them in the process.

"That's not true."

"I swear it is," Perico managed to say. "Don Aurelio's foreman came and they reached an agreement."

"For how much?"

"That I don't know."

The boy ran out without explaining anything further. The two men felt something had failed. The older man thought that Antonio had betrayed his people, as the men from the capital had done when they came during the time of the Republic to call them out on strike. There was no danger then. Standing on a bench in the plaza, they spoke to the workers who applauded and followed them. And nothing happened—nothing except for the fact that the Republic was finally lost and the war came to establish "order" again.

There were also scabs during those strikes, but they didn't get off so easily. It occurred to him that Antonio, on the other hand, could take great advantage of being the first to give in, without troubling himself about

Negro, who had been in jail for three days, nor Calero, nor all his comrades who were risking their necks for him and with him. Why had he gotten mixed up in this in the first place? Hadn't the years given him enough experience? Neither the war nor the denunciations nor the executions had cured him.

Juan had no such memories. He trusted Antonio and didn't think he was capable of doing such a thing. He was ready to accept any explanation he might give him, as long as he wouldn't have to take him off the pedestal he had placed him on. Nevertheless, the word "betrayal" kept popping up in his mind. Or maybe strikes were always like that, in which case they had no meaning. Why all the beatings, the trip to the mountains, the threats, and the words?

Paco slapped his old felt hat on his head.

"Let's go."

His stepson followed him without asking any questions. The old man walked with great strides, repeating an impressive list of insults aimed at the supposed scab.

They reached Antonio's hut in less than half an hour. They had passed the bullring and the Pino district without realizing it because they had taken a shortcut by jumping over the wall of the abandoned schoolhouse.

There was no light inside the cabin with its mud walls and straw roof. In the working-class sections everybody goes to bed before midnight. Only gentlemen can afford the luxury of going the rounds of the bars at those hours. Paco pounded on the door. He mauled the sheet of wood for five minutes until he almost broke the door down.

Antonio's voice came out of the depths of a deep sleep.

"I'm coming."

He appeared in the doorway in white shorts and a

carbide lantern in his hand. His eyes were still half closed.

"Why, it's you! Come on in."

He gestured to them to enter with that natural hospitality of his people. Paco and Juan stepped across the doorway without saying a word.

"Speak softly because the others are sleeping," Antonio asked.

The seven members of the family were distributed on the bed and two mattresses placed over empty boxes. There was Antonio's wife, his son, a disabled uncle, and the two brothers who were still at home. An empty place for Pedro was nowhere to be seen, whereas the spot where Antonio had been lying was still vacant. It would soon be occupied, though, when the nearest person to it rolled over in his sleep.

Paco had great respect for women and children and he therefore didn't raise his voice.

"You're a dirty scab."

Antonio looked at him in surprise.

"Don't pretend you don't know what I'm talking about. We found out that you're going to work for Peláez tomorrow."

"He's paying what we're asking."

"That's a lie. You just don't want to lose the job. All the boss has to do is shed some crocodile tears or threaten to never call you again till the end of your days for you to stab us in the back."

Antonio began to wake up.

"I swear that it's true. Matías, the foreman, came to see me. He had a letter signed by Don Aurelio promising us the eighty *pesetas*. It's what we're asking for; all we have to do is take it."

"And screw the rest of us, right?"

"After this the other landowners will all give in. They're sure to."

"And me without anything to eat."

Antonio felt trapped. On the one hand he had to go. It was a good lesson for the other landowners. On the other hand, his comrades would see his suffering end and they would call him a traitor and stop the strike.

"The foreman called the same ones he calls every year."

"How about Don León's and Don José's foremen? Will they call us? No, friend. They won't call us now or ever, because we've attracted too much attention to ourselves."

"I have, too."

"And look how you've ended up."

"I swear I'm not a scab."

Paco almost believed him, because Antonio never lied. Besides, a scab is usually frightened.

"All right. We'll see tomorrow. Let's go."

He and Juan returned the way they had come. They jumped the wall again, taking care not to be seen by the dog, and walked through the plaza, keeping close to the walls.

The men watched Peláez's work crew file out of town. Thirty workers left for the fields with their tools on their shoulders. Antonio tried to explain to the others.

"If we stay we'll be in the wrong. It's like breaking our word."

But the others wouldn't listen to him. The only thing they could see clearly was that Antonio and the others would collect their wages that afternoon, while they stayed behind and pretended they were tougher.

"I tell you we have to go to work. We have to go, because our boss has guts and he's going to pay what we're asking. I know as well as you do that he's had problems with the others. But it's not right for us to leave these fellows in the lurch either," continued Antonio, addressing the others who were going to work with him. "The only way out that I can see is for us to share and share alike until the strike's over."

But those who were going to do the work didn't agree with that.

"It's our backs that are going to hurt tonight."

"Remember that the only reason we got the eighty is because we all stuck together. They have a right to share in what we earn, because they all tightened their belts like the best of us."

"All right. We'll give them the thirty *peseta* difference between our old wage and what we'll be getting now."

"Antonio's right. If it wasn't for us, you wouldn't have gotten anything."

"There are five kids, my father, my mother, Antonia, and me in my house and we've had to make do with two rolls and three tomatoes at each meal. Today is the end of that! We're going to eat!"

Juan went over to Antonio.

"If you screw us, you'll all regret it."

It was getting late. Those who were going to work began to leave. Antonio stayed behind a moment.

"Hold on a while longer. They're beginning to give in."

His comrades called him to come along.

"Don't do anything for less than eighty until tonight."

Two Civil Guards crossed the plaza. Their rifles were on their shoulders and they were wearing their regulation shoulder belts. Nobody made a move.

Chunga began his daily speech from his chair in Largo's doorway.

"I told you so. Let this be a lesson to the know-it-alls. In my time, when strikes were really strikes, we all went back to work together. And we wouldn't even give the time of day to anybody who went back sooner. Nobody's ever been able to beat the bosses."

The men listened to him, and some of them began to think he was right. The workers in the plaza broke up into two groups, those who agreed with Chunga and the others. Pelao, Paco, and Juan were left alone in the middle. They began to talk in little groups about going back to work for whatever they could get.

"That would show Antonio. It would teach him not to play around with us."

"You think he wasn't telling the truth?"

"He's swallowed shit just like anybody else."

"But he's one of the first to go back to work."

Juan approached one of the groups.

"What do you say, revolutionary, are we giving up already?"

The boy shrugged his shoulders.

"Look at him. He doesn't even dare answer."

Paco called to him. "Let's go."

As always, the old worker wanted to back down. Pelao opposed it.

"Antonio had his reasons for going. We have to keep the others from going to work. If we leave them alone they'll go like sheep to the slaughter, without even waiting for the bosses to come to them."

"Now they're not even afraid of us."

"We'll see about that."

Don León stopped his car in front of the watchman's house. He usually didn't drive up there because the road was bad and it was bad for the car, but this was a special occasion.

"Pacorro."

The watchman, who was also his foreman, came up to Don León holding his cap in his hand.

"Yes, sir."

"You're going to the plaza to look for men."

"Have you decided to pay what they're asking, sir?"

"No, imbecile! The one who's paying is that fool Don Aurelio."

"But you know they won't come."

"That's none of your business. You'll do what I tell you to do and nothing more."

Pacorro didn't fancy the idea of facing the workers. They didn't like the foremen. They regarded them as scabs and stool pigeons for the bosses. Ever since the trouble started he had been very careful not to leave the fields. He had heard that the workers were feeling very rebellious, that they had beaten some people up and other things. But a job is a job. He swallowed hard.

"Yes, sir."

"Get in."

Pacorro obeyed, putting his cap back on. He always took it off when he greeted his superiors, but after that he could cover up his bald spot without being disrespectful.

Don León started the car and it lurched off. He was in a bad mood. The car stopped near the curb halfway down San Nicolás Street.

"Tell them that we're paying sixty *pesetas*. If they protest a lot, you can go up five. But only if they protest a lot. Convince them that Antonio and the others made a deal with their boss and that they're getting the same pay as before. Emphasize that it was all just a maneuver on the part of the revolutionaries for political prestige. And take them straight to the vineyard. I'm watching you, remember. You'd better carry it off."

Pacorro was trembling as he walked toward Puerta de Jerez.

Rocío left her car on the highway. It was impossible to drive to the Atalaya through that mud hole. The

little well had overflowed, as usual. The foreman saw
her coming from his house. At other times he would
have gone down to meet her, but now was no time to
bend over backwards.

"I wonder what she wants?" he murmured.

Petra, his wife, heard him as she was cleaning chickpeas on the stone bench.

"What do you care? Do what she says, and you'll be
on the safe side."

"You know very well that I can't go into the vineyard."

"She knows it too."

"They're scared of the possibility of mildew. She's
capable of spreading the sulphate herself."

"What do you care?"

"If she goes into the fields I'll have to go too, or I'll
be out of a job."

"Then go."

"Then I won't be able to set foot in town. Antonio's
boys don't play around."

"Then don't go into town. It's just as well, consider-
ing what you do there, spending money and drinking
wine. You'd be better off if you never saw the town
again."

The foreman shook his head. This visit was going to
bring trouble. Rocío was just a few yards from the
house.

"Go on. Say hello to her."

The foreman turned his back on his boss and pretended that he was working. Without realizing what he
was doing he picked up a brand new hemp basket and
a needle to sew it. They were the first two things he
could put his hands on.

"Señorita! I didn't see you."

"You've seen me since I stopped the car."

"I swear . . ."

"Never mind. Come along with me."

The foreman turned pale.

"Where to?"

"To Puerta de Jerez."

"But . . ."

"If your mistress tells you to, just do it."

"All right . . . I'm going to change my clothes."

"I don't have that much time. Come as you are."

The foreman quickly threw his straw hat on the table and put on his Sunday hat. It was a felt hat in very good condition that went well with his mended jacket and coarse cotton pants. He followed his boss to the road.

"You could have come down. It would have saved me the trouble of climbing the hill."

The foreman smiled idiotically.

"It doesn't matter now."

Juan was defending his position.

"We're winning. Wait a little longer and you'll see how they give in."

"Don León or Don César, for example."

"Yes, tell us how you'll shove it down their throats."

Pacorro had arrived at a good time, but he didn't know it. He went up to Chunga. The old man had the reputation of being a pacifist.

"Good morning, old-timer."

"Good morning."

"I wanted to ask you something."

"Go ahead."

"Don León told me to come."

"Is he going to pay what we're asking?"

"No, that's the problem. But he wants me to take him two hundred men."

"There aren't that many here."

"Then as many as I can."

"It's not going to be easy for you. People are not in a very good mood."

Pacorro made an eloquent gesture. He already knew that was the case. Some of the men recognized him.

"There's Pacorro."

"Don León's going to pay? That's not possible."

"Let's see what brings him."

Pacorro found himself surrounded. To defend himself he put his back to the wall behind Chunga.

"Come on, you little bastard, spill it."

"Tell us what bug your boss has up his ass."

Pelao and Paco were the only ones who realized how dangerous any offer, no matter how small, would be. If Pacorro was afraid, it meant that he couldn't offer eighty, but the fact that he had come at all showed that he intended to offer something a little better than they were paid before. They pushed their way to the front of the crowd.

"Come on. Talk fast, because we don't have time to waste."

"My boss says that he'll pay you up to sixty-five *pesetas*."

It was a *duro* more than he had been authorized to offer, but he felt that his skin was well worth a *duro*.

"Is that true?" asked Lechuzo, his eyes shining. Sixty-five *pesetas!* It was more than he had ever earned in his life.

Juan cut him short.

"We said we weren't going for less than eighty."

"But that depends . . ."

"The offer shows good will."

The men, who had united when they saw Pacorro, divided into opposing groups again. The foreman felt he was on solid ground.

"Are you coming then?"

Lechuzo stepped forward.

"You can count on me. Between the rain and the strike I haven't made a *céntimo* for seven months."

He was followed by Juanillo, Perico, Tuerto, Mulo . . .

"You're screwing Calero and Negro."

Nobody listened to Pelao. The two prisoners were in jail "because they wanted to be there." And Antonio was out making money with Peláez. The number of men on Pacorro's side grew.

Many of them ran home to get their tools.

Rocío crossed San Nicolás Street.

"What in the world is Alvarez doing, hiding over there?" she wondered aloud.

Everyone knew the green Land Rover with the brand painted on the door. Don León wasn't a cattleman, but he had a brand for his sheep and he used it as a coat of arms.

Her foreman shrugged his shoulders, thinking to himself that Rocío knew perfectly well what Don León was waiting for. He felt like a guinea pig, but he kept his thoughts to himself.

They parked in the plaza. The argument between the two groups had become more violent. It was impossible for an outsider to tell what they were arguing about, above all when one looked at Pacorro who, reassured by the men's attitude, was staying in his corner.

"How many do we need?" asked Rocío.

"From fifteen to twenty."

"Wait here."

The foreman was astonished. That woman was going to enter the plaza knowing what the situation was and what might happen to her.

"Be careful, Señorita."

"Don't worry. I know what I have to do better than you do."

Stopping a few yards from the workers she put her

hands on her hips and shouted: "I need twenty men right now."

It was a high voice, different from the rest. They all fell silent. Pelao walked over to her, leaving his post in front of Pacorro.

"Nobody here is going to work for less than eighty."

Pacorro wanted to say something, but Juan and Paco held their hands over his mouth.

"Who said anything different?"

The leaders' attitude changed little by little. They were prepared to be aggressive and now they didn't know what to do. The enemy was turning into a friend right under their noses.

"Are you going to pay that?"

"Naturally. Otherwise I wouldn't be here."

Pelao realized that her offer was going to play a very important role in the future of the strike.

"Hey, twenty of you! Here's another one who's going to pay what we're asking for."

Those who had taken Pacorro's side moved away from him. They had to stand pat, because it was now clear to them that if they did, they would win. Antonio and the others were right.

"I want three of you right now. Paco, who comes every year, Juan, and you."

The three men lowered their heads. If they left, the others would be at the mercy of the first person who arrived.

"No, neither Juan nor I . . ."

"If you three don't come, I won't pay."

"We knew it," said Lechuzo. "It was all decided beforehand."

But Lechuzo's protest was not successful. His neighbor effectively shut him up by punching him in the mouth.

"Come on, make up your minds. I'm in a hurry."

Pistolero stepped forward. He was a blond boy,

about sixteen, small and thin because of undernourish-
ment.

"You can go with her. We'll stay here."

One by one the men offered to take their leaders'
places.

"Don't worry. We won't let you down."

"There will always be one of us to take somebody
else's place."

Mulo, who had gone over to Pacorro's side more because he had momentarily lost hope than because he
was against the strike, turned to his comrades.

"I'll break the neck of the first one who works for
less."

Don León was getting impatient. He had parked his
car in an alley in order not to be seen, but the children
recognized him. Two of them—children are not afraid
to do anything—stuck their tongues out at him as they
went by. Pacorro's proposition might anger the men, he
thought, and a group of angry men, certain of their
strength, are capable of doing many things. His only
defense was to run over them with his car. Some of the
workers would be injured and when people are injured they file complaints. Then there'd be a trial,
something he wanted to avoid at all costs. Of course he
could have the matter covered up, but sometimes that
was a very expensive process, much more expensive
than raising wages for an entire year.

From time to time he started the motor and inched
the car forward to see if his foreman was coming with
the workers.

It was incredible—almost an hour! It must be a violent argument. Perhaps they had already killed Pacorro,
and if they killed Pacorro, they would kill him too. All
that had to happen was for the ball to be set rolling,
and then it would crush them all.

He started the car in second and drove through town

faster than he should have. When he got home he ran inside as fast as he could, without even bothering to lock the car, sure that there was a mob close behind him.

Pacorro was left alone with his back to the wall. Even old Chunga, the protector of law and order, had abandoned him. He didn't dare move lest someone notice him. The Santo Domingo crew had left and those who stayed behind sat down, prepared to wait for their comrades to come back or for a third visit from the landowners.

They were talking about Rocío.

"She came alone. She's not afraid of us."

"It proves she's acting in good faith."

"I always said that I preferred to work for her. They don't push you at Santo Domingo the way they do other places."

"On the other hand, that bastard Alvarez sent his foreman instead of coming himself. Some man he is."

"And his messenger too. Just look at him. He doesn't even dare move."

"Hey, you, motherfucker. Are you going to stay there all afternoon holding up the house?"

"Beat it!"

Pacorro began to run toward the street where his boss had been waiting for him. He didn't realize that Chirlo was waiting for him on that very corner with open arms.

"Where are you going in such a hurry?"

Pacorro tried to run in the opposite direction, but Mulo cut him off.

"Ahhhh . . . nowhere. Don León is waiting for me down there."

Chirlo burst out laughing.

"He's not waiting for you now. He ran away like a rabbit."

Pacorro tried to pull himself together.

"All right, fellows, a joke's a joke."

Mulo knocked him flat on his back. Pacorro began to cry.

"Leave me alone, for my children's sake."

"We're doing it for the sake of ours."

"We already told you not to come around here offering us less money than we're asking for."

"The boss sent me. I didn't want to come."

Mulo hit him again. Pacorro's ears rang.

"This is so that you'll know that we're better men than your boss. Next time it'll be a one-way trip."

Mulo tried to hit him a third time, but Chirlo caught his arm.

"That's enough. Now run and tell your little master all about it."

Pacorro didn't wait to be told twice. He went down Belén Hill as fast as he could and in five minutes he was at Alvarez's door. It seemed to him that hours went by from the time he rang the bell until they opened the door. Panting for breath, he asked for his master.

Weeds had invaded the vineyard. Antonio began to clear them away with four others who had brought their hoes with them. The others carried the packs filled with sulphate.

"We've got to work hard. We want them to know we can do a job well."

They worked without talking, only standing up to wipe off the sweat, until the foreman reminded them of the time.

"Time to smoke."

They sat down on the ground wherever they happened to be, taking advantage of every moment allowed them.

Ciriaco took out a bag of loose tobacco.

"Does anyone have cigarette papers?"

They looked in their pockets. Juanelo found four wrinkled papers in the bottom of his jacket pocket.

"These are all there are."

"Give them to me."

Ciriaco rolled four cigarettes, being careful not to tear the paper.

"There's one for every five men."

The baskets were opened at lunchtime. Bread, salt, and tomatoes. The foreman called his wife.

"Bring them a bottle of olive oil."

"You're crazy."

"Do what I tell you to. The boss told me to give it to them."

The woman went into her house. There were two bottles in the kitchen. One was for everyday use and was half empty; the other was only opened when Don Aurelio came by. She took his bottle.

The men poured it liberally on their bread. They worked better that afternoon because their stomachs were full.

"Now let them say that we don't do any work."

Antonio contemplated their work with the satisfaction of both another worker and a boss.

Don Aurelio arrived at five o'clock. It was time to be paid. One by one they received their envelope. It was the first money that had been won by the strike.

"Thanks very much, Don Aurelio."

But the day was not over.

"You're old hands in the vineyard," said Don Aurelio. "You know better than I do what grape-growing is like. If we don't spread the sulphate fast, everything may be lost. And, if there's no harvest, you'll be hurt as much as I will. You'll lose your jobs and I'll lose money. Remember that I risked a great deal yesterday afternoon, so don't let me down."

Antonio spoke for them all.

"If what you want is for us to work extra hours, we can't. There are others waiting in the plaza and we'd be taking work away from them. But that doesn't mean that we don't appreciate all you've done for us."

Ciriaco didn't agree. Four or five *duros* extra would come in handy, if for no other reason than because the money could be shared with the others.

"Nothing's going to happen if we stay here an hour longer. It won't hurt anybody."

"We can't get much done in an hour, but something can be saved."

Antonio turned to Don Aurelio.

"I have just one thing to ask you. Don't make us stay overtime today. I swear that we'll work double tomorrow."

Peláez let them go.

Juan prepared the sulphate. They were also working hard at Santo Domingo. The foreman walked away from the workers. The strike had separated him from them. He didn't have anything to say to the workers and there was no need to say anything to make them work harder. Rocío had stayed at the vineyard. She sat on the porch and watched from a distance. She gave no orders, but everyone was aware of her presence and it made them feel even more obligated.

When time came to break for a cigarette, she took out a pack.

"I had a feeling you wouldn't have any tobacco."

That afternoon the workers expected her to ask them to work overtime.

"I'll see you tomorrow. I'll expect you at eight o'clock."

They left, counting their money as they walked down the road.

Don Luis was waiting at City Hall. He had closed the doors and sent the attendants home. The only person left in the broad hallway was an old, half-deaf attendant who couldn't understand why Don Luis didn't let him go home too.

Alvarez burst into the office without giving the poor wreck time to announce him.

"Now we've got them. They beat up Pacorro."

Don Luis called the judge, interrupting his reading of an edifying book of religious meditations.

"What's the matter?"

"They beat up Pacorro."

The judge didn't know who Pacorro was.

"He's Alvarez's foreman."

"Who did it?"

Don Luis lost his patience.

"Who do you think? The strikers."

The judge lowered his eyes to the book: "All roads lead to the Lord." God always put the phrase at hand that he needed for choosing his own road.

"Do you know their names?"

"No."

"So?"

"It was in the plaza. We can swear out a complaint against everyone who was there."

"All right. Bring in the victim."

Don León took Pacorro to the courthouse, but the judge wasn't in his office because it was late and he had gone home. They had his secretary take the typewriter to the little room furnished in nineteenth-century style in the judge's house.

"In a case like this, any time is the right time."

Pacorro told his story.

"Apparently you know perfectly well who hit you."

"Yes, Your Honor, it was Mulo and Chirlo."

Don Alberto didn't want him to be so precise. He motioned to his secretary, who continued the questioning.

"Tell me what their names are."

"I've already told you."

"I want their baptismal names. Nicknames are no good here."

"You can ask anybody. That's what everybody calls them."

"We're not going to bother half the town because of you."

Pacorro picked up his cap to leave.

"No, wait, you have to sign the paper."

"But . . ."

"I told you to wait!"

Pacorro was left standing in the middle of the room with his cap in his hand. The gentlemen talked to each other as though he wasn't there.

". . . a vague accusation. The mob jumped on the boy . . . He couldn't recognize anyone. He just knows that they beat him and that he reached the home of Mr. Alvarez more dead than alive. Mr. Vázquez will make a statement as witness . . ."

The secretary continued writing. With that paper anyone could be arrested. The worst agitators would be removed. They all liked the idea. All of them, that is, except the foreman. If his master hadn't promised him those thousand *duros,* he would never have taken the chance. Besides, he wanted to get those two toughs, not the others. A thousand *duros,* five banknotes that were of no value to him, because he would never be able to come to town again. Things always have a way of leaking out.

The secretary removed the document from the typewriter and handed it to Don Alberto who read it under his breath and passed it on to Don Luis.

"That's fine."

They put a pen in Pacorro's hand.

"Sign it."

"But . . . don't they say that you should read things before you sign them?"

"Sign it, I said! The people who should read it have read it. They've memorized it by now."

He signed. When he was out in the street he realized how heavily five sheets of paper can weigh on a man. Nobody looked at him, nobody knew anything. However, when his cousin Carlos came over and invited him to have a drink, he felt ashamed.

"I have to go home soon. With what happened this afternoon, God knows what state I'll find Clara in."

"Come on, just one drink."

"No, I tell you."

"We should have a drink because of what happened at the plaza. It was nothing. You did what they told you to do and we did what we had to."

"Were you there?"

"Yes, a little way away because I didn't want them to confuse me with the scabs."

"Why didn't you defend me?"

Pacorro was looking for someone to blame for what he had done. He wanted to be able to say: "I denounced them because they mistreated me, because my own relatives turned against me." It was very important to him.

"I had nothing to do with it."

"I'm your cousin."

"But you don't seem like a worker."

"I work for wages just like you do."

"It's different."

"If they hadn't done it . . ."

"What do you mean?"

"Well, nothing would be about to happen."

Carlos smiled.

"What do you think is going to happen? A war?"

"No, you're all going to jail."

"Nobody knows anything."

"The Civil Guards saw it."

"Don't be foolish. There wasn't a single Guard around all morning. Unless you said something . . ."

Pacorro swallowed hard. He was afraid.

"Me? I swear by my children that I didn't. Don't you think I know what you'd do to me?"

Carlos slapped him on the back.

"Come on. We all know that you wouldn't do a thing like that."

And he ordered another round. Pacorro drank slowly. It was his turn to pay and all he had with him were the green banknotes. No worker has bills that color toward the end of the month. He racked his brains for the best way to keep from taking them out without making his cousin suspicious.

"Put them on my bill."

The boy who was tending bar did so, surprised that someone with a steady job didn't have enough money to pay for a round.

Carlos put his arm around his cousin's shoulders.

"Let's go to Largo's place. I want you to make up with the boys."

Pacorro held back.

"All right, I'll drag you over if I have to. Matters like this should be settled while they're still fresh in everybody's mind."

Mulo leaned on the bar.

"Here he is. He's sorry for what he did."

Pacorro tried to hide. Chirlo called him over.

"Don't be afraid. What happened this morning was just a lesson we had to give you, but we didn't mean

anything by it. As far as we're concerned, it's forgotten."

And he held out his hand. Pacorro shook hands, but
his heart wasn't in it. They offered him a drink. He
drank and tried to be careful not to talk too much. He
thought every glass would be the last. He kept saying
goodbye, but they wouldn't let him go. They were sorry
that they had hit him so hard. He had always been a
poor devil and they wanted to make up for it.

Pistolero was standing at the other end of the bar,
not taking his eyes off Pacorro, who was thinking that
he had seen the boy somewhere.

Pistolero came over. Now Pacorro remembered where
he had seen him. It was at the Havana bridge on the
way to the courthouse. He took the offensive.

"Why are you staring at me?"

Pistolero faced him.

"Because I saw you this afternoon."

"Well, I never saw you."

"You were going into the courthouse with Don León
and the mayor. You were there more than an hour."

"So what? We had to go to take care of matters relating to the vineyard."

The workers had formed a circle around them. They
were listening intently, because a lot was at stake. Carlos
thrust his fist in his cousin's face.

"If you told them something!"

"But what do you take me for? I'm no stoolpigeon."

"If you are you're going to get it."

"We went because of the boundary question. You
all know that Don León cut off the road to Trebujena,
because he said nobody was using it."

"So? Is it going to be opened or not?"

"I don't know . . . We had to make some statements."

"What did you say?"

"What could I say with the boss there? I said it was his. I've been working for him for a long time and I make good wages."

"You've given him a few yards as a gift."

"More than that. That was a wide road."

Pacorro agreed resignedly.

"That's not good, because we all need the road."

Mulo ordered another round. Pacorro agreed to have one last drink.

"I'm half drunk already. I'm going."

Carlos accompanied him as far as the crossroads. Pacorro leaned on him, shaking noticeably. His legs were weak, but it wasn't because of the wine.

The complaint was lying on the post commander's table. Impressed, he reflected that a man becomes a judge for good reason, since he himself, being just a simple officer, would never have had such an idea.

He called in Private Pérez, who knew a great deal about the town through his fiancée. In fact, he was waiting to be transferred to another post so that he could get married. A Civil Guard can never serve in a place where he has relatives.

"Give me the name of some of the most rebellious."

Pérez thought rapidly as he stood at attention. Rebellious? Who's rebellious? People who protest because they don't have enough to eat? Common criminals? The question probably had to do with the strike organizers.

"I don't know them, sir. They all look alike to me. They're quiet, and they don't bother anyone."

"The other day we talked about somebody named Antonio."

"There are so many with that name."

"Núñez told me that he was making trouble."

Pérez shrugged his shoulders.

"He must know something that I don't know."

The captain slammed his fist on the table.

"It's your duty to know them too!"

"Sir . . . I . . . I've been on duty . . . I don't know anybody."

"Your fiancée must know them."

"My fiancée doesn't know them either. She's not from a country family."

"Dismissed!"

Pérez clicked his heels smartly.

The captain called the brigade commander. He was an old soldier who had served through the period of the struggle against the guerrillas and kept, in the bottom of his suitcase, a list of the Civil Guards who had died in the line of duty during that time. He was right. Those men, victims of their sense of duty, deserved a better fate than just being forgotten.

"Sir!"

"Pérez didn't want to give me names."

"I'll give them to you. Juanelo and Pirri."

The captain started in his seat.

"One of them is at sea and the other works in the wine cellars. They don't have anything to do with this."

"They were with the guerrillas in the Forties. It's possible that they're the brains behind the whole affair."

"There aren't any brains here! What I need are culprits. Do you understand?"

"A few that will serve as an example to the rest, you mean."

"Exactly."

"I'll look for them, sir."

"Oh, and put Pérez on night guard duty on the beach."

"Yes, sir."

The brigade commander was pleased with that order. Pérez was the black sheep of the barracks.

"I want to teach him to understand me when I ask him something."

"Yes, sir."

The brigade commander withdrew, leaving his superior deep in thought. Now the law could be applied. All that was needed was a plan.

They separated at the entrance to town.

"You fellows go to our district. You go to Pradillo and look for Pelao."

"Right."

Antonio continued toward Puerta de Jerez.

"Good afternoon."

It was Pistolero.

"Everything's going well," he said. "Juan and the others are working at Santo Domingo. I'm in charge of everything."

Antonio patted him affectionately on the back. They went on to Largo's place and took a table.

"All right, boys, the time's come to divide it up."

Each one of those who had worked kept thirty *pesetas* for himself.

"We have a right to eat too."

The men who had been working at Santo Domingo arrived. They counted all the money and, when it was divided up, each one received five *pesetas*.

"That's not enough to even begin with."

Chirlo had an idea.

"We'll spend it on bread, and share whatever other food we can buy."

His idea was accepted unanimously.

The wives of those who had worked in the fields were making their own calculations.

"What do you think? Should we pay the store or the loan shark first?"

"I'm going to begin by paying the Ocaso funeral parlor for the burial policy. You never know what might happen and I haven't given them a *céntimo* for months."

Salvadora thought that the best would be to spend the 160 *pesetas* that her men had earned on food and fill the bellies of her whole family. At least they would all eat well for a day.

Juan and Paco came home late. They were tired, dirty, and in a bad mood. Salvadora was upset because the fish was getting cold and the meat had almost dissolved from being boiled so long.

"You had to be late on the one day when you had something good to eat. How stupid I am, to kill myself for you. Drunkards, spending the whole day in that tavern. It'd be good riddance if it burned to the ground. Hand over the money!"

Paco gave her fifty *pesetas*.

"Is this all you have?"

Juan looked in his pocket for the ten *pesetas* he had intended to keep to buy tobacco.

"And the rest? Did you spend it all on wine?"

"I tell you there isn't any more."

Salvadora threw the money on the floor. She needed to have her hands free to pound first her husband and then her son on the chest. The stew was boiling away without anyone noticing.

"Sons of bitches! Bastards! You were supposed to bring one bill and twelve *duros* home. Where did you spend the bill?"

"All right, that's enough. Stop bothering me."

Juan went over to the pot while his parents were quarreling and took a good helping of broth and meat in the tin can that served as a plate. With the can in his hand he lay down under his blanket and calmly ate his supper facing the wall.

"My mother always told me it would be like this!

It's my own fault for having married a man from such a low family as yours."

"Be careful, or I may forget that you're the mother of my sons."

Paco was not a violent man, but he wouldn't tolerate anyone insulting his dead family.

"Here I am sacrificing myself and you two throw the money away in the street."

Her husband was tired and wanted to go to sleep. And in order to sleep he had to shut Salvadora up or she would spend the whole night complaining, driving him to the limit of his endurance, as she had done on other occasions. Therefore he grabbed her by the hair and pulled her around a bit, being careful not to really hurt her.

"Be quiet or . . ."

Salvadora understood that it was no night to serenade him. Filled with dignity, she went over to Luisillo.

"Wake up, son. We're not wanted here."

The child followed her, half asleep. Whenever his parents quarreled he always had to go out at night. He was the favorite son and neither parent wanted to leave him with the other when they walked out on each other. Juan got up to give his mother a kiss.

"Goodbye, son."

"I'll see you tomorrow."

"No! This time you can stay out for the rest of the week," Paco said. "I think it would be better."

Salvadora slammed the door. It was cold in the street and she felt abandoned. She picked up her child and wrapped him in her shawl.

Juan poked his head out.

"Poppa, should I go after her?"

"No, son, it's better for her to be away for a few days. It'll calm her down. Otherwise we'll have a battle every night."

"Who is it?"

"Your sister. My husband—the murderer—threw me out of the house."

Sinforosa opened the door of her hut. Those visits were not unusual, so she gave it no special importance.

"Come in. You can sleep in your regular place. Did you bring the boy?"

"What did you think I was going to do, leave him in the hands of those savages?"

"All right. He can sleep with you."

Sinforosa went back to bed. She had no children, so her sister's arrival didn't bother her in the least. They were very close, especially since their mother's death.

Pelao and Antonio waited for the moon to disappear.

"Damn it!"

Antonio looked at the almanac.

"It'll go down at 0.30 hours."

He read with great difficulty.

"That's impossible. There's no hour called 0.30."

Antonio scratched his head. Manolo was right.

"The main thing is that it'll go down."

"But suppose the zero is tomorrow morning? The sun will already have come out."

Antonio ripped the page for that day out of the almanac and put it in his pocket.

"The sun rises at 5:45. Since five o'clock can't be zero hours, it means that the moon will set in the middle of the night."

Pelao drank another glass. The bottle was empty.

"It'll be a dry wait."

When midnight came, Cayetano announced that he was closing up.

"Come on, stay open a little longer."

"I wish I knew what you two were doing at that table for so long. You look like you're planted there.

You've been drinking the same bottle for the last three hours."

"That's none of your business."

Cayetano got angry.

"I'm the boss around here."

"You or the Guards?"

"Right now, I am. I close up when I feel like it."

Antonio didn't want an argument. He drank the little that was left in his glass, the swallow he had left for the end.

"Let's go. Good night."

Cayetano closed the door. He didn't want customers around while he was cleaning up. He spent half an hour arranging bottles and "preparing" wines for the following day. His helper was sweeping between the tables.

"What's the date today?"

The boy looked at the calendar.

"The 25th."

The 25th? The 30th he had to make the second payment on the coffee machine. He opened the drawer to count what he'd put aside. There wasn't enough. He took a grimy notebook from the bottom of the drawer. It contained names of customers and sums of money. More than four thousand *duros* that he wouldn't collect as long as the strike lasted.

"Those bastards could have gone back to work by now."

The boy didn't answer.

"Hey, you. Doesn't your father work in the vineyards?"

"Yes."

"Then tell him to go to work. Say that I told you to tell him, because I need money."

The boy continued sweeping, seemingly deeply interested in the broom and the way the sawdust was moving across the floor, soaking up the liquid that had been spilled there.

"Did you hear me?"

"Yes, sir."

Antonio imitated the hoot of an owl. An identical sound came out of the jail.

"Calero."

"Here I am."

They spoke in very low voices.

"I've got tobacco and two letters for you."

"Wait."

A piece of twine was lowered down the side of the building. Antonio tied a small package to the end.

"Don't go away. I'm going to send something down."

"There's also something for you, Negro."

Negro was on the ground floor. He leaped up to the window and stuck his hand through the bars with some difficulty.

"Give it to me."

The hand disappeared into the cell again with the package. At the last minute Pelao had added two pieces of cheese to it. Calero's voice came from above. They were holding him incommunicado in the women's cell.

"There it goes."

Antonio saw a white piece of paper being lowered down the side of the building. It had been a good idea to wait until the moon had gone down.

"Tell the others to keep holding out."

"We will. How are things?"

"The same as usual. It's always the same in here."

"Beatings?"

"Not yet."

Pelao, who was hiding on the other side of the street, whistled. Antonio barely had time to turn his back on the jail and take a few steps away. The two Guards, with their cloaks over their shoulders, walked by only inches away.

"So long, and look out."

"So long. Good luck."

Private Núñez turned back.

"Where are you going?"

"I didn't like the looks of that fellow."

Private Pérez held his arm.

"Leave him alone. After all, what difference does it make to us?"

Núñez persisted.

"What's your name?"

Antonio was startled to hear the Castilian accent. He hadn't heard the sound of the Guard's boots on the cement of the sidewalk.

"Antonio Cabeza de Vaca, at your service."

"Your papers."

"I don't have them with me, sir."

"Let's go to your house, then."

"The fact is that they're not at home, either. I lost them."

"People don't lose their papers."

The Guard was speaking softly, as they always do when they really intend to hurt you.

"I requested the card two months ago. I just went to be fingerprinted."

"Show us the paper the corporal gave you."

"I've already told you I lost it."

"Come along with us."

Private Pérez didn't like to make arrests.

"Leave him alone. Our job isn't to patrol the streets. The brigade commander sent us to the beach."

"Do you think I want to get rheumatism? He'll be pleased that we made a catch like this. Tomorrow we'll be able to choose our own beat."

"This fellow isn't anybody. I know him very well. He's just a poor guy who's got nothing to do with anything."

Núñez smiled coldly.

"I hope you're not protecting criminals. We know that everyone is under suspicion now."

"I'm not helping anybody, but I know the trouble-makers. This man isn't one of them."

"He was in the plaza the other morning."

"It must have been someone else."

"No. You know I never forget a face."

"You weren't there."

"The owner of the place in the middle of the plaza told me about him."

"The damned stoolpigeon," Antonio muttered.

Núñez guffawed.

"Do you want more proof than that?"

Pérez lowered his head.

"Let's go."

The three figures walked toward the barracks. The Guards' patent-leather hats shone as they passed under a streetlight. Pelao disappeared down a dark alley where streetlights hadn't been installed yet.

Eight

Don Antonio Vázquez was giving a dinner. A dinner for very important people, including the governor. The guests discussed the situation as they were drinking their after-dinner coffee. It would not have been good-mannered to do so earlier.

"And that's what's happening."

The governor's expression demonstrated his concern. He had not heard about what was happening in San-lúcar. The mayor, in fact, had kept him from learning about it. A strike is always unfortunate. If it lasted, he could always have the local authorities removed, and the weakest link would be the first to go.

"A bad business."

Don Luis realized that he ought to say something.

"I didn't want to take severe measures because the press is always on the lookout for something like this, and everyone knows that in Madrid they don't like things like this to be publicized, especially in other countries."

The governor frowned.

"The least you could have done is warn me in time. We would have taken emergency measures by now."

"For example?"

"Administrative arrests. Without any fuss or trials, based on the law of public order."

Don Luis swallowed hard.

"I took the step of arresting two agitators. They've been in jail for several days."

"I don't like anyone to overstep my authority. I'm the only one who can make arrests or decide who should be arrested."

Don Luis lowered his head. The governor's tone softened.

"What are the agitators' names?"

"Juan Moyano, alias Calero, and Luis Ponce, known as Negro."

"The legal basis for the arrests?"

"The first because of his wartime record. The other one was caught making speeches in the fields."

"Good. Send me a note reminding me to take legal proceedings against both of them. Oh, and I'll send you several signed warrants with the names blank so that they can be used against whomever you think best.

Don Luis expressed his gratitude for this show of trust.

"In any case, there's no need for this to reach Madrid. That's why it's good to nip it in the bud as soon as possible. Be very careful with people from out of town. It has to be resolved before the end of the month, and among ourselves."

Calero lay down on the blanket that took the place of a mattress. His bones had ached since the day he was arrested. He ate the piece of cheese while he reread the letters. His family was well and the boys were holding out.

"They've got balls."

The captain jumped out of bed.

Corporal Pérez was standing at attention, trying not to look at the huge bulk lying by his commander's side. The captain's wife was the one responsible for the poor lanky-haired maid's having dared to take him into their bedroom.

On the day the strike had begun the captain's wife had ordered her maid:

"If you learn something or if someone comes, tell me no matter what time it is. Even if it's in the middle of the night."

Moreover, the corporal seemed very important to the maid.

"Do you realize what this means? The governor!"

"And they didn't even let you know."

The captain's wife was indignant. When there were problems, they didn't care what time it was when they called him, but when he could talk to someone important, no one remembered to call him.

"Hurry up, get dressed and run after them."

"They've probably already left."

"He was at Don Antonio's house five minutes ago, sir."

"Wait for me outside."

Corporal Pérez saluted the pajama-clad figure smartly.

The captain's wife took his dress uniform out of the wardrobe.

"No, woman! That's going too far."

His wife insisted. The captain put on the uniform, but he refused to buckle on the yellow leather strap.

"I know what I have to do. The black one is enough. Besides, nobody asked me to horn in on this meeting."

"Put it on! You're not going to let anyone undercut you."

The captain's wife wanted him to be promoted to colonel. In other times she had dreamed of seeing him put on a general's sash, but the years came more quickly than the promotions. It was impossible now for him to climb higher than major without powerful recommendations, if he should even make that.

The captain ran down the stairs, almost breaking his neck in the process. The maid was waiting in the patio with her nightgown showing under her muslin robe.

"Should I do anything?"

"Go to bed!"

The maid closed the door after him.

The governor was leaving his host's house. He turned his head when he heard the clatter of boots on the pavement. The three-cornered hats were the only thing visible in the night.

"Is anything happening?"

The post commander snapped to attention.

"All's quiet, sir."

"Then will you tell me why you're running so fast?"

The captain didn't know what to say. Corporal Pérez helped him out.

"We're inspecting the guard posts."

"And you're behind schedule, naturally."

The captain nodded. He seemed unable to think in his chief's presence.

"That is negligence unbecoming an officer of the Civil Guard, above all taking into account the present situation. I will see that it is noted on your service record."

The commander raised his hand to his cap and saluted, waiting without batting an eye for the official car to leave. Corporal Pérez followed his example.

The residents of Sanlúcar were left alone. Don Luis turned toward the commander.

"That was dumb."

"Come on, Don Luis, don't be silly."

It was different with Don Luis. The commander had no reason to be afraid of him. They saw each other every day. They needed each other and they had shared in business deals more than once.

"We're all going to have to pay for the consequences of this bit of idiocy."

"But . . ."

"Yes, I know. The posts haven't been inspected since the war either by day or by night, and no one has been the wiser. Not before you began to run around tonight, that is."

Without saying anything else, Don Luis got into Alvarez's car. Don Antonio put a friendly hand on the officer's shoulder.

"There's no need to be worried. I'll make sure it's forgotten."

The captain was grateful. Toño, as his friends called him, felt sure that the favor would make it possible for him to get several wagons of contraband wheat past the Guards. He wasn't mistaken.

What no one understood was the excess of zeal on the captain's part. Corporal Pérez didn't speak to even his most intimate friends about the matter. It was also to his interest that it be forgotten.

Dawn came. Calero heard the locks open. Núñez, Private Pérez, and Corporal Pérez entered his cell.

"Let's go."

Negro was with them, handcuffed. They also put handcuffs on Calero. It was the first time.

"What's this for?"

"So that you won't escape."

"When am I going to be taken to court?"

"You're still going to have to enjoy our company for a while. You're here on order of the governor."

Calero was experienced in these matters. He knew that once he was taken to court they couldn't beat him. He would have the same status as the other prisoners and they would have to leave him alone. But when the orders came from above it was different.

108·

He said nothing else, because it wasn't the right time to argue the point.

The brigade commander examined Antonio. About thirty years old, tall, dark—one more.

"They caught you in the act."

"They caught me because I didn't have my papers. All you have to do is look in the register. I applied for my card more than four months ago."

The officer shrugged his shoulders. He wasn't interested in that. There were three orders for administrative arrests on the table. One of them was blank.

"What's your name?"

"Antonio Cabeza de Vaca, at your service."

The officer filled in the space.

"Why were you at Puerta de Jerez three days ago talking to the workers?"

"I think I have a right to talk to my friends."

The officer changed his tone.

"Remember that I'm like a father. I wouldn't like to have to hit you, but your father didn't like to do it either when you were a child and played pranks. Who told you to go on strike?"

Antonio drew back.

"We're not on strike."

"A strike is when people don't go to work when they're called, as you're doing now."

Antonio scratched his head.

"You mean that workers are the only ones who can strike? Can't the bosses strike too?"

The officer looked at him with curiosity. What could the man be driving at?

"Look, it's what we're always saying. If not working is striking, then not hiring us must also be striking. So the bosses have been striking all winter and nobody said anything to them."

The officer laughed. His prisoner wasn't a bad fellow, just a little stupid.

"If you're not hired in the winter, that doesn't hurt the vineyards. On the other hand, if you don't go to work now the harvest may be lost. And that's bad for the national economy."

"Unemployment is bad for us, and we're part of the national economy too, aren't we?"

The officer didn't know how to answer.

"It's different . . . The foreign exchange that the sale of wine brings is for everyone, for the entire nation."

"Not for us."

"It's also for you."

"When we're hungry we're hungry and nobody gives us anything."

"But the highways get repaired."

Antonio gestured dubiously.

"Yes, the foreign exchange creates highways, dams, irrigation projects . . ."

"I don't have a car," said Antonio. "But if we want water, we have to go to the fountain for it. And the fountain was there when my grandfather was born."

This was getting complicated. The brigade commander took refuge in his authority.

"It's a fact that you're striking, and striking is a crime."

"No, sir. It's just that we don't feel like working in the spring. Let them call us in January and see if we go to work."

The door opened. Corporal Pérez stuck his head into the room.

"They're ready in the stable."

"Tell them to wait. I'll be there soon."

Corporal Pérez closed the door carefully.

José Armada called the maid. He wanted his breakfast. José Armada's wife wanted her breakfast, too. At ten o'clock a broker was arriving, so he had to be at the wine cellar a little before in order to "prepare" himself. That was why Don José was getting up so early.

Caridad entered the dining room with a pitcher in either hand. Milk and coffee. The bottle of brandy and two glasses were already on the table. Brandy is good for the stomach. The Armadas had had a glass of brandy with breakfast ever since they were married.

Don José was in a worse humor with every succeeding day. He didn't talk any longer. He croaked.

"Bring me the newspaper."

"Bring me the toast."

He felt like talking that morning. And his wife was his best audience.

"Did you know they're still on strike?"

She nodded, without ceasing to spread the colored lard on her bread. When they had guests they ate only butter, because lard reminded them of the old times in the store, when they lived among sacks of saffron and ledgers of money they had loaned. An agreeable and distant memory that they only indulged in privately.

"This can't go on."

His wife agreed.

"Say something," he insisted.

"You should all do whatever has to be done."

"Whatever has to be done! Whatever has to be done! And what is it that has to be done?"

"I don't know."

"You could come up with an idea, at least."

"Put them all in concentration camps, force them to work."

"That could be done during the war. It's not allowed now."

"Well, then, convince them."

"Very simple. I suppose people are in the mood to

listen! You women are all the same—idiots!"

Señora Armada shrugged her shoulders. Why did he persist in asking her opinion on the matter if he knew perfectly well that she didn't understand anything about men's affairs?

Don José bit into the little loaf, getting lard all over his mustache.

"Let's go!"

"Where?"

They crossed a large patio. There were clothes hanging in the windows. Several of the Guards' children were playing war between the whitewashed columns. A woman was washing clothes in a tub.

The brigade commander opened a large door. Half a dozen horses were eating in the wooden trough. The straw was dirty with manure and the stable smelled of urine and animals.

Corporal Pérez was standing at the rear of the stable with two other Guards. Antonio couldn't see Calero and Negro until they placed him next to them against the wall, as they do when prisoners are going to be shot.

The brigade commander asked for a chair and sat down facing them.

"You are all here by order of the governor. You know what that means."

Neither Negro nor Antonio had the vaguest idea of what it meant. The officer realized by their reactions that they didn't understand. The governor had arrested them, and that had something to do with government, they reasoned. Therefore it followed that it was an arrest like any other, as when someone is caught stealing a sack of straw for a mattress.

The officer continued his speech.

"This means that you're not going to court. That is, that you won't be released until the governor himself, who gave the order for your arrest, releases you."

He paused. It was important to see what effect this had on the prisoners. They showed not the slightest reaction however.

"In a word, you're going to be here for quite a while if you don't behave properly, and that means cooperating with the police by answering all questions truthfully."

This produced the same result as his previous remarks.

"Well, I don't know if you realize that you can only stay in the jail here in Sanlúcar for one month. After that you go to Cádiz. Have you ever been there? And from Cádiz to the Puerto. How many ever return from the Puerto, right?"

Calero knew that route. He had traveled it when he was arrested a year after the war ended. ("You ought to be shot!") He was just a boy then, less than twenty years old. He had spent the next fifteen years in jail without ever knowing why. Now he felt chills and tremors in his legs. He made an effort to control himself because he didn't want the others to notice.

Cádiz: a cell below sea level with light entering through a little window which also let water in during storms. The walls were damp and covered with mold. No one could stand it in the Cádiz prison for more than six months. He was there a year. The only reminder of that period he had was a pain in his side whenever the weather changed. He had been young and strong, and that was why he didn't end up spitting blood like the others. And the Puerto? It was by the salt beds, in an old convent building. It was bad, but it was like a divine blessing to be transferred there from Cádiz.

The others' only thought was that they wouldn't be able to see their families so far away. It was easy in Sanlúcar. All they had to do was pull themselves up to the windows. Somebody was always passing by. Somebody who would signal to them and then they wouldn't feel lonely.

The officer got up. It was better to be standing during interrogations. The height gives one a certain superiority. With his head low, like a bull about to charge, he pondered which method to use on the animals before him.

The hobnailed boots were muffled by the manure. Private Pérez came in carrying two bull whips and a rusty chain that clanked noisily. The men listened to the iron links clanking together. Corporal Pérez picked up a brush for currying horses that was lying on a shelf.

The officer turned suddenly to Negro.

"Who told you to go on strike?"

"No one, commander."

The officer hit him.

"Do you think we're fools?"

He rested his hand gently on Antonio's shoulder.

"Son, you have no reason to be involved in this mess. You're working, you have a family, and you've never been in this barracks before. Tell me who organized the strike and you can go home peacefully."

Antonio bit his lips. It humiliated him that they thought he might be a stoolpigeon.

"If I was working, why did you pick me up?"

"Because you didn't have your papers."

"All right, then this can be cleared up quickly. If you look in the register you'll find my request. In any case, if you want to ask me something, ask me about my papers. I don't know anything about anything else."

Calero had had his doubts about the boy. He was new to these things. But now he was sure. Antonio wouldn't talk.

The officer was furious because he couldn't tell Antonio that they had never entered his name in the reg-

ister, because no one had ever bothered to register the
names that the Jerez police gave them after issuing
identification cards. Nor could he admit that they
wouldn't have felt like doing it even if they were supposed to and that the whole matter of the papers was
just a pretext.

"You're here by order of the governor. That's different."

"The governor must have some reason for arresting
me. I don't what it is. You tell me."

"Because he damn well pleases, do you understand?"

Corporal Pérez's answer wasn't the right one but it
seemed like a good one to the brigade commander for
the simple reason that there was none other to be given.

"Then just because a gentleman in Cádiz whom I
don't even know feels like it, I have to rot in jail. Is
that the law?"

Corporal Pérez threw him to the floor. Antonio lay
there on the dirty straw.

"Leave him to me!"

The officer agreed and sat down in his chair to watch
the spectacle. He preferred others to beat the prisoners
so that he could watch and become excited by their
writhings. Corporal Pérez knew this, but the others
couldn't understand the gleam that appeared in the officer's eyes with the very first blow, nor why he gradually became paler. Many times the brigade commander
asked himself what his life would have been like if he
hadn't entered the Civil Guard. A lowly murderer,
probably, appearing in the newspapers, like those he
occasionally arrested.

Private Núñez hung the chain from a hook in the
center of a beam. It could hold the weight of a man
hanging from it. They handcuffed Antonio, and Núñez
and the corporal between them lifted him into the air.
He was left hanging in the center of the stable, a short

distance from the rears of the horses. Calero knew that
that was called "the swing."

"Leave the boy alone," he said. "I'm used to it."

He was standing near Antonio with his hands held
together by the handcuffs and his feet apart. Corporal
Pérez forced him back to his place with a blow from his
whip.

Then he turned to the boy.

"We know that you've been mixed up in the trouble.
That you've beaten people on the roads and other
things. If you tell the names of those who were with
you, we'll let you go."

Antonio didn't answer. The corporal hit him at the
waist. His body swung to one side.

"Tell us what these two had to do with the strike.
They've already been caught and nothing worse can
happen to them."

"I don't know. They're not my friends. I just know
them by sight."

"In that case, why were you just outside the prison
at dawn? Why were you talking to them?"

"I wasn't talking to them."

"We heard you."

"Because I damn well felt like it . . . like the governor."

Núñez hit him and then Pérez hit him. Antonio
swung from one side of the stable to the other, hanging
from the "swing." His wrists stopped hurting. He
couldn't see. He felt nausea, but no pain. Not even pain.

Private Pérez asked for permission to leave. His
stomach was upset and he didn't want to throw up in
front of his commander. The officer denied his request.

"You've got to get used to it, kid."

"With all due respect, I must tell you that you're
acting like savages."

The brigade commander looked at him coldly.

"I suppose you're not anxious to take his place."

Private Pérez hid among the horses. He opened his mouth and vomited bile.

"Someone has to talk to Peláez."

"What for? He's been working his fields for two days. The harm has already been done."

"He's a Jew. He studied the figures and saw that it was to his advantage. He never will have a conscience nor a sense of duty such as we have. We shouldn't let him step all over us."

"Just as there's a law that regulates the minimum wage, there must be one to regulate the maximum."

Don Mariano was not very sure about it.

"I don't know, but I don't think there is one."

"What are you waiting for? It's your obligation to find out for sure. You have to know the law before you can apply it."

"I'm neither a lawyer nor a judge."

"But you have control over labor matters."

Don Mariano called the page. He wrote something barely legible on a paper napkin.

"Take this to the labor union. Give it to my secretary and wait for an answer. And have her type it out. It's very important."

Corporal Pérez had a flask of vinegar brought to the stable. The women of the barracks had dissolved a kilogram of coarse salt in the liquid. They were used to doing this.

"This is the best thing there is for sores."

Calero, Negro, and Antonio were lying naked on the floor. After the "swing" they had been beaten on their joints and on those other parts of the body that policemen know well. Corporal Pérez sprinkled the three bodies with the mixture.

"Turn them over."

Núñez obeyed.

Deep groans filled the stable. Private Pérez listened from his corner. His rifle was close at hand. For a moment he thought that it would be better to kill them. Right then and there, so that they wouldn't suffer any more, so that they wouldn't make them suffer any more, and—why not?—he would also fire on the brigade commander and the corporal. But he didn't do it. Lack of energy? Fear of the consequences? Afterward he recalled that he had put out his hand to pick up the weapon and something had stopped him. Something he couldn't identify.

Beli was working. She was preparing statistics, numbers that no one would ever read. The carefully written pages were stored in the archives. Her chief didn't even bother to look at them when he signed them. Beli knew it and still did her work conscientiously, never losing hope that some day these papers would be of some use. They described the rate of unemployment, families lacking necessary calories, houses deteriorating . . . figures that only she knew.

Don Mariano always arrived at two o'clock. "Is there anything new?" At three o'clock he would leave, "since there's nothing new." At night he would spend another hour in the office. His friends would come to see him. "There's a worker outside who says that . . ." "I don't have time. Tell him to come back tomorrow." "Don X is here." "Tell him to come in."

The page ran in.

"This is from Don Mariano. I have to wait for the answer. It has to be typewritten."

Beli read the note. No, there were no laws that limited the maximum salary. To satisfy her conscience she examined several volumes of labor legislation. Then she drew up a complete report. She wrote of rights and of strikes. For once she was sure that what she wrote would be read. She especially advised her chief to be cautious in this matter.

Beli was with them, with the agricultural workers. It was her chance to help them and she had every intention of not letting the opportunity go by.

Don Mariano read the report carefully. His secretary belonged to that category of human beings whom he admired without understanding them. Her advice was good and her ideas were right. He was obviously paid to defend the workers, whether he liked the role or not. The first wrong step could cost him his job, and without the job there would be no more food on the table or tailor-made suits.

He fanned himself with the papers before speaking. He had to think about what he was going to say, because the landowners were very influential.

"No, there is no provision in the law that can be applied against Peláez."

Don César threw his cigar butt into the street without bothering to see if anyone was in the way.

"It's clear. We can't fire them without severance pay. They, on the other hand, can stop working when it's to their advantage. They leave us in the lurch when we need them most, after living at our expense a while! And we'd better not forget to pay for their insurance, the widows' and orphans' fund, and vacations or we get the book thrown at us . . ."

"If it weren't for our class, Franco wouldn't be in power today. The bastard, the traitor!"

"Careful, someone might hear us," Don Mariano interrupted. "If a comment like that were heard by people higher up, we'd never be able to convince them that we're right."

This calmed Don León down. He let off his remaining steam by damning the people.

Nine The small landowners gave in.

"The others, with their wine cellars, can hold out, but if we lose the harvest we'll go under."

Small crews of men left Puerta de Jerez that morning. Three hundred more began to earn wages. "There'll be enough for everybody today," Pelao commented.

Those who stayed behind made bets as to which of the big landowners would be the next to give in. They mentioned important names: Vázquez, Alvarez, Blázquez, Argueso, Domec of Jerez, Mérito, González, and also Terry y Caballero of Puerto de Santa María. They figured out how much those firms were losing and how much they had left. And they judged the men.

"Don Carlos González isn't a bad man. The trouble is that the others won't leave him alone."

"Nor Don Manuel."

"But Don Manuel isn't in the wine business any longer."

"The Domecs could afford to pay, with the money they have."

"Them? They wouldn't even give you the time of day. They'll give you charity if you ask for it, but don't even mention wages."

"And the ones around here?"

"They should all kick off."

Rumors arrived to the effect that they weren't working in Chiclana either. It was said that the fields of Huelva were empty and that Moriles and Montilla would join the strike.

"This year they won't even have enough wine for mass."

They were no longer alone. There was strength in unity, the older men said, and the younger ones dreamed of victory. More salaries and then . . . land for everyone.

"I don't want them to give me anything, but it doesn't seem right to me that they should get four thousand *duros* per *aranzada* when they don't even give us half a banknote. It would be better for us all to cultivate the land. They'd also have their share, because no one wants them to starve to death."

They also talked about the men who were in jail.

"A fellow they call El Tato has been in the Jerez jail for three days."

"My cousin, the one in Conil, was called to the barracks. My aunt wrote me about it."

"You have to be brave in war, don't you?"

The young men wanted to be heroes. The wage question was secondary. Now their sights were set higher.

"And let the chips fall where they may."

The governor had closed his office to visitors. He didn't want to listen to anyone's complaints nor waste time. If the present situation continued there was no way to keep Madrid from hearing about it. One group of exporters' representatives had presented him with some very interesting figures. They showed the amount of foreign exchange the state would lose if the grapes were not picked.

The workers, on the other hand, had written him in the language of the people, without so many numbers or words, warning him that they were prepared to "go all the way." The letters had come from Cádiz.

And the denunciations were piling up. The land-owners sent in names and addresses without rhyme or reason. "His father was a Red," or "he fought with the Reds," were the most common accusations. He would have acted on them if there had been fewer of them, but it was impossible in such quantity. A hundred or two hundred arrests could be made, but not five thousand.

All of this had caused the governor to cancel visits, hiding his head like an ostrich.

His secretary knocked timidly at his door.

"Who is it?"

"A letter from Madrid, Excellency."

"Come in."

The secretary left an open envelope on his desk.

"His Excellency Don . . . , Civil Governor of the Province of Cádiz." It came from the Ministry. It was not an official document, just a private letter from the secretary, a good friend of his. The governor had gotten his post thanks to influence in high places, and he had no intention of losing it.

"My dear friend: News of the labor situation in your area has reached us here. I haven't been able to find out who could have been so badly disposed toward you as to have made the trip for the purpose of putting you on the spot, although we suspect who the man is.

"The minister is very upset. He hopes that you will be able to resolve the situation yourself, because he would not like to take it to the Council of Ministers. Apparently this person is prepared to take the matter to the Generalissimo himself. I don't have to tell you that the foreign press would find the problem of great interest.

"You know that under the present circumstances it is impossible to contemplate a violent repression. In view of this, you should try to settle the matter as quietly as possible. Remember that raising the wages in one area of Spain would be an international propaganda coup that would not do too much harm to our economy.

"Best regards . . ."

The governor called in his secretary.

"I suppose you read this letter."

The secretary was an old hand when it came to the vicissitudes of office politics. He knew that his zeal in this case would be regarded as an indiscretion.

"No, Excellency, I just looked at the beginning and realized it was a private matter."

The governor was thinking that his friend should have written him at his home address. Then he remembered that he had never sent him the address after moving into the new building.

"That's all right. In any case, not a word."

"I won't say a thing, Your Excellency."

The governor pondered the best way to solve the matter. He was expecting a large delegation of landowners to arrive on the following day, and he was no longer able to support them. It was unpleasant to have to turn them down, though, because money is influence and he might need them at some future point in his career.

"Tell the gentlemen we're expecting tomorrow that I won't be able to see them. And call the local delegates of the striking towns. Tell them to come with one or two spokesmen from the social section of the unions."

"When should they come?"

"At the same time we were expecting the others."

"I don't know if Your Excellency realizes that there isn't even time to write the letters summoning them to the meeting."

"If there isn't time, then invent it. That's an order."

The governor's military spirit brooked no obstacles.

"Yes, Excellency."

The secretary closed the door softly. When he reached his desk he pressed a button.

His secretary entered timidly.

"By order of the governor . . ."

"Should I tell the clerks to stop what they're doing? If not . . ."

"Of course!"

The endemic inactivity of the governor's office disappeared. Typewriters began operating at top speed. It was an urgent matter.

The letter arrived at three o'clock. The word "Urgent" stamped in red letters just under the governor's letterhead on the envelope caused the old attendant, the only person in City Hall, to run as fast as he could. Don Luis wasn't at home or in the club. Someone told him that he had seen Don Luis leave for Bajo Guía with some other gentlemen.

The attendant considered taking a taxi, but he didn't earn enough and the mayor wouldn't want to pay for it either out of his own pocket or out of his official expense fund, in spite of the urgency of the matter. He trotted along the highway for a mile or so in the May sunshine, and then took a shortcut along the beach. His dirty grey uniform with its gold chevrons made a strange contrast with the river.

The last five hundred yards were the hardest.

"And what if on top of all this he isn't there?"

Don Gaspar Núñez was leaning on the arm of Don Luis. Don Gaspar was an authority. Even Alvarez and Don César respected him, although Don César a little less than Alvarez. They were the same age, but Don César carried his years better. With his silver-headed bamboo cane under his arm, Don César, conscious of his physical appearance, set the pace for the rest.

Don Gaspar was no longer able to go down to Divina Pastora Street to pick out the prettiest girl. On the other hand, he . . . Don César contemplated the group with his malicious little eyes and listened. He was biding his time until he spoke.

The men were discussing the weather and women and comparing the past to the present. Don Gaspar recalled the year that he went to Madrid. Don Luis reminisced about the day he was made captain, thus taking a spectacular leap in rank.

"I was just a brigade commander at the time. We were defending a hill when the captain, who had a stomach ache, put me in command of the battery . . ."

Don Luis always talked about the war. Before 1936 he was a sales clerk in a hardware store. Thanks to the war he had acquired what is commonly known as "a future."

The others paid little attention to his story. Why bother? They knew the mayor's reminiscences by heart. Don Gaspar tried not to trip as he walked, carefully avoiding the stones in his path. The sun and the voices provided an uninteresting background.

Don León walked half facing the speaker with his hands behind his back, trying to adopt a respectful attitude. He always affected profound respect toward old men. He knew how to learn things beneficial to himself from those mummies, forgetting the rest.

Juan Llamas was in the rear of the store. There were only a few customers, including three tables occupied by strangers.

"The mayor is coming," a waiter warned him.

Juan buttoned his jacket. He looked in the mirror, trying to pull himself up taller than his five foot four. Seen from the front his hunchback couldn't be noticed.

Juan Llamas looked for a black tie. He always wore a
tie with his blue shirt when Don Luis came in.

There were many in his wardrobe. Half of them
should have been thrown away, but his wife insisted on
keeping them as "souvenirs." He took the first one he
put his hand on. As he tied it he discovered a greyish
stain, probably deposited there during his last spree.
Lobster sauce. There was no time to change it, so he
tried to hide it with a broad knot.

The notables had picked a table in the center of the
room. They couldn't see the beach and could hardly see
the sea from there, but it was the table most easily seen
from the street.

"Good day, gentlemen."

Juan greeted each of his guests with a little bow. His
position as owner of a restaurant living off the public
had greatly developed his own natural gifts for servil-
ity. Two-faced, cringing, and hypocritical, he treated
each customer as the customer expected to be treated,
taking special care to observe class differences. The
mayor, for example, was an outsider, a good customer
but not a steady one. Don Gaspar and the others were
more important, because they were the ones who, in
the final analysis, chose the mayor.

"What do you have?"

Juan recited the menu. Fish soup, flounder, crayfish
. . . the same as usual.

"Some magnificent shrimp have arrived. I kept them
for myself."

The shrimp were brought to the table with several
dozen crayfish. The house gave them three small bottles
of wine. Three different brands. Everybody was pleased.

"Bring me a large bottle of *solera*."

The waiter trotted toward the storeroom. They had
to keep Don César happy.

Juan served the table personally, a distinction that
the worthies appreciated. His grotesque face looked as

though it had split in two. It was his way of smiling.

Don Luis was peeling an enormous crayfish.

"It'll all be over soon. With what the governor gave me this afternoon, I'm going to order fifty arrests."

The wine producers approved.

"The only way to make a burro move is with a stick," said Don Gaspar.

They unanimously approved what they regarded as an eminently intelligent observation.

"They're rabble. They don't understand any other language."

A group of men who unloaded the fishing boats were leaning on the railing that separated the outdoor terrace —a little island of luxury jutting out into the sand— from the rest of the world. They didn't have anything else to do until the boats came in, and it comforted them to see others eat. There were some children among them sucking their snot—half naked, brown beach children, with faces like old men and shrunken bodies.

They bothered Don Luis. He called the waiter.

"Yes, Don Luis?"

"Isn't there any way to make that trash move on?"

"It's a little difficult. They always stand there looking at the dishes until they begin to auction the fish."

"Well, try."

The waiter called his boss. Juan turned toward the men.

"Haven't you ever seen anybody eat before?"

Gamba had had one glass too many that morning and he had a lot to get off his chest.

"What we don't see is food in our homes. We'd forgotten how much a man can swallow."

The mayor had them call the police. Ten minutes later Nabito arrived, perspiring in his blue uniform. He stood at attention as smartly as he knew how in front of his chief.

"Remove all of them!"

Nabito politely tried to convince the men to move on.

"Go on, boys, you're bothering them."

Nobody budged. The mayor frowned. Nabito didn't want to lose his job because he was useless for farm labor.

"Please, for my children's sake."

"The street belongs to everyone, doesn't it?"

They called the Civil Guards who were on duty. With their three-cornered hats and green uniforms their mere presence was sufficient to cause a general exit.

Nabito approached the table.

"Don Luis, your orders have been carried out."

The mayor smiled.

"With some difficulty, I see."

Nabito felt uncomfortable without knowing why, since he hadn't understood his chief.

"Find out the name of the one who talked back to me and go to the station. Get all the information you can about him and bring it to me this afternoon."

Nabito stood at attention.

"I don't think that we should allow them to be disrespectful to us."

Don César agreed. When you give them an inch, they take a mile. That's how the war began.

"It's like a bullfight. You have to defend your terrain."

Nabito went to Bigotes' bar. Cabezas was behind the counter. He was in luck. Cabezas knew everything and everyone.

"Who was the fellow who talked back to the mayor?"

"Gamba."

"What's his real name?"

"That I don't know. He lives on Rubiño Street. They'll give you his name there."

Nabito went to the workers' neighborhood, reflecting

that work in the fields was more comfortable. There one didn't make enemies or live isolated from people. For the first time he felt nostalgic about the risky days when he carried contraband through the swamps with his father. Tobacco, chickpeas—anything was good to take to the city. They traveled on moonless nights. During the day they hid their packs in the bog and spent their time catching birds. Pigeons and ducks fell into their nets or their hands. They had to walk carefully, without making any noise. When the bird wasn't watching they leaped. One more in the sack!

Afterward they lit a fire in the first good spot they found. They always had a little salt and olive oil, and with that the roast was complete. The worst was the water. They had to get it at the homes of friendly Guards, because they couldn't trust them all. There were days when they only had half a liter for the two of them. Their tongues swelled up, their mouths felt rough and rasping, and they couldn't eat.

Without realizing it he had reached Rubiño Street.

Juan Llamas was writing down the number of servings that were being taken out of the kitchen. The other tables were full now. A quiet day had turned into a busy one.

The watchman poked his head into the rear of the store.

"We're going to begin the auction."

"How many came in?"

"Half a dozen."

"I can't go now. I have a lot of work."

"Tell me what you want and I'll put it aside for you. There aren't many crayfish."

"Wait for me."

"All right."

The watchman drank one glass of wine and then another. The outfitter and the sailors were getting impatient out on the beach. The fish were on the sand and other boats were arriving, lowering the price they would get for their catch.

Juan went over to the mayor's table.

"If you don't want anything else, I'll go to the beach." Don León answered for them all.

"Thank you, you can go."

The watchman gave the order to begin. Juan pointed to two boxes of crayfish. The auctioneer began the sale.

"Sixty, fifty-nine . . ."

He spoke so fast that no one could understand him. Juan raised his arm.

"Fifty—going once, twice, three times . . ."

The boxes were carried up to the bar. Alfredo had also tried to buy some. He made his bid just before Juan did, when the price was around seventy-five *duros*. He was sure that he had shouted loudly enough, but they pretended they didn't hear him. He needed that box because he was expecting customers and had to serve them. It wasn't easy to make money with a bar when City Hall helped his competition financially. Alfredo owed money on several loans and he was having a hard time of it.

"Sell me two dozen. A family ordered them from me and I can't disappoint them."

"Buy from another boat."

"No others have come in."

"You should have bid on these."

"I did and you know it."

The dwarf shrugged his shoulders.

"That's your problem. I need them more in my place than you do in yours."

Alfredo walked away. He knew that the auction was rigged and he also knew that it was useless for him to protest. The beach didn't belong to everyone. Llamas,

Carrasco, and Manuel the watchman were the owners.

The attendant reached the dock with his shoes under his arm. He hid behind the cement posts to put them on again. Then he took the long way around so that he would arrive by the highway. He stopped at the fruit stand beside the Carmen chapel and asked if they had seen his boss.

"I think he's at Llamas' place."

The woman answered without looking at him. The attendant walked on under the arcades, taking advantage of the shade.

The mayor was drinking coffee. There were several empty bottles on the table. A waiter was removing the remains of the lunch.

The attendant took off his cap and stood behind Don Luis with an absentminded look on his face. It was no time to interrupt the mayor. He was telling a very interesting story.

". . . when her husband came in, Petra didn't know what to do, but Celedonio thought fast. He jumped through the window with his pants under his arm."

Don César laughed maliciously.

"Another cuckold."

"An outsider."

"Petra always liked men."

"You're telling me."

"Well, whenever I wanted something . . ."

Don César was angry.

"Then you've made me a cuckold too, because I've known her for more than ten years."

"You too?"

Don Luis and Don César always talked about women. The attendant cleared his throat. Don Luis turned around, angry because someone had overheard a story which was so incompatible with his official position.

"What is it?"

"An urgent letter from the governor, sir."

"Excuse me," Don Luis said to the others. He opened the envelope and his face showed surprise and indignation.

"Call Don Casimiro Ruiz immediately. Tell him to come to my office within half an hour."

"Where should I call him from, sir?"

"From any telephone. Or look for him. But get out of here."

The attendant didn't wait for him to repeat the order. Don Luis asked for the bill.

"Send it to me at City Hall."

His meals were always put under "official expenses."

"What's the matter?" asked Don Gaspar, uneasily.

"Look."

The three vintners read the order. It was brief and unequivocal, without the slightest sign of cordiality or friendliness.

"This is madness."

"Madness or not, it has to be obeyed," asserted Don Luis, who had already stood up.

"We're going with you."

Don Luis hesitated. It wasn't a good idea.

"I'll go alone."

"In that case, take my car."

Don Luis ordered the driver to take him to City Hall as fast as possible.

He had to wait in his office for a quarter of an hour before the attendant announced the captain's arrival.

"Tell him to come in."

The captain installed himself comfortably in an armchair and lit a cigar.

"Should we make some more arrests?"

The mayor handed him the order he had just received.

"But . . ."

"No buts about it! It has to be done immediately."

"But we 'interrogated' them."

"Both of them?"

"All three. Another one was brought in last night."

"It makes no difference. You have to let them go."

"But they're not in very good shape."

Don Luis nodded. He knew that already. It was only to be expected.

"The main thing is not to let them go to a doctor."

"Or rather, for no doctor to give them a certificate."

Don Luis picked up the telephone.

"Connect me with Dr. Teruel immediately."

Dr. Teruel was an important man. He had just entered the School of Medicine when the war broke out. He became a Falangist and left for the front. However, it was in the rear guard that he won the stripes that brought him a medical degree as soon as the shooting had stopped, after he had completed—with a minimum expenditure of effort—one of the crash courses for veterans. It was a program initiated to cover the many vacancies left in the profession by the death or exile of the Red intellectuals. He completed his internship in the Sanlúcar hospital, and then got his degree and became director of the hospital. He was made a councilman during the last elections at the express desire of Don Luis, who placed absolute trust in him.

He had never had a private practice, because his professional failings were too well known. Fortunately for him his connections brought him a larger income than other well-known doctors received from their patients.

He was absorbed in an exciting detective story when the telephone rang.

"Hello."

"Is that you, Bartolo?"

"Yes. Who's speaking?"

"This is the mayor."

"Hello, Luis. What can I do for you?"

"It's a rather delicate matter. It would be better for you to come to my office."

"When?"
"Right now."

Juan Llamas sat down at the table. His work was finished and he could rest for several hours. Hidden behind his glasses, he seemed even smaller alongside his fat, flamboyant wife, Francisca. They were married during the black market years when the hunchback was beginning to acquire the golden touch. Juan was above suspicion because he knew too much. His little body was everywhere. He put his malice at the service of the power structure, while his sadism caused him to dirty his own hands more than once. Sometimes it was simply for the pleasure of killing, while other times he did it to ingratiate himself with his peers and get rid of "charlatans." When the "grand fiesta" was over and he went back to civilian life, he felt very nostalgic about the days when he had had his pistol in his hand. But in time he became reconciled to peace.

Francisca knew of his past when she agreed to marry him, since her father had been one of the victims of "Itchy Finger," as Juan's friends called him. He was the one who fired the *coup de grace,* who executed the sentences passed by mysterious courts in the castle cells, who denounced people . . . It wasn't until after 1940 that he stopped coming home at night with red stains on his shirt—the blue shirt of the Falange—and a roll of banknotes in his pocket.

Francisca raised her head from her plate. It was only then that she noticed the stain on his tie.

"What do you have on your tie?"
"I don't know. I put on the first one I could find when Don Luis came and I didn't see the spot until after I'd tied it."
"It looks like blood."
"Blood?"
Juan took off his tie to look at it. It was one of the

first ones he had bought. Or perhaps it was the one they gave him when José Antonio died.

He got up from the table without excusing himself. He went to his room and carefully hung the tie up in his wardrobe.

Whose blood could it be? The lame man's? Paco Veleta's? The blood of that child of fourteen or of the sixty-year-old man? His face disappeared in the mirror and instead he saw the empty eyes of the dead and the eyes of those who were about to die. He saw how that stranger—a young lawyer—whom he had tortured to death had writhed on the floor. He died without saying a word, without speaking. And he had to do it! What was it for? Oh, yes, it had to do with the truck. Why had he kept him from leaving the barracks? Hadn't he read the order from his superior officer? When all was said and done, what difference did it make to him whether the regiment ate or not? Was it Don Pedro Mata or General Calderón who had given the order? The young man was still in the mirror. "You idiot, no one wanted to kill you." The face of an old man appeared in his place. An old man with a child's voice who said, "Kill me if you want to, but leave my mother alone." The old man was dead and the child was too. One was superimposed on the other, blurring the outlines of their features. A child with white hair and an old man with big eyes. A stream of blood came out from between the woman's legs. The barrel of his pistol was covered with blood. He hadn't killed her. The woman lived for three days. Why did she insist on dying? The barrel wasn't so long. Juan had pulled the trigger just as he had so many times before. The woman opened her eyes. "Murderer!"

"I'm not a murderer! I'm not a murderer!"

Francisca and Cabezas managed to get him into bed, holding his arms and legs down.

"He fights like a condemned man."

Cabezas smiled.

"He *is* a condemned man."

Francisca agreed. Juan opened his eyes and looked at them.

"What are you doing here, sticking your noses into my business?"

Cabezas disappeared. Juan got up and threw a chair at his wife, who managed to nimbly sidestep it.

"You were shouting. We came up to see what was the matter with you."

"What did I say?"

"I don't know. We couldn't understand what you were saying."

Juan calmed down.

"Well, I'm sorry. Go down to the store. I'll be there right away."

That was his first attack.

"You don't have to worry as far as the hospital is concerned."

"There are doctors who don't belong to the hospital."

"I'll take care of the ones who work for social security."

The captain was worried. The whole business, which had seemed so clear, was beginning to look ugly.

"There are still the private doctors."

They went over the list. López, Don Braulio, Bunell . . .

"Don Braulio has applied for a job working with the social security office in Jerez. Bunell needs me for a recommendation. There's just López left."

"What can we do?"

"He's a very strange man . . . very troublesome."

"Wasn't he working for social security too?"

"He quit."

"Because he wanted to or because they fired him?"

"Because he wanted to, slamming the door behind

him! He's the type who says that it's a doctor's job to cure people and who persists in respecting the Hippocratic Oath."

"Casimiro, can't you do anything?"

The captain shifted uneasily in his chair.

"You don't have to worry about Antonio and Negro. If it weren't for Calero, nothing would happen. But Calero knows the law . . ."

"That means that only one of the three may go to the doctor."

"No, he's too afraid. There's his past. He'll never live that down. But he may advise the others to. And it's a sure thing that they'll do what he says."

Teruel had a brainstorm.

"The only way to issue a certificate is at the hospital. If it can't be done there—and it won't be—then the doctor has to have official stamped paper, since it can't be written on just any paper. It's possible that López has two or three sheets of official paper, but no more, since his patients usually bring what they need with them. Without that paper, the only thing he can do is have his statement notarized."

Don Luis smiled.

"Don't worry. The notaries are my friends. They won't sign anything I don't want them to even if Franco himself asks them to do it."

"In that case, all we have to do is make sure López doesn't have any official paper."

Teruel called Ocaso, Inc., which held the semifeudal privilege of selling official paper in that town, a distinction bestowed on it by the medical association.

"Don't sell a single medical certificate until I tell you to."

"Yes, sir."

Ten "Good afternoon, doctor."

The man had come carrying his child in his arms.

"Sit down."

The boy let his head fall on his father's shoulder.

"What's the matter with him?"

"We don't know. He's stopped eating and he gets attacks that leave him in very bad shape. He gets all red in the face."

"Are you covered by insurance?"

The man nodded.

"Why don't you go to your doctor? It would be cheaper."

"I have gone, but he doesn't know what's the matter with him. He gives me all kinds of medicine, and the boy just gets worse."

Don Vicente examined the child.

"I think he's nervous. Didn't you get an analysis?"

"No, sir. They didn't send me . . ."

The telephone rang. López motioned to the man to be quiet.

"Hello?"

"Good afternoon, colleague."

Teruel's voice sounded the same as ever, hoarse and happy. Teruel had no worries. Other people's worries didn't bother him and his own were quickly resolved.

"I have a small problem. It's very silly, really. I've

run out of official paper and the mayor asked me to
send him ten medical certificates for his policemen immediately."

"The fact is that I only have four sheets, and that's
just by chance."

"I'll just have to make them do. Can you send them
to me?"

"It would be better for you to come for them. You
know I don't have anyone here."

"I'll send a boy with my card."

"All right."

"Good, captain, now all we have to do is release the
prisoners."

The post commander sighed. Such a good job done
for nothing, and all because of the scruples of the officials in Cádiz.

"We'll set them free now."

Teruel put the certificates away.

"I assume that neither Juan Carlos nor Alonso will
let me down . . ."

"They've been told. Sanlúcar can get along without
a notary for a day."

The captain called the barracks.

"If I go I'll have to make a lot of explanations. It's
not good for discipline."

Corporal Pérez answered the telephone.

"But . . ."

"Personally and immediately! They can't remain in
prison any longer."

The corporal would have preferred to have been able
to give that mission to someone—anyone—else.

The authorities left for the Café Martínez.

Damián Cura was drinking his beer as he did every
afternoon. Don Damián never drank wine because the

smell of it made him sick. From the day his father had bought "El Puntal" from the princess he hadn't left the wine cellar. He was stationed among the casks from morning till night, on the lookout. The workers were more afraid of him than they were of his brothers, because he had trained himself to hear the slightest sound.

"Hey, you! What are you doing?"

"Nothing, Don Damián."

"Well, I'm paying you to do something. If you don't like it you can clear out."

No matter how far away he was, he never missed the "glu-glu" that the must made as it ran through the funnel and the scratching of the *alpargatas* on the floor.

Don Damián opened the newspaper. Unimportant news. He ran through the headlines rapidly, stopping when he reached the account of the bullfight.

"For El Cordobés, two ears and a tail, and ears on his second . . . El Puri, booed by the crowd on both."

Don Damián read with great difficulty. His father had been concerned with preparing his sons for the business world, not with making them gentlemen. Until he had become a landowner and a wine producer, Don Damián's father had been a donkey trader. Going from one country fair to another he never missed a deal, no matter how shady it was. With practice he learned how to straddle the fence better than his contemporaries. He didn't need the war to make money. When he was finally old and wealthy, Suero decided to get himself a wife. For months he had to bear the humiliation of seeing himself rejected by the family of the woman he had chosen.

"A Bermúdez married to a gypsy! That can't be."

But the Bermúdez family was ruined and Don Suero was swimming in money. The marriage was celebrated with great pomp and the only thing lacking at the party was the bridegroom's relatives. Actually, he was the first to admit that he didn't know them. He had once had news of his mother, but so long ago that he had forgotten where she lived.

Don Damián and his brothers were born of that marriage. Old Suero lived long enough to initiate his sons into the secrets of life.

The story of that love affair was told and retold in the town because it was remembered by the sentimentalists as the most moving event of all time. Don Suero was afraid that his sons would believe the popular version of what had happened, and that would be bad for their future education. So he brought them together one afternoon in his office with its mahogany furniture and an old book bound in parchment, but neither pen nor paper, because the old man had never learned to write. "The truth is I didn't marry for love. Your mother was ugly and stupid. I didn't like her, but I was looking toward the future. I'd made a lot of money, but money can be lost. The important thing is to get one of those names that allow a person to be a social climber. Once you're on top it's very difficult to fall down again. It was a small step, I admit, but it was one that will aid all of you."

And so it did. They all made good marriages.

Don Damián finished his beer. The church clock struck six. The foreman called the men together.

"Quitting time! That's all there is for today."

The workers stood in single file in front of their boss. Don Damián put his hand in his pocket.

"Take it and sign."

The workers took the coins and signed the same receipt that they signed every night: "I have received the amount of sixty *pesetas* for one day of work as a temporary laborer in the Bodega Cura, Inc., thus settling my account with the house."

It was Marciano's turn. Marciano had never worked

there before and he counted the money before signing the receipt.

"You made a mistake. There are only twenty-five *pesetas* here."

The others laughed, and so did Don Damián.

"Be quiet, son. The fellow that went before you got less."

Marciano didn't accept the system.

"I won't sign."

Don Damián kept his head.

"It's the custom of the house. You'll be luckier another day."

"It may be your custom, but I get paid what I'm owed."

The foreman came over to the new man.

"Don't make trouble. If you behave there's always work here. That's the good thing about this job. No matter how little or how much, we always take something home."

Marciano threw the coins on the floor and walked out of the wine cellar. Don Damián paid the others.

"Hey, you, wait."

Tobías was the man he trusted most. And after Tobías, the foreman.

"This can't happen again!"

"I thought he was all right. They recommended him to me on the street he lives on."

"You have to keep your eyes open, you fool!"

The foreman lowered his head.

"I'll forgive you this time, but you two have to keep a complaint from being filed at the labor union, one way or another."

Tobías wasn't intelligent, but he understood his boss. He and the foreman left the wine cellar together.

Don Damián poured himself another beer. He had more than five hundred workers who were not covered by insurance and did not collect a minimum wage or vacation pay. A labor inspection would ruin the firm. Five hundred fines, five hundred debts for back wages. The system was well organized, but if inspectors came from outside they could set wheels in motion with all the consequences that entailed.

Corporal Pérez called the jailer.

"I've come for the three prisoners."

The jailer accompanied him to the cell.

"When they brought them here they could hardly walk."

"Well, now they'll have to get a move on!"

Antonio had collapsed on the floor. His whole body ached. The cold tiles made him feel better. There was a water bottle by his side left by the Guard.

"That's all I can give you without special permission. Those are the rules," the Guard had said.

He closed his eyes when he saw the corporal. This wasn't a dream like the ones he had when he managed to sleep. He was back in the cell and they had come for him. The "swing" again. It occurred to him that he would die hanging there, and the dead feel no pain.

"Get up."

He tried to stand up but was unable to.

"Help him."

The jailer lifted him up, taking care not to hurt him.

"Stop your wool-gathering. We're in a hurry."

Calero and Negro were in better shape. They had been beaten less because the Guards had expected to get less out of them. Besides, they were used to it and knew how to avoid the dangerous blows. Between the two of them they carried their friend to the door.

"Now, beat it."

Calero didn't move. Negro and Antonio looked at him in surprise.

"What are you waiting for? Let's go."

"Don't move."

Corporal Pérez hadn't counted on that.

"I told you to get out."

"And just between you and me, don't you think that I know what the law says about shooting escaping prisoners?" Calero answered.

The corporal was getting impatient.

"You were freed by order of the governor."

"Show us the order. Then we'll go."

"Don't be stupid. I told you to get out!"

Calero remembered Traga. Traga had never done anything. He had met him in jail, where they were in the same cell. He told Calero things about the Nationalist front, where he had served in the Falangist zone. He had followed General Calderón through Andalusia, but then he had committed the error of thinking for himself. One day he asked why they had been ordered to fire on seminary students. The regiment was standing in formation in front of the general, and they all heard him. He couldn't forget those boys. The Reds had sent them over from the other side because they didn't know what to do with them. A cloud of blood had covered the cassocks.

"Aim, fire."

And the rows of men fell. They fired point blank without wasting a bullet. The ones who were behind raised their hands to show they weren't carrying weapons, and then they also fell.

The general didn't like the question. Without giving a reason he ripped off his lieutenant's stripes and medals—he had won them in battle, with red ribbons indicating special valor. Then they sent him to jail on a charge of espionage.

Traga wasn't afraid.

"It'll be proven that I didn't do anything. My parents have influence. They're probably already pulling strings in Madrid."

One afternoon they were walking around the prison patio. Traga was talking about how stupid war and killing were. He told how they forced him to kill and how he discovered that a murderer can never be a hero.

Two Falangists called him.

"Carlos Altozano! We have an order for your release."

Traga asked for permission to say goodbye to his friends.

"I'll help you all," he promised Calero. "It's not just to keep you in prison just because you defended your ideals."

Traga left. They heard the shots inside. The Falangists called two prisoners to drag away the body.

"He misunderstood. He was trying to escape."

The men in the patio took off their caps in sign of respect.

A lawyer explained to him that that was the "escape law."

"We'll not go until we see the order."

Corporal Pérez decided to consult his superior. The prisoners waited inside the prison.

"They think that we're trying to apply the escape law to them."

The commander swore.

"Well, we can't show them the order. A paper like that would give them all kinds of ideas."

"What are we going to do?"

"I'll go with you."

The sun was going down by the time they decided to give them a paper saying that they were free. It was

an ambiguous document, since it was difficult to explain
how someone can be freed when he never entered jail
legally in the first place.

They had to carry Antonio. He could barely move
his feet. He was delirious and trembling with fever.
Calero realized that Antonio was in very serious condition. Holding him up as best as they could, they
reached the plaza. On the corner of San Antonio Street
they met Juan and the others.

"Help us."

Mulo and Chirlo carried Antonio. Two others helped
Calero and Negro.

Manolo was playing with the other children. They
had found a puddle where they were making mud balls.

"Don't worry, nothing will happen to him."

The boy hadn't lifted his eyes from the ground since
the day they took his father away. On the one hand, he
was ashamed because his father was in jail. Adults had
always told him that jail was for bad people and criminals. Even Antonio had told him every day: "If you do
that you'll end up in jail, and that's very bad." "If you
do this other thing I'll call the police to take you away."
"Police are for locking up bad people." On the other
hand, he was afraid they would kill his father. Manolo
loved him very much and he knew that the Guards beat
people. Of course, his father had never been a bad man,
but he wanted to see him again so that he could ask him
if he was really bad or if the others were the bad ones.

"Look."

Manolo glanced around. A monster was approaching
his house. Two very strong men were carrying him, and
two other monsters were following him. The child ran
to hide in his mother's skirts.

"Mama, I've seen the Devil."

At that moment Antonio entered the room. His wife recognized him. She was already prepared. One of the Civil Guards' wives had told her that they were beating him.

"Put him down here."

Encarna pulled the blanket off the mattress. She didn't cry, even though she thought he was dead. The others came in with him.

"We came to accompany him. We'll go home now."

They weren't in much better condition than her husband.

"Take them home as fast as you can and call a doctor."

"They're already looking for one."

Four of the most reliable workers took charge.

"What do you think, should we get one doctor for the three of them, or three doctors?"

"Three doctors. That way they'll cure them faster."

The best place to look was the hospital.

"Is the doctor in?"

"No, there's no one at this time of day."

"Call him. A man's dying."

"Why didn't you bring him here?"

"He's in very serious condition."

The male nurse looked for a pencil to write down the address.

"What street does he live on?"

"Mesón del Duque, at the end."

"The doctor isn't in Sanlúcar."

"There must be others."

"They can't come. They're all seeing patients at their offices."

"All right, but there must be someone."

"Of course, but not at the hospital."

"We don't have a telephone. Can we use this one?"

"No. It can only be used by the doctors on the staff."

"Then you call. Don Vicente López, perhaps."
"I can't call, either."

They had no alternative except to walk to the other side of town to look for the doctors.
"You go to López's office. We'll see Don Braulio and you go to Blanes, Negro's doctor."
"But the only thing he knows about is childbirth!"
"It doesn't matter. If you find him, take him to see Negro."

Don Vicente was reading. Fortunately there were no more patients and the telephone was not ringing. He didn't expect any emergencies. López was very familiar with the state of people's health in Sanlúcar. April was usually a quiet month. Someone knocked on his door. Don Vicente knew it was his wife by the way she knocked. He liked her to sit by his side in the armchair that was there especially for her, but Clara thought she was in the way. According to Don Vicente that was a complex for which she had to be treated. He told himself every day that he would set aside time for therapy but he never did.
"Come in."
"Someone is here to see you."
"Who?"
"A boy from the other side of town. It seems that it's very urgent."
Don Vicente got up.
"Bring me my bag."
Chirlo was waiting impatiently.
"He's dying, doctor."
"Who?"
"Antonio."
"Which Antonio?"
"The one who lives on Mesón del Duque Street."

Don Vicente remembered him. He had come many times with his son Manolo, a weak child who was going to cost his family a lot of money.

"What's the matter with him?"

"They beat him."

"What do you mean, *they* beat him?"

"The Civil Guards."

The events in town rarely penetrated into Don Vicente's world. His patients had vaguely mentioned a strike. They were just chance comments that he paid little attention to. Now he realized that he would have been better advised to listen to them.

Don Vicente took what he needed. Bandages, alcohol, camphorated oil.

"Is the doctor in?"

The maid appeared on the porch overlooking the patio without opening the screen door.

"What for?"

"A sick man."

"Where?"

"Mesón del Duque Street."

"I'll see."

The maid looked for her employer throughout the house. He was in the wine cellar measuring the degree of acidity of some musts. He had purchased forty or fifty casks full at harvest time to make some money selling them.

"I'm not in. I'm not in for anyone. I already have enough to do during visiting hours. At the end of the month I'll have just as much money whether I go or not. Nobody is going to pay me for the bother."

The maid returned to the patio.

"He's out."

"Shit!" Mulo was furious. "It's because we're poor. If we came with our wallets full of money you'd see

how fast he'd come out."
The maid shrugged her shoulders.
"Why tell me about it?"
"Tell him that it's very urgent, that the man is dying."
"I'm not going to tell him anything. That's all I need, to get bawled out because of you."
"Why don't you do it? You're from our class. You live on my street."
"I don't have anything to do with it."
The maid disappeared with that air of superiority of people who don't have many chances to humiliate others.
"She'll hear about this."
Juan tugged at his companion.
"Leave her alone. Let's find another doctor."

Don Vicente López went over to the mattress.
"What a mess!"
He began to work on Antonio slowly and carefully. There were cuts all over his face and body. Two ribs were broken, and the collarbone was dislocated. Don Vicente reflected that it was a pity he couldn't move him to a hospital, at least not for the moment. Antonio groaned.
"You'll have to grit your teeth a little, my boy."
Encarna helped him silently.
"More gauze."

The others came in at a run.
"There's no way to get a doctor in all of Sanlúcar."
Paco asked them not to shout.
"Is he dead?"
"No, Don Vicente López is treating him."
They breathed easier. With Don Vicente, people only died of old age.

Eleven

Don Mariano burst into the club. The members, who were getting a breath of fresh air in the chairs out on the sidewalk, followed him in.

"Is Don Luis here?"

He hadn't come.

"What's the matter?"

Don Mariano left without answering.

Don Luis had taken refuge in Blázquez's office. The labor union official found him there finishing a bottle of vintage sherry with his host and preparing to forget the worries of the day. Mariano's arrival didn't please him in the least.

"What brings you here? I hope it's not another problem."

"An order from the governor. I have to go to Cádiz tomorrow with the representative from the social section of the grapeworkers' union."

"What for?"

"I don't know. It seems a little strange to me."

"Do you need anything for the trip?"

"A car . . . and the representative."

Don Luis was frightened.

"Didn't you people name one yourselves?"

"On the contrary. Imagine, the elections last year were almost legal."

"So what?"

"The representative is named Antonio Cabeza de Vaca."

"I don't see what his last name has to do with it," Don César interrupted. "We know that it was a great family, but the old towers fell down a long time ago. It won't bother anyone."

"Don't you two understand?" Don Mariano shouted. "Antonio Cabeza de Vaca was arrested last night by the Civil Guard."

"And he was interrogated this morning."

"Exactly."

Calero and Negro washed themselves.

"I wonder how Antonio's getting along."

"Not very well."

"Let's go to his house. Don Vicente is there, and he'll take care of us properly. We shouldn't call him, because Antonio can't be left alone."

"We have to do something before that."

Calero and Negro went to the courthouse with Pelao, Mulo, and Juan.

"I tell you it's not open."

"It's always open for a complaint. And if it isn't, you'll see what happens."

"Is the judge in?"

"One moment."

The maid closed the door, leaving them outside. Those rooms were not his office, but his home. She knew this very well.

"There are some men at the door. Two of them are in bad shape."

"Do you know them?"

"One is named Ponce and they call him Negro. He lives on my street."

The judge looked at a note. Luis Ponce had just been released from jail.

"Tell them to come back tomorrow."

The maid passed on the message. Don Alberto continued his meditations. That day was dedicated to Christ's painful ordeal with Anas, Caiphas, and Pilate. It was his favorite meditation. He felt better when he contemplated those unjust judges.

The maid returned.

"They say that if you don't see them immediately they're going to Cádiz."

"Tell them to come in."

The judge left his book on the little table beside his armchair. He looked for a copy of *Camino* on the bookshelf. As a member of Opus Dei, he liked to find one of Father Escrivá's maxims for every moment of his life. These thoughts were his best guide in doubtful circumstances, when the good was not easily discernible because it was hidden by sentimentalism and human considerations.

The judge returned to his armchair. The men appeared in the doorway preceded by the maid. Really, they hadn't been treated very well.

"May we sit down?" asked Calero, who could hardly stand up.

"If I were just a man and were not invested— anointed, so to speak—by the office of judge, I would allow you to do so, but out of respect for the authority which I represent, I must order you to continue standing."

Calero and Negro leaned on their companions.

"What have you come for?"

"To file a complaint."

"This is not the time. Come back tomorrow."

Calero acted as spokesman.

"By law there has to be one night court in a town of forty thousand inhabitants. If Your Honor will tell us where this court is, we have no objection to going there."

The judge cleared his throat.

"There ought to be one but apparently there isn't," Calero continued. "In any case, we'll file our complaint. If not here, we'll exercise our rights in the capital, making it clear that we weren't able to do so in Sanlúcar."

"I see that you know the law."

"Unfortunately, I've had to learn it, Your Honor."

The judge cleared his throat again.

"You're right. There is, in fact, a night court. Since this is my home, please go to my chambers and wait for me there."

"Yes, sir."

Calero fell onto the wooden bench.

The judge called his maid.

"Tell them to find the secretary immediately, no matter where he is."

Then he picked up the telephone.

"Find the mayor and connect me with him."

The telephone operators called all the bars in town. They were told at the Colón that he had left there with Don César.

"Is the mayor there?"

"Who's calling?"

"The judge."

"One moment."

Don Luis answered the telephone.

"They've come to file a complaint."

"What do you intend to do?"

"I can't throw them out because they're prepared to go wherever they have to and one of them knows what he's doing."

"Do you have any ideas?"

"Are you sure about the doctors and the notaries?"

"Of course."

"In that case, don't worry. I'll take care of it."

The judge waited for the secretary to arrive. Since

he didn't want to waste his time he read a few sections from his book, the source of his inspiration in the administration of justice.

Don Vicente finished bandaging his patient. After washing his hands in a basin that Encarna had prepared, he called Paco.

"Go to the notary and tell him to draw up an affidavit. Tell him that I need it as a doctor."

"What if he's not home?"

"Go to the house of the other one, the old one."

The judge left the two little books on one corner of the table. The desk to his right was occupied by his secretary, who had brought a typewriter. He hadn't carried a load like that for quite a few years. There was always an attendant to do it for him every morning.

The five men stood in the middle of the room.

"Let's proceed systematically. Who are the complainants?"

Calero and Negro stepped forward.

"Give your names, nicknames, addresses, numbers of your identification cards . . ."

Negro didn't have his card.

"In that case it's going to be difficult to file the complaint."

The secretary didn't like the proceedings. He felt that things could get out of hand and that it would be worse for everyone.

Calero interrupted.

"That doesn't matter, Your Honor. You can fine him, but his address and the other information are enough for the complaint. As for documents, here's one."

It was his welfare card. In towns where social services hardly exist, the municipal government hands out a great many rose-colored cards which, even though they are quite useless, lead the bearer to think that he is covered by some hypothetical medical protection.

"Against whom are you making the complaint?"

"Against the brigade commander of the Civil Guard at this post, and against Corporal Pérez and Private Núñez."

"For what reason?"

"For ill treatment."

"What proof do you have?"

Negro took off his shirt, showing a back covered with coagulated blood and whip marks.

"And how am I to know if the Civil Guard did that? It could have happened in a street fight or some accident."

"We have witnesses."

"Very well. Bring them forward."

"These three men and, if you want us to, we'll bring more. The whole town knows about it."

The judge waved his hand.

"No, there's no need for more," he said to Calero. Then he asked the witnesses: "Did you see with your own eyes how the Civil Guard beat these gentlemen?"

"We weren't in the stable when they beat them," Pelao said, "but we know they did it."

"By 'they' do you mean the ones named in the complaint?"

"Yes. It's always the same ones who beat the prisoners."

"I asked you if you had seen them being beaten, and you tell me that you weren't in the stable. Therefore you couldn't have seen it, and you add that 'it's always the same ones who beat the prisoners,' as though you had spent your whole life in the barracks."

The judge leaned back. The room was silent. Suddenly he pointed at Juan.

"You!"

"Yes, sir?"

"Were you ever arrested?"

"No, sir."

"Then how do you know who beats people in the Civil Guards' barracks? Answer me!"

"I . . . sir . . . the others . . ."

Juan was totally confused. Pelao was too, but he was more aggressive.

"Look here, Your Honor, I was with Antonio last night when he was arrested, but I managed to slip away. He didn't have a scratch on him at the time. Today I found him just outside the jail and he was in worse shape than these fellows are—he was half dead. I don't believe any other prisoner beat him or that he fell down the stairs, because if he'd fallen the bruises would have been different. Besides, it would seem strange if all three of them had fallen down the stairs, wouldn't it?"

The judge smiled benevolently. Benevolence is an effective weapon when dealing with the people.

"The only thing that is clear in this whole affair is that you have no concrete evidence to offer. You didn't see what happened in the barracks or in the jail or anywhere else. You don't know what happened and yet you claim to be witnesses. No, that's not legal."

"Your Honor, allow me to point out that this is not a trial," Calero replied. "We're filing a complaint, or, rather, we're trying to file one, and to do that all we have to do is make the complaint. It's better if there are witnesses, but it's not essential. Besides, we have the two witnesses who are required for a trial. He and I saw them beat Antonio, Antonio and he saw how they beat me . . ."

Don Alberto had the feeling that something had gone wrong in his system. Either this worker was not like the others, or Father Escrivá was going out of fashion. Inwardly he cursed his good friend the post commander for his lack of prudence. Everyone knows that it's possible to beat people without leaving marks.

He gestured to his secretary to leave the room. When he was alone with the men he came down from the dais. He pointed to the red sofa at the other end of the room, inviting the men to sit down. They obeyed.

"Do you want a cigarette?"

Calero took one, and the others followed suit.

"Let's look at the facts calmly and realistically. You don't get anywhere by making a complaint. You know that the Civil Guard, which was formed to maintain order, is governed by special laws which do exist, even though they are not divulged and you don't know what they are. If the brigade commander thought it was necessary to employ some physical corrective measures to keep you from going down the wrong road, that was his right."

"No, sir," cut in Calero. "The law says that they can't beat prisoners, and furthermore that they can't lock people up for more than seventy-two hours without taking them before a judge. They held two of us for several days and treated us just as they pleased."

The judge smiled.

"But there is also a law which permits provincial governors to issue orders for preventive arrest of individuals who may be a threat to public order. You were arrested under this order."

"That's fine, but there was no reason for them to beat us the way they did. Antonio is half dead."

"You're exaggerating."

"Come look at him."

"I can't. As you very correctly pointed out, there has to be a night court in large towns. I'm now on duty."

Calero knew the judge had scored a point.

"All right, my sons, I think the best thing would be for you to forget this incident and forgive those who transgress against you, as Jesus Christ told us to do."

Pelao leaped up.

"Fuck all this talk of Jesus Christ! I wouldn't care if old Whiskers bandaged us himself. We have to swallow our hunger and everything else because of him, and in his name the same people who walk in religious processions with symbols of authority break our backs! Either Christ is for everyone or he's for no one. He also said, 'Thou shalt not kill,' and 'Do unto others as you would have them do unto you.' He was great, but here where everyone loves him so much and is so Catholic they don't give you anything to eat or even let you live in peace."

The judge's expression changed.

"Do you know that I could send you to jail right now for saying that?"

Pelao shrugged his shoulders.

"What difference does it make? One injustice more or less isn't a big deal, when we'll get it in the neck in any case. Those of us who speak out won't be overlooked, even by mistake."

The judge softened his tone.

"Don't worry, I forgive you. I realize that you're young and impetuous and still aren't able to see the logic behind the events that have caused the authorities to act this way toward you. Calero, Negro, and Antonio were not beaten in order to hurt them. Quite to the contrary, it was done to protect the peace we all enjoy, so that you can go to work without fear of war, so that nothing can halt Spain's development and, most important of all, so that they themselves will see their error and take the road of eternal salvation."

Pelao blew up.

"He's fucked us! Our eternal souls . . . ! So that I can go to work! I knew that all the time. And so that I'll put up with the fifty *pesetas* until I die in some corner."

Calero saw that the judge was getting exasperated.

"Pelao!"

"What?"

"Go home."

"Why?"

"I'll tell you later."

"What if I don't want to go?"

"Go anyway."

Calero had authority. Pelao was used to obeying him. Without knowing how he had gotten there, he found himself in the street walking home. Halfway up the hill he turned toward Antonio's house.

"Both notaries are out of town, Don Vicente."

Don Vicente López took off his glasses.

"I figured they would be. Where can I find a telephone around here?"

"In the parish house."

López smiled.

"I'm not interested in that one."

"Maybe they'll let you call from Cayetano's bar."

Don Vicente went to the bar.

"Of course you can use the phone, doctor. You don't even have to ask."

"Connect me with Don Juan Carlos," Don Vicente asked the operator.

"He's not in Sanlúcar," she replied.

"I don't want to speak to him, señorita, but to his wife."

"One moment."

Cayetano made his customers quiet down. When they knew that it had to do with Antonio, there was a respectful silence. Not even a fly could be heard buzzing in the stillness.

"Is your mistress in?" asked Don Vicente.

"Who's calling?"

"Pedro Domec of Jerez."

"I'll call her."

"Beatriz," he said when she answered.

"Oh, it's you, Vicente. I thought it was someone else."

Her voice was trembling. She had lied on many occasions, but never as outrageously as she was going to lie now.

"I know your husband's there."

"No, he left Sanlúcar."

"It seems that the other notary is also out of town."

"I don't know about that. They called him from near Chipiona to make out an affidavit. It seemed urgent, so he left."

"At what time?"

"I . . . I don't remember."

"Do you know that it's against the law to leave a town without a notary? There's an association to keep that type of irregularity from occurring."

"Look, Vicente, tell that to Juan Carlos tomorrow."

Beatriz hung up.

Don Vicente realized there would be no notaries in Sanlúcar for two days. He called Ocaso to ask for official paper.

"Do you want it for a death certificate?"

"No, I want the other kind."

"We have it on order, but it hasn't arrived yet."

"I need it urgently. Tell me as soon as you receive it."

"Don't worry, Don Vicente. I won't forget."

He returned to Antonio's house. His patient was in no condition to be left alone.

Calero was bored. He wanted to go to bed and stop hearing stupidities. The judge talked and talked, offering them one cigarette after another. Verses from the Old Testament, bits from the New Testament, advice, but not one word about the complaint.

The secretary had gone to sleep in the waiting room. Juan and Negro were yawning.

"Very well, my sons, I think it would be better if we went to bed in view of the hour. Think it over carefully, and come back tomorrow if you still want to file the complaint."

"No, sir. We're going to file it right now."

"But one of your friends left."

"Didn't you say my friends were no good as witnesses?"

The judge called his secretary.

"Write what these gentlemen tell you to."

Calero spoke with a firm voice. An hour later the matter was ended. They read the statements carefully before signing them.

"Good night, Don Alberto."

"Good night."

They went to Antonio's house after leaving the courthouse.

The secretary was looking at the papers with a frightened expression. He had never written down such a damning series of truths before.

"What are we going to do with this?"

The judge took the papers.

"You can go. I think it's time."

The secretary understood that he was in the way.

"Good night, Don Alberto."

The judge reread the sheets carefully. There was no doubt—the workers were beginning to wake up. If anyone higher up saw these documents it would cause a great deal of trouble, enough to make half the officials in the province lose their jobs.

With a weary gesture he tore them in half, then in four, then in six . . . Before leaving he filed the entire matter in the wastebasket.

Twelve

Don Mariano went to the labor union office with Don Luis. One by one they went through the books and pamphlets that contained the rules governing the election and replacement of representatives. There was nothing in Antonio's conduct to justify removing him from his post.

"Who goes in case of illness?"

"Another representative, who has to be chosen from among the other spokesmen for the workers."

"Who are they?"

"Juan Cabeza and Pelao for the grape workers' union. They're also among the strikers."

"So they've gotten too smart for us."

"Not all of them. We have two who are very cooperative. Tobías, who works for Damián Cura, and Pacorro, who works for León Alvarez."

Don Luis didn't know them.

"Which one do you think would be better?"

"Tobías. Remember that Pacorro was beaten up by his fellow workers and he filed a complaint against them. He wouldn't be a good representative in this case. We have to go strictly by the law now."

But before they could find a substitute they had to eliminate the person who already held the post. Neither of them could come up with a convincing formula.

The judge was the person who knew most about the

law in the town. They went to his house.

The maid opened the door in her nightgown. Her employer had been working late in his chambers and she was tired.

"Is Don Alberto home?"

"He's at court with some men who came to file a complaint."

They went in.

The maid knew the mayor and therefore she didn't mind leaving them alone in the living room. They might take something, but, as they say, "he who robs a thief . . ." The maid considered all government employees thieves, but that didn't stop her from admiring them profoundly.

Don Mariano had time to smoke five pipefuls of tobacco and Don Luis had a good nap. The judge found him snoring loudly when he walked in.

Don Mariano got up to greet him.

"But, at this hour?"

"It's very important."

Antonio didn't regain consciousness. His breathing became more labored and Don Vicente asked the hospital for an oxygen cylinder, but they wouldn't send it to him.

"Besides, it's almost empty," the attendant confessed.

A car was needed, so they woke up Piolo.

"You have to go to Jerez for oxygen."

Piolo got dressed as fast as he could.

"Where can you buy it?"

"Ask in the pharmacy."

Just in case, Don Vicente gave him a prescription describing what was needed down to the smallest detail. Piolo carefully put it away in his wallet. It was a very important piece of paper.

He wanted to see Antonio before he left.

"Is he in very bad condition, Don Vicente?"

Don Vicente didn't answer, and neither did Encarna. Manolillo, who didn't understand what was happening, had gone to sleep clutching his father's legs.

"People like that shouldn't be allowed to live."

Everyone agreed. They all knew whom he was referring to.

"Hurry."

"Don't worry. I'll make it as fast as the car can go, because nothing is worth more than a life."

Manolillo woke up and began to cry. He wasn't used to seeing so many strange faces in the house. His mother took him in her arms to lull him to sleep again.

"It's very simple. Get a document certifying that he's sick."

"Who has to issue the document?"

"The social security doctor."

They called Teruel, who in turn advised Blanes.

"You have to make it out without seeing the patient. Say flu or tonsillitis, what difference does it make?"

Blanes didn't want to. He smelled smoke in the matter and was afraid of getting burned.

Blanes didn't work as much as Don Vicente did. He had more than enough time to learn all the local gossip. He knew that the Civil Guard had severely beaten someone, that strange orders had arrived from the government, and that the prisoners had been released.

"Isn't he one of those who were arrested?"

Teruel lied.

"Absolutely not. He works for César Blázquez. He's one of the workers who are at Campo de Andévalo and he doesn't want to have him brought back."

Blanes shrugged his shoulders. After all, the machinations of the authorities made no difference to him.

"All right. Send me a letter saying all this and I'll

give the certificate to the bearer."

Teruel promised to send it immediately, but first he called the courthouse.

". . . this can get me into a lot of trouble."

They had to convince the doctor. Letters are always compromising. Don Alberto sent for his secretary.

Casimiro Ruiz was sleepy, but his wife, Regla, nonetheless made him describe the scene at the courthouse in full detail.

"I don't know why, but it seems to me that the complaint is already in the wastebasket," he concluded.

"Don Alberto is a slippery bird."

In Regla's language, the word "bird" was a sign of admiration. Birds earned money, rolled around on four wheels, and gave away mink coats. They were the ones who became governors, ministers, and other very important persons. She knew this very well. She had been married for ten years, ten years of listening to her husband discuss what really went on in his office.

She had seen how Don Claros, that white-bearded old gentleman who made so much of his honesty and the fact that he never received anything other than the wages that were due him, retired even though he was five years short of the minimum age. However, Don Claros had never been on the high court and had spent his life going from one town to another, while Don Pedro, the Asturian, had barely lived five years in San-lúcar. And yet they had taken him to Seville and then to the Supreme Court. What a good man Don Pedro was! He never forgot to send people cards on Christmas or their saint's day.

Of course Don Pedro had been lucky. First, the accident when the child was run over. What was his name? Well, it didn't matter; he was just another kid. Sebastián Armada was frightened and Don José was even

more frightened. The indemnity and the fine would
have been colossal if it hadn't been for Don Pedro.
Why did Antoñito have to take the car that afternoon?
Precisely when the streets were most crowded and when
the most children were playing in them. It was raining
and he didn't have a driver's license. At any rate, it
cost him almost as much to cover it up as it would have
to pay the fine and the rest, but they avoided scandal,
which was the main thing. And then came the question
of Mariquilla's estate. The girl was very nice. She was
sorry for her when Casimiro told her "everything was
arranged." What a beautiful deal! Deals were always
beautiful to her when they involved millions.

She remembered the lawsuit very well. Mariquilla's
parents had made her uncle Manuel her guardian. The
parents had spent years saving their money. When
Manuel had to turn it over to the girl, he wasn't able
to show how he'd spent it and Mariquilla sued him.
She would have won if it hadn't been for Don Pedro,
but Don Pedro knew what he was doing and Mariquilla
didn't. "It's not necessary to bribe anyone in court,"
she always said, and she didn't offer anything. She
would have won the suit if she had promised more
than her uncle. Regla was on the verge of warning her,
but she didn't dare. Her husband had told her: "Be
careful she doesn't find out what's happening." Her
husband also knew how to make it in the world.

The court secretary fell asleep while meditating on
these matters.

"Don Casimiro! Don Casimiro!"

Regla woke up.

"What's the matter?"

"The judge has sent someone for him. He's to come
right away."

Regla helped the maid and Casimiro opened his eyes.

"Again?"

Beatriz returned to the living room. Juan Carlos was nodding beside the fireplace. He was a young man, and looked like a movie star.

"Vicente López. For an affidavit."

"I hope you told him I was away."

"Naturally."

"Did he ask for Palomo?"

"They had already been to his house. Of course they didn't find him either. I told López that he had probably gone to the country to draw up some papers."

"Good."

The notary closed his eyes. He didn't feel like talking. He didn't like to have Vicente López mixed up in the matter. Vicente didn't come from Sanlúcar, and he had his own ideas and knew his profession. His profession and the law. He might try something. Of course, just one man without authority or an official position would find it very difficult to make himself heard. Even if he should manage to reach someone higher up, they wouldn't read his letters or take his complaints seriously.

Juan Carlos was an ambitious man. His notary business was too small for him. He dreamed of becoming a minister of state and of having money. He had completed the first stage of his plan and was rapidly advancing through the second stage. It would be a shame to spoil it.

It had been a good idea to ask to be sent to Andalusia. His Catalonian colleagues had been surprised. They didn't think it made sense to leave a summer resort where deeds and drafts abounded for a town lost at the mouth of the Guadalquivir River. He had felt a momentary panic when they notified him that his transfer had been approved. Going to a town run by local bosses has its drawbacks. One has to snap to when they give the word, and political bosses are fickle, but it's always easier to make it in a place like that than to get ahead where the majority rules or good will prevails.

The first days were hard. They rented a house without water; Beatriz complained constantly about the lack of the conveniences she had enjoyed in her province; they were ostracized by the closed society they encountered. Those were the heroic days of getting about on foot and seeing clients in their best room where they put the most presentable furniture they could afford to buy. But on the other hand, neither he nor she ever went out poorly dressed. They kept up appearances from the very beginning.

Little by little they established themselves. To do so they had to go without many necessities. It cost money to invite people out, and the money was only available through the strictest daily budgeting. Juan Carlos knew how to be agreeable and flexible. He had ideas. He was born to be a corporate lawyer rather than a notary. His accurate advice, his blindness when engaged in shady deals, and his unconditional support of the authorities and the powers-that-be were a great help to him.

First he bought that hole and furnished it decently, and then he bought a Versailles. He didn't want a new car because the people of the town were beginning to talk and cars stand out too much. Of course, other things stand out too, but "nobody pays them any account," as the people around Sanlúcar say.

That summer he acquired La Condesita. It was a big, modern, Andalusian-style house with a porch and a garden. All that was missing was a swimming pool, and he was having one built.

The furniture and the ancestors came from the antique shop. People still recognized the latter, because they were pictures that had been in the store for a long time. Above all the painting of the child, who was gradually transformed into "Grandfather Nicholas." Time causes people to forget.

He wisely decided not to "discover" ancestors earlier than the first part of the nineteenth century. He would always be able to expand his genealogy, and it was obviously not a good idea to present himself as a descendant of the Cid in a town where the best families had such short family trees themselves.

His dreams of grandeur were what produced the name of his country home. And as time passed, popular speech would bestow nobility on him also. "He's the owner of La Condesita," people would say, "of La Condesita . . . el condesito . . . el conde." And count he would remain, by a process of etymological deformation that seemed inevitable.

But there was the ugly affair of the strike and the prisoners. And there was Vicente López.

Juan Carlos got up. He spent the rest of the night thinking of how to ruin a doctor's career and his reputation.

The secretary went up the alley counting the steps. He didn't like this job. It was like sticking his head in the lion's mouth. What doctor did they think he was going to find there? It was obvious—Don Vicente.

He had barely entered the street when he noticed that something very serious was happening. Men were pacing up and down and smoking nervously. From time to time they stopped and looked through an open doorway into a lighted room. Women whispered together in groups, looking as though they were going to stay where they were, in spite of the late hour. Some of them recognized him. They fell silent and their eyes were bright with undisguised hatred.

Casimiro walked down the middle of the sidewalk, not looking one way or the other.

"Does Antonio Cabeza live here?" he asked.

Vicente López lifted the sackcloth curtain that served as a door and came out into the patio.

"Yes, sir."

He had completed his mission, but it wasn't wise to leave without saying something to justify his visit. They had warned him about that in advance.

"I want to speak to his wife."

Don Vicente stood his ground in front of the secretary.

"You can't just now."

"The judge sent me."

"What for?"

"I have something to tell her."

Don Vicente called Encarna. Casimiro motioned to the doctor to leave them alone.

"I'm sorry, but I don't see why I should."

The secretary cleared his throat.

"I've come . . . to find out how your husband is. The judge is interested in his condition."

"They kill him for me and now they're worried about him! To hell with all of them. I hope the same thing happens to them."

López quieted her.

"It's curious how interested our authorities are in the matter," said Don Vicente to the secretary. "Four days ago there were three prisoners in jail. Four days ago they were beating them and the judge wasn't interested in them then."

The secretary looked around him. The men had surrounded him. He sensed that the slightest slip could set off an explosion. Or just a word or gesture on Don Vicente's part. The secretary was afraid. The best thing was to leave.

"That's fine, gentlemen . . . since you don't want anything . . . At any rate, if you need something, call Don Alberto. He'll be very glad to help you."

Mulo stepped forward.

"Help us to do what? To die?"

The secretary turned around. He walked slowly out

of the house. Once in the street he walked faster. When he reached the silent part of Sanlúcar, the section of the town where nothing ever happened, he began to run. He didn't look over his shoulder, even though he heard footfalls behind him, because he was afraid of falling.

Tobías and Fernando hid in an alley. They had been following Marciano from bar to bar for hours. Someone drew nearer. They flattened themselves against a door.

"Good evening."

Fernando answered with a grunt.

"It was Piernas. Do you think he recognized us?"

Fernando didn't reply. It was possible that he had recognized them, in spite of the darkness. Men from the country have good eyesight.

"How long will it be before the bar closes?"

"At least an hour."

Marciano already had been in Carmelo's place for more than thirty minutes.

"Do you think he's drinking?"

"I don't think so. He's flat broke."

"It would have been a good idea to get him drunk."

"How?"

"By buying him drinks."

Fernando laughed out loud.

"Do you have any more bright ideas? The last thing we want is for people to see us with him."

"Who was it?"

The secretary was breathing hard. He was very tired.

"Don Vicente López."

Don Luis hit the table with his fist.

"I thought so!"

"What are we going to do?"

The judge shrugged his shoulders. When one has to choose between a labor boss and a mayor, the mayor is always better.

"Actually, you have more of a stake in this than we do. You were the one who let them beat him."

"I didn't know anything about it."

"Well, you should have. Antonio has an elected post in your organization."

Don Mariano realized that they wanted to leave him holding the bag.

"No, absolutely not! You're the judge, you ought to know what's going on in the jail, and you, Luis, ought to know what happens when you send people there."

Yes, they all had dirty hands, including the governor.

"There's only one way out of it. We have to get the matter of the certificate settled without letting López know about it."

The secretary went for Dr. Teruel.

A light was still on in the home of the hospital director. Don Bartolo Teruel was waiting impatiently for them to call him to the courthouse. The bell rang and Don Bartolo pulled the wire that opened the grating in the front door.

"They told me to tell you to come. They're at the courthouse."

Don Bartolo put on his jacket and picked up two certificates before leaving.

"Go for Dr. Blanes. He lives on Madre de Dios Street."

"What if he's asleep?"

"Knock until they answer the door and bring him with you. Give him this letter if you have to."

Resting the paper on Casimiro's back, Don Bartolo wrote: "This is an order. It will be to your advantage to see us immediately."

Teruel went on his way alone. His steps echoed in the street. Two workers walked quickly by.

"Good evening."

The men looked up and recognized him. They didn't answer.

Marciano sipped his wine a little at a time. Carmelo had bought him a drink, just as he always did when Marciano had no money. Carmelo was a good man. He had worked outside the country for three years and had had some rough times, but he returned with enough money to set up a bar. Now he was living comfortably, but he never forgot the bad times. Whatever money he had was always at the disposal of whoever needed it. That was why people said he'd never be rich.

"Why should I put it away in a drawer? I can't take it with me when I die."

Marciano was telling what had happened that afternoon. The others were listening attentively. They knew the way Don Damián and his brothers cheated them, but they didn't know that they could protest in the labor union about it.

"You'll file a protest no later than tomorrow. If you want to, I'll go with you." Carmelo had learned a lot while he was abroad.

"But things aren't the same here as they were there," Bala said. "I think the best thing he can do is keep his mouth shut. These things always end up badly."

Bala was a prudent man. He had been very cocky when he was younger, but the years had taught him that you can never beat the system, because it's always the little man who pays.

Marciano got angry.

"And let them keep stepping on us all our life?"

"What we need here is unity," said a boy who always made the same comment without ever convincing anyone.

Carmelo agreed.

"If we always spoke out together, the way they do in

other countries, there wouldn't be anything they could do about it."

"But the strike hasn't gotten us anywhere."

"Keep your shirt on. It's still not over and there are some who are already earning eighty *pesetas*."

"You're right. And we'll all win in the end!"

Bala shook his head. Those boys didn't know very much about life.

"Will you give me another drink on credit?"

"It's on the house," replied Carmelo. "Let's see if it makes you think more clearly."

Blanes arrived with the secretary.

"You can leave, Casimiro."

The secretary made half a bow.

"May I go home?"

They looked at each other. Yes, he could go home. Don Mariano closed the door and locked it, putting the key in his pocket.

"What now?"

"We need that certificate."

Blanes smiled. He had made a lot of points in a short while.

"It's dangerous. I insist on seeing the patient."

"I've already told you that he's in the country."

Don Luis interrupted.

"If you haven't told him the truth, then it's better for you to do it now."

Teruel didn't like to dirty his hands in front of his subordinates.

"In the last analysis, I'm the only one who doesn't have anything to do with this. So if you're going to start giving orders, I'm leaving. Let's see if you can get along without the medical association."

That was impossible, and Don Alberto knew it better than anyone else.

"Do you remember Gringo?" he asked Teruel.

Teruel turned pale.

"Gringo? What Gringo?"

"That boy who died of peritonitis in the hospital waiting room. I believe I have the family's complaint around here somewhere. You know how much I like papers . . ."

"I don't know anything about it. I never had a patient with that name."

"His real name was Luciano Ordóñez. He was short and dark, about twenty-two years old. They took him to you 'because of the pain.' You diagnosed the case rapidly and correctly, but the boy had neither insurance nor a welfare card. You asked the family for five hundred *pesetas* for operating expenses. That was stupid, since they obviously had no way of getting that much money. The mother and brothers spent several hours looking for it, nevertheless, and when they returned to the hospital there was no further need for it."

"But I didn't have anything to do with that. I only diagnosed the case—Velázquez was the surgeon."

"And he still is in spite of everything. As hospital director it was your duty to make him operate and certainly to remove him from his post and file a complaint with the medical association when he didn't."

It occurred to Teruel that he could always blame his aide for it, but in that case Velázquez would also talk. Eyes burned with silver nitrate to cover up malpractice, shipments of quinine that were never used because at that time quinine was worth money and there was a great deal of malaria . . . In short, many things . . .

"If we start remembering things . . ." Teruel said.

Don Alberto didn't back down.

"We can all remember things, all right, because we've known each other for too long. But we'll all go down together, not just one or two of us."

His tone of voice showed that he meant it. Don Alberto was ready. Blanes contemplated the scene with amusement.

"It seems as though I'm about to be taken in by . . . 'Society.' "

Don Mariano nodded and the tension lessened.

"Exactly."

"It's a piece of luck . . . that I won't accept without immediate results."

Things were now becoming clearer.

"Are you interested in the position of ophthalmologist? That was the way I got in."

"At any rate, it's always a steady salary."

"Let's talk no more about it. From tomorrow on you'll be the official ophthalmologist."

"But that's your position."

"I'm going to resign. I don't have enough time for it."

"I think you ought to do it right away."

They brought a typewriter. Teruel wrote to the provincial health director. He really didn't want to, because those *pesetas* came in very handy, but under the circumstances it was well worth the sacrifice to solve their immediate problem.

"Date it next week."

They admired Blanes' prudence. The letter referred to him as the man most suited to occupy the position, and also stated that he needed a second source of income. The doctor put the document away in his inside coat pocket. He preferred to mail it himself.

"What illness should we put down?"

"It seems that he's seriously ill."

"Tuberculosis?"

"No. In that case he ought to be in a sanatorium."

"An acute attack of gastroenteritis."

Teruel agreed. Gastroenteritis could be a symptom of worse things.

Carmelo looked at the clock.

"I've got to close up. I've already been fined twice this week. They don't play around with me."

His customers drank up. Five minutes later the tavern was empty. Marciano walked toward his house with Tobías and Fernando following him.

"We're getting close to Trasbolsa Street. If only no one's around . . ."

"He's almost home!"

"They're all asleep at his house. Don't think that they're sitting at the window waiting for him."

Tobías and Fernando were wearing *alpargatas,* and yet it seemed to them that the noise of their footsteps filled the street. They walked on tiptoe.

Don Mariano went to the office of the labor union with the certificate in his pocket. For a few minutes Sanlúcar echoed with the roar of two motors, Blanes' motorscooter and Don Luis' car.

Don Mariano crossed the deserted patio. He always felt afraid of empty houses, and that night everything seemed filled with phantoms. He looked for blank summonses in his secretary's desk.

He sat down at the typewriter and laboriously began to fill out the first one.

Thirteen

"Hey, Marciano."

Marciano turned around.

"Good evening."

"We want to talk to you."

"Well, I don't want to talk to you. I don't like shits."

"You were very good this afternoon. Someone should have talked to Don Damián like that a long time ago."

Marciano said more gently: "What do you want?"

"We want to take you to Tripa's house. You know who he is, the wine racker who was with you. Among the four of us we're going to draw up a complaint. We'll be your witness."

Marciano was a good and therefore trusting man by nature. Consequently, he didn't imagine for a moment that he was falling into a trap. On the contrary, he was proud of himself. He had raised his voice and, although he had thought that no one had listened to him, it had served to awaken the conscience and dignity of others.

"Let's go."

They crossed Piojo Plaza and walked down the street to the Pastora Theater. A little farther on was Gómez's saw mill and Pirri's place.

"Let's go this way."

They left Falón Hill. The unpaved road passed by the edge of truck gardens. They heard an animal run by and a dog howl. These were the usual noises of the countryside, and therefore Marciano paid no attention to them.

"Where does he live?"

"Over there, near the beach."

The three men walked on in silence. Suddenly Fernando stopped dead.

"I heard someone groan down there. It sounded like a child."

Marciano cupped his ear in order to hear better. The three men listened in silence.

"I can't hear anything. It's your imagination."

"I swear I heard something."

"I hear it now. Don't you?" Tobías asked.

"Let's see what it is."

Marciano jumped over Pitas' stone wall. It was a new wall, just a few inches high. He let himself slide down the muddy bank to the edge of the bog, where he tried to see if there was anyone in the water. Tobías and Fernando followed just behind him.

"I don't see anything."

The two friends jumped on him. Marciano tried to defend himself but Fernando hit him on the back of the neck and he fell to the ground.

"Into the water!"

The cold water brought him to his senses. He instinctively moved his arms and tried to grab the reeds that grew on the edge of the bog. The sandy bottom dissolved under his feet.

"Bastards!"

Tobías and Fernando hid in the reeds.

"Let's be careful. Somebody might see us and recognize us."

There was no danger. The road was too far above them for anyone to see what was happening. Marciano shouted for help. He couldn't get a firm footing nor could he float. He had only a few seconds left. The bog was swallowing him up just as it had swallowed many others. There was no way to get out of the bog without help.

A whirlpool formed around him and Marciano felt something pushing him down. He gradually let himself fall into the black hole. It was black and open . . .

Fernando was pushing on the boy's back with a thick reed.

"Be careful! He can hold onto it."

"No, not any longer."

They waited a while, just in case. The body rose to the surface.

"Let's get out of here."

The east wind erased their footprints in the sand.

Piolo's car raced into town.

"Look out! You're going to kill somebody."

Piolo didn't answer. He had to deliver what he was carrying, and fast. Blowing his horn constantly so that people would get out of the way, he reached Antonio's house.

Several boys came over to help him. The oxygen tank was very heavy. They carried it into the room.

"Is Don Vicente here?"

Piolo didn't trust people who knew a great deal. He was afraid that the druggist had deceived him.

"Yes. Did you bring the other equipment?"

Piolo went to the car to get the package while Don Vicente prepared the oxygen. Antonio was gasping and felt a piercing pain in his chest, as though something inside were transfixing him.

Don Mariano left the union offices with the paper in his pocket. He had also typed the envelope. The waste-basket full of paper up in his office testified to his lack of skill at the typewriter. For the first time he realized that it wasn't an easy job to be a typist.

He went down San Jorge Street before going home. The messenger who worked for the union lived in Number Five. Don Mariano knocked on the small door that opened onto the landing of the stairway.

"It's upstairs. The third door on the left."

The woman accompanied him in her slip. That gentleman looked as though he were important, and she didn't want to lose the chance to help him. They banged on the door for several minutes.

Chivato wasn't married. He lived with Petra, a girl who slept less soundly than he did.

"Who is it?"

"Wake up Chivato. It's urgent. It's Don Mariano."

The representative was very impressed with the sound of his own name. As for Petra, the name was associated in her mind with their food. She proceeded to very rudely awaken the little man who occupied the other half of the mattress.

"Come on, get up. Don Mariano's here."

Chivato pulled on his pants. He buckled the belt without bothering to button them up. Then he opened the door a crack and Don Mariano handed him the envelope.

"Deliver this right away."

It was three o'clock in the morning.

"Now?"

"Yes, and no excuses."

Don Mariano left and Chivato went back to bed.

"Look out! You're going to get into trouble."

"I'm not breaking my balls for anybody."

The woman hit him and he seized her around the waist.

"Come here."

As soon as he had her in his arms he realized that he didn't want her, but he had already begun the game. He was sleepy, very sleepy. But of course, being sleepy was no excuse for not performing well as a man.

He went out into the street rubbing his eyes. The sky was getting light. The first workers were on their way to their jobs, but the "unemployed" ones had still not gone to the plaza.

Chivato looked at the address on the envelope.

"At least he's not far away."

Irene heard a cry. Then another. She looked out of the window of the hut, a small square cut into the straw. "Criminals," someone cried. Then, "Help me out of here." It was a clear voice that was getting weaker but was still easy to understand. Irene woke up her mother.

"Someone is shouting over at Brinca bog. He's saying something about criminals."

Paca sat up in bed. She heard the cries and was frightened. That afternoon she had sold four pigs and the whole town knew about it. It might be a trick to make them open the door and then steal the money.

"Did you lock the door?"

"Yes."

"Check the bolt and don't you dare open it!"

Irene obeyed.

"It's shut."

"All right, then. Go to bed and don't open the door even if someone knocks."

"But Ma, there's a man shouting for help out there."

"Don't ever trust men."

Irene went back to bed. The cries continued for a while, and then there was nothing. She thought she heard two other voices.

"Ma, there are others."

"That's why I told you not to open the door."

Tobías entered the building, taking care not to make any noise. Fortunately there was no light in the patio or on the stairway. He opened his door. It was made of cardboard because they didn't have enough money to buy any other material. His wife was sleeping. He took his clothes off in the darkness because he didn't want to turn on the light. It could be seen from the outside no matter what precautions were taken. He dropped his clothes on the floor and made his way toward the bed. An empty bottle rolled over the tile floor.

"Shit!"

Tobías stood stock still. The noise didn't wake anyone up. He pushed his wife to one side to make a place for himself on the bed. She was drunk, as usual, and drunks sleep soundly.

It was six o'clock when Chivato arrived. Tobías, who had awoken at dawn, heard the strange footsteps. They crossed the patio and then came up the stairs. Someone knocked at the door. He looked for a corner to hide in. There was another knock at the door. Alberto, his youngest son, got up.

"I'm going to answer the door."

Tobías motioned to him, but the child didn't understand.

"Does Tobías Blasco live here?"

"He's my father."

"Give him this."

Chivato left the letter with the child. It occurred to him as he went down the stairs that if it was urgent he ought to have asked for Tobías. He went back up.

Don Damián woke up very early. The whole family got up early.

"Bring me some coffee."

His wife obeyed. She was a lady, but she knew how to serve her husband. Don Damián had his habits. "Bringing coffee and pressing pants are things you can't tell a maid to do." That was why Doña Marcela took his coffee up to the bedroom every morning.

The cook was up. This kept the mistress from having

to call her and saved her the usual morning scolding.

"Señora, Fernando is here. He says he wants to see the master."

"Tell him to wait."

Doña Marcela announced the visitor.

"Ask him if something has gone wrong."

His wife went downstairs again.

"He says nothing's wrong."

"Then tell him to go to the wine cellar and wait for me there."

Fernando went to the wine cellar. It was early and he was tired. He went into the little office and lay down on his boss' bed. The night's "work" gave him a certain authority. He was thinking that his boss would no longer be able to scold him or fire him. The idea that Don Damián would be afraid of him, his foreman, amused him, but of course it wouldn't be a good idea to get him too worked up, because Don Damián was capable of anything. Someday Fernando might be in Marciano's shoes, and that wouldn't be amusing.

Tobías took the blue envelope. A summons for him to appear in court, probably. They had certainly uncovered the matter quickly. He turned the letter over in his hands, wondering if it was better to read it and waste time or to escape immediately. The truth was that Tobías barely knew how to read, and he didn't want to ask a neighbor to read the letter.

Someone knocked at the door again. Tobías woke his wife up.

"Open the door and find out what they want."

"What for? Can't you do it as well as I can?"

"Do what I tell you!"

His wife got up.

"What do you want?"

"I want to know if Tobías Blasco is in."

"There he is."

The door was standing wide open and a finger was pointing at him. Tobías didn't say anything because his voice stuck in his throat.

"Don Mariano, the head of the union, sent me. I brought a letter, but since it's urgent, I wanted to know if you were at home."

Tobías was still more terrified. Without knowing what else to do, he handed the letter to the messenger.

"Read it to me."

Chivato looked at him, surprised at such ignorance. Then he ripped the envelope open.

"It says that since Antonio is sick, they've named you to go to Cádiz in his place as representative of the social section. You have to be at the stop at eleven o'clock."

Tobías breathed freely. They didn't know anything, but . . .

"What happened?" he asked Chivato.

"Nothing, it's just that they went a little too far with Antonio in the barracks."

That morning César Blázquez felt the devil in his flesh. Mass had done nothing to calm him down. He felt as strong as a boy and he forgot everything—the strike, the vineyard, and the wine cellar. He even forgot his secretary, a short, unctuous man who was always trotting by his side.

"Manuel!"

"Yes, Don César."

"I'm not going to the wine cellar today. Take care of everything."

"Whatever you say."

Don César turned at the next corner. He went around two blocks and then took the same street he had left. There was no need to publicize the excursion. At the bottom of Belén Hill was Turco Alley. A long time ago a certain Turkish merchant had given his name to the place. Like many others he had come to San- lúcar in search of fortune, bringing with him a veritable Allah's paradise. The men of the town learned the way to his house, pointing it out to merchants and soldiers who were passing through on their way to the Indies. Those houses thrived and survived the centuries thanks to the prosperous trade which, even though it is not mentioned in the autobiographies of any of the great figures of the world of finance, was the beginning of many fortunes.

The only remaining trace of Oriental times was the old inn, today Doña Mary's house.

It had windows with iron gratings on the outside and lattice shutters on the inside, a large door studded with bronze nails in the style of noble houses and, on the other side of the door, a patio covered by a thick grapevine.

That was where Don César was going when a wrin- kled woman cut him off.

"Don't you want to see your son?"

Don César pushed her to one side with his cane. The past was a bother. Once it's left in the confessional it's forgotten by God and, presumably, other men. It also seemed to him that this woman had no connection with the Macarena he remembered, which was all the more reason why she shouldn't bother him.

The woman insisted.

"I don't even have enough money to feed him."

Don César threw a *duro* on the ground.

"Take it and don't bother me. I'm in a hurry."

The woman picked up the coin and went into a door- way.

"How time passes," Don César mused.

He had met her more than ten years before. The girl was only about fifteen at the time. She was dark and had green eyes and a willowy figure, as they said in such cases. She lived in the poor section of town, where his wine cellars were located.

He had called his foreman, Botas.

"Do you know who that girl is?"

"She's my daughter, sir."

Don César ran after her for quite a while, but Botas, who knew his boss from way back, tried to get her out of his reach.

"I want to see your daughter, Juan."

"She's not here. I sent her to Trebujena."

"Bring her to me. It'll be better for you."

"She's not here, I tell you."

Don César couldn't stand it. When he wanted something, he had to get it. He talked about Botas at the club.

"I'm going to have to fire him for taking advantage of his job. Now he wants to pay overtime. You know how people get ideas when they've been working in one house for a long time."

The foreman left. For months neither he nor any of his family could find work in Sanlúcar. Don César was making sure that he would have them where he wanted them.

In those days people didn't emigrate, so the family went hungry.

One day Don César found Macarena in the street playing with the other children. She was thinner and he wanted her more than ever.

"Do you want me to show you the wine cellar?"

The child tried to run away, but Don César grabbed her around the waist.

"Come with me. I have a ham hanging in my office. I'll give you a big piece."

When Botas found out about it he wanted to kill Don César. His friends convinced him that it was better to file a complaint. However, they paid no attention to him at court.

"Your daughter violated by Don César! You don't even know what you're saying! That girl has been playing around with half the town!"

"That's a lie! Have the doctor examine her."

"We don't want doctors here, just witnesses."

Botas committed suicide. He loved the girl dearly and couldn't stand the shame.

His widow had to take care of the children. Macarena continued going to the master's house for several months. He gave her some food and a few *pesetas* for sweeping the enormous rooms. One day he tired of her.

"When Macarena comes, tell her that I don't want her around here any more."

The doorman carried out the order, but Macarena was waiting for him on the doorstep.

"Don César . . . I'm expecting a child by you."

Don César shrugged his shoulders. The girl's mother appeared in his office that afternoon.

"I'll talk, and it'll be the biggest scandal you've ever seen."

"But woman, what do you want me to do? Don't you know that I'm married?"

"I'm not asking for that. Give us something for the child."

"You know that your daughter has been going around with other men. God knows whose child it is!"

"That's not true, Don César."

He gave her five hundred *pesetas,* which was a great deal of money at that time.

"I don't want either of you to bother me again."

Later he learned that Macarena had become a prostitute. His conscience pricked him slightly, so he went to confession.

"Father, the girl I told you about has become a prostitute."

"Did you have anything to do with it?"

"No, father. You already know everything that happened."

"That's all right then, my son. Rest easy. People will follow their natural inclinations, no matter what you do for them."

He met her in Doña Mary's house several times. She had moved to the alley with the child. Sometimes he went to bed with her.

She lost her good looks very rapidly, and the Madame fired her. Then she began to work on her own among the laborers, but people who don't have much aren't able to pay much. Macarena went from bad to worse.

The most disagreeable part of it all was being accosted in the street. He didn't want to denounce her because his wife might find out about it. The matter had been covered up very carefully. The other girls had turned out better. They didn't dare bother him; they just greeted him from a distance. Only God knew how many children he had sired in his long life.

"Babies are made before you know it. It's the woman's fault, because they enjoy themselves when they ought to hold back."

As is customary in Spain, pleasure and conception were linked in the vintner's mind.

He didn't stop in the patio to listen to the musical flow of the water. Those who had built the fountain for the customers' pleasure were dead and gone by now. It went unnoticed by the new visitors, who were only concerned with tangible pleasures. Today they were of another, more practical race, that wanted to touch flesh and "hear less talk."

He went into the little nineteenth-century-style salon where the mistress of the house received her customers. She got up and embraced him warmly. Don César's face was buried in the vast mound of flesh.

"I'm certainly glad to see you," she said. "With all this nonsense in the fields that keeps all of you busy we're always alone now."

"You know I never forget you. No matter what happens, I always find time to come even though it's only for a moment."

Doña Mary smiled coquettishly.

"I have something just for you."

Don César sat down on the drawing-room sofa. It wasn't comfortable, but he liked it. He had one just like it in his home, but his wife wouldn't let him use it. It was for visitors and she took great care of the yellow satin upholstery.

"Let's see what you have."

"It's very expensive," said Doña Mary, with religious unction.

"How much?"

"Two thousand *pesetas*."

"No, I'm not interested."

"I'll show it to you anyway."

Doña Mary left and returned with a little gypsy girl with big eyes and a half-formed body. She wasn't a child, but she wasn't a woman yet, either. Just the point at which Don César liked them.

He pointed at the girl with his cane.

"This, two thousand *pesetas?* You're crazy."

"My God, Don César. You haven't taken a good look at her."

"Five hundred and that's all you'll get."

"Child, take off your blouse."

She obeyed.

"What do you say now? You don't see things like this every day."

Don César was getting excited.

"I have to see some more of her."

The child let her worn skirt fall to her feet. There

she was in the middle of the room, like some circus animal. She felt ashamed and cold in spite of the heat, but she didn't say anything, trying to preserve her proud and distant attitude.

"I'll go as high as eight hundred."

"Don César! Remember that things have gone up. I do have some at that price, but they're not untouched."

Don César's little eyes were shining.

"Well, find me another one."

"All right." Doña Mary turned to the child. "Go on, get dressed and go up to your room."

The girl ran out with her clothes under her arm.

"Come on, Mary, I'm a good customer. I give you more business in the course of a year than anyone else."

"I know that, Don César. If I could, I'd be delighted to, but the parents have to get theirs, and I'm not going to pay them out of my own pocket."

"You'll make something on the deal."

"I swear by my daughter who's being educated by the nuns and whom I love more than my own life that I'm not making a *peseta* on this."

Don César shook his head.

"I'll call another one if you want me to. Pili, for example. Do you remember? She's the blonde that you liked so much."

But Don César was hooked.

"No, she's already been pawed by too many people."

"Juani then . . ."

"Can't you come down a little? I'll go as high as a thousand."

"Impossible. If she were mine I'd give her to you for nothing."

Don César put fifteen hundred on the table. Doña Mary slipped the bills between her breasts.

"Send her to my room."

Don César slowly climbed the marble staircase.

Fourteen

It was after nine and only five men had arrived. The foreman was impatient.

"Where are the others?"

Piojito stepped forward.

"They're not coming . . . It's because of Antonio . . ."

The foreman didn't like jokes.

"You're paid what you ask for here. It's not right to play a dirty trick like this on Don Aurelio."

"Some of us have already gone to tell him. We came in order not to let him down entirely, but the fact is that Antonio's worse."

The foreman didn't know anything about it. They had told him that the boy had been arrested and he had looked for someone else to take his place.

"They beat him. He was never very strong."

The foreman took off his cap.

"That's all right, boys. We'll do what we can."

Don Aurelio had one defect which he had never tried to hide. Don Aurelio would have liked to have been born a woman. That was why he was wearing a rose satin housecoat with slippers of the same color when the three workers came to his house.

"What's happening, my sons?"

Fortunately the three men had been up all night by Antonio's side and didn't feel like laughing.

"We came to tell you that today five men will go to work in your fields. Antonio is worse."

Don Aurelio knew less about it than his foreman.

The judge was in the courtroom taking care of minor matters. Slander, fights, petty robberies. A morning filled with boring work. Hearings were held two days a week. There was no originality either in the crimes or in the witnesses' statements.

Corporal Pérez arrived with a sheaf of papers.

"I need to see Don Alberto."

The secretary looked him straight in the eye. He always looked straight at people he considered his inferiors.

"What for?"

"We found a corpse. We have to move it. Here are the preliminary findings."

Corporal Pérez left the papers on the desk. A death is interesting when it takes place under strange circumstances. The secretary entered the courtroom.

"It looks like murder . . ."

Don Alberto lifted his eyes from his book. He found the statements of those who were testifying boring.

"Tell the corporal to wait."

Court was adjourned.

Tobías was smoking as he sat on the edge of the sidewalk. He was waiting for Don Mariano. The church clock struck eleven-thirty. He was thinking that with the money Don Damián had given him he would be able to smoke for a long time. "And don't go around blabbing about it." Tobías didn't intend to say a word.

The sun was heating the cement. He got up and went toward the bar.

"Don't give me new wine. I want the best manzanilla."

The tavern owner laughed.

"And what are you going to pay for it with?"

Tobías handed him a thousand-*peseta* bill. The workers whistled.

"Did you rob a bank?"

"Work . . . just hard work."

The bartender held the bill up to the light. It wasn't counterfeit.

Don Mariano appeared at twelve.

"Are you Tobías Blasco?"

"Yes, sir, at your service."

"Get into the car."

Piolo rubbed his eyes. He hadn't slept all night and now he had to drive to Cádiz. When they called him he said no, but Don Vicente convinced him that he ought to go. "See if you can find out something. Very strange things are going on. It's not a bad idea to be up on what's happening."

"Tobías is a rat," protested Piolo.

"That's why you ought to go. He wouldn't say a word to us."

Don Aurelio Peláez parked his car at Puerta de Jerez.

"Where does Antonio live?"

The men shrugged their shoulders. One can never trust the rich.

"It's so that I can see him. He used to work in my fields and I heard that he's sick."

"Mesón del Duque. We don't know the number. You'll see the people standing outside."

Ciriaco went over to his boss. He didn't like to let people down and it seemed to him that they'd done it that morning.

"You're not going to hold it against us, are you, Don Aurelio?"

"No . . . I can't . . . Tomorrow I'll pay you the wages you lost today. I've got Antonio's here with me."

People spoke well of Don Aurelio on the street.

"He looks like a fairy, but he's a brave man."

An argument was taking place in the governor's office. Present were the president of the district council, who was a big landowner and wine wholesaler, the mayor, and the two biggest landowners in the province. They couldn't reach an agreement.

"I can't see any other way out. No matter what we do it's useless."

"They'll have to compensate us in some way."

"Possibly we'll get an increase in the price of wheat."

"That's unlikely, very unlikely. They don't want to touch the price of bread."

"Or a tax cut."

The president of the district council was nervous.

"If I lose my position and the others lose theirs, what will happen? The positions will be taken by strangers who won't make the slightest effort to defend our interests, and will even be capable of undercutting us. One has to know how to lose a little when it's a question of gaining a great deal."

"You're the one who has most to lose if you get booted out. You haven't helped us at all."

"More than you think. Haven't my reports warded off the most disastrous measures? We're able to conceal what we earn. It seems to me that that's quite a lot."

"It would be the same with someone else in your post."

"I don't think so. Remember that I own land too, and that it means more to me than my position."

The governor called in his secretary. He wanted to end the pointless discussion.

"When there's only one road it's useless to discuss

which one to take. Within an hour the minimum wage in the vineyards will be eighty *pesetas*."

The landowners left his office. The governor gave a sigh of relief.

"They're almost worse than the others."

The president agreed.

"Let's see, Angel, write this down."

The secretary waited with his pen poised.

"At a meeting held in the office of the governor for the purpose of coping with the situation created in this province by the increase in the cost of living, and fearing that this would lead to the disruption of law and order . . . I don't think it's necessary to explain it any further, do you?"

The president of the district council agreed.

"Let's go on. It has been agreed unanimously by the union authorities as well as by the representatives of the local delegations, including both the economic and the social sections of the unions . . ." The governor hesitated. "Reverse the order. It will sound better to some."

The secretary revised what he had written.

"What were we saying?"

"The social and economic sections . . ."

"Oh, yes. We have agreed to raise the wages for seasonal laborers in the vineyards to eighty *pesetas* a day. The effort that Andalusian landowners are making on this occasion to improve the lot of their workers is worthy of special note, since they cannot afford to do so. The meeting was held in an atmosphere of perfect cordiality on the part of all present, and this agreement was greeted with general acclaim. Etc., etc."

"Does Your Excellency want me to draw up a full report?"

"Yes, and try to think up a reason for our not meeting in the union hall."

"Because of the problem of public order . . ."

"That seems all right to me."

"Is that all, Your Excellency?"

"Yes. See that it's published in the morning papers. It should be made known as soon as possible. We may be inspected, and I don't want them to find any irregularities."

The secretary went out.

"Well, I think we've finished."

"We still have the meeting."

"That's not important."

The governor looked at his watch.

"Let's go."

The two authorities went to the conference room. They found the provincial head of the local unions waiting for them at the door.

"Are they all here?"

"Yes, and everything is in order."

Don Vicente left a message for his wife.

"Don Vicente said that he wouldn't be home today, either," the maid told her. "If there's something urgent, they should get in touch with him on Mesón del Duque Street."

"I'll eat alone, then."

Clara was used to it. Ever since they had been married she frequently ate lunch and supper alone. "I warn you that I didn't study medicine in order to get rich. If I'd wanted that I would have become an engineer or a crook. I'm a doctor because I want to take care of the sick. They come before anything. Even before you." She had said yes. Clara was bored but she never complained. She understood Vicente's work and tried to help him.

She went into the little room where the medicine was kept. Another package of samples had arrived and they had to be put away properly.

The court went to the bog. Marciano was floating on the green scum. His mother was leaning on Private Pérez's shoulder and crying. Private Núñez was trying to console the father.

Don Alberto proceeded with the investigation.

"Are there any witnesses?"

Irene's mother has told her not to get involved, but . . .

"I heard him shouting last night."

The judge looked at the girl warily. Ignorant people have a great deal of imagination.

"Where did you hear it?"

"I live over there."

Irene pointed to the hut, less than fifty yards away.

"Why didn't you go out to see what was happening?"

"My mother told me not to open the door."

"Where was your mother?"

"With me."

"Tell her to step forward."

The woman was frightened.

"It's nothing, señora. Just a simple statement."

"We were afraid. We live alone and we had just finished selling the pigs. There was money in the house, something that almost never happens. There isn't any there any more, because I took it to the bank early this morning."

"Didn't you see the corpse when you crossed the road?"

"You were already here. I didn't think I was needed."

"What were the shouts like?"

"He asked for help and called someone criminals. Then we heard two other voices, but we couldn't understand what they were saying because they were speaking in very low voices."

Their neighbors were also questioned, but they lived farther away and they had more experience in these matters. They didn't want to have anything to do with the Guards.

"No, we didn't hear anything."

Corporal Pérez confirmed the fact that the man had been murdered, and he was put in charge of the case.

The men didn't go to the plaza as they usually did. The word that came from Antonio's house was clear.

"We won't be seen in either the plaza or the bars until he's out of danger."

The people filled Mesón del Duque and the adjoining streets. It was a human sea that flowed toward the wounded man's door. Pelao, Calero, Negro, and the others stayed there and informed the rest. Don Vicente didn't want to say that he had lost hope, but Encarna knew it. Some sixth sense had warned her.

The rest of the town seemed deserted. Some of the bars closed because their owners were in the Barrio Alto. That's what the signs on the doors said. The Guards didn't dare stop them.

Don Luis crossed the wide street. The palm trees waved in solitary majesty in Cabildo Plaza. Two women hurried by on their way to the Cuesta. A group of children were sitting on the benches in the center of the plaza. They were silent, like the men. Two automobiles broke the silence. The tension increased. Don Luis noticed that he was becoming apprehensive.

His first visitor was Don León Alvarez.

"I don't know what's happening, but there's something strange in the air."

Don León agreed.

"How is the business of the grapes coming along?"

"Badly."

"Well, patience."

Don León cleared his throat.

"I suppose you've come to ask me about something."

"Yes, of course. I've been told that Mariano left a while ago for Cádiz with a workers' representative. Is it something important?"

"I don't know. But I can say that he was summoned by the governor."

"I suppose that it was to impose order."

"Yes, surely. They didn't tell me anything. I know as much as you do."

Don Luis sent off his unwelcome visitor with a few slaps on the back. It was no time to clarify things. What for? They would read the news in the papers. He would stay out of it and keep his hands clean, as usual. The letter from Cádiz was categorical. Things had to be resolved immediately, "and without violence."

The others kept coming after Don León. Gaspar, César, Diego, Damián's brother, Antonio . . .

Don Luis greeted them and offered them cigarettes.

The attendant came in to announce another visitor.

". . . There are also two women with a child in their arms. They want a welfare card."

"Tell them to wait and have the gentleman come in."

"Don Aurelio Peláez is here . . . There are two of them."

"I know, two women. Have Señor Peláez come in."

"It's incredible!"

Even in the most dramatic circumstances Peláez's gestures revealed a profound timidity.

"I'm talking to you about the affair of Antonio Cabeza de Vaca, the boy they arrested the other day. In following the governor's unfortunate orders, naturally."

"You're wrong, that's not the way it was," replied the mayor. "The Civil Guards surprised him while he was talking to the prisoners through the jail windows. You know very well that it's against the law."

"It makes no difference. The arrest of the others was equally inexcusable."

"Calero and Negro? That's water under the bridge."

"Water under the bridge or not, it requires an explanation."

Don Luis became angry.

"An explanation of what?"

"Of the beatings. There's no law allowing a man to be beaten to death."

The mayor pretended to be surprised.

"I didn't know anything about it."

"You're lying. You knew it as well or better than the rest of the town did."

"I swear I didn't. Besides, it's nothing to get so worked up about."

"Antonio is dying. It's shameful that wretches like you can bring this town to such a pass. I intend to lodge a complaint. I'll go to Madrid. I'll do whatever is necessary to end these abuses."

"My dear friend, I'm the mayor, not your servant."

"All of us pay your salary. As a result, you should be the servant of us all."

"I don't want to argue with you."

"Very well. I'll see that this matter reaches the courts."

Don Luis' expression changed. His initial smile gave way to a look of extreme severity.

"I'd advise you not to."

"I'm a free man, and I don't need your advice or anyone else's."

"A free man! Nobody has forgotten the position you took. Nobody will forget that you marked yourself by paying too soon. Or do you think that will be forgotten?"

Peláez turned slightly pale. Don Luis pointed to a large chair, reserved for high-ranking visitors. With his stubby index finger and a voice that he tried to make conciliatory he began to dominate his visitor.

"Sit down, Aurelio. Come on, calm down a little."

Don Aurelio obeyed. The mayor began to feel an almost sensual emotion as he regarded his well-intentioned victim who was feeling timid and uncomfortable and didn't dare to renew his impetuous indictment.

Without conviction, Don Aurelio spoke in an almost pleading voice in order to cover his retreat.

"At any rate, I'll do as I please."

"Think about the risk you're taking."

"The others are risking just as much."

"You don't have any witnesses."

"And where do you intend to find any?"

"In our position and with money, my friend, you know that we'll have no trouble finding some. On the other hand, you . . ."

Don Aurelio slowly stood up and left without saying goodbye. He realized that he had just been bluffing. How could he who, when all was said and done, was just a son of ordinary people, oppose the omnipotent masters? He put on his hat. For the first time he would have liked to have had another father. A father with a name. A father who could have made him invulnerable now. That way no one could shout at him. The great men would have to treat him as an equal. And he could pay the workers whatever he pleased. Yes, indeed. But Don Luis knew his background as well as everyone else. That background that made him feel timid before slaves and masters alike. Because there he was, neither on one side nor the other, hesitating and lonely, indecisive and strange. He walked on slowly and clumsily, with his head down and his hands in his pockets. A fresh breeze blew the brim of his hat back from time to time. He walked faster. He crossed the street. Suddenly he felt an irresistible desire to cry.

The governor was presiding over the meeting. For the first time in his life he hadn't written down his speech. This was too intimate a gathering for such formality.

"Gentlemen, we called you together in order to officially approve the new union agreement. As of today the workers in the vineyards will receive a minimum wage of eighty *pesetas*. Are you in agreement?"

The provincial representative stood up.

"Of course, Excellency. We are in agreement and very grateful."

"Since we have not heard anyone oppose the proposal, the agreement is unanimously approved. I hope you will now sign it, and tomorrow it will be announced in the press."

The representatives signed in order of rank, and at one o'clock the meeting was over. At the same moment an attendant was registering the official report at the post office.

"Whew! I didn't think I'd get here on time."

The postal clerk smiled.

Corporal Pérez worked diligently. If he were able to solve the crime it would mean a good notation on his service record, and a good record was very important, above all in this absurd situation. If Antonio died there might be trouble, and a good job on this case would make his superiors forget that he had had a hand in the beating. For once people talked freely.

"He left alone, just before I closed up," Carmelo said. "It must have been about one o'clock in the morning, or maybe a little earlier, because I'm always careful to close up on time now. He'd drunk two or three glasses of wine. I have his bill written down right here. He told us that he didn't have any money because he didn't want to take Don Damián's."

"Don Damián pays what he feels like paying. Marciano knew his rights and didn't like it," Bala added in a burst of courage.

"Yes, he was telling us about the fight they had in the wine cellar. He was going to file a complaint with the union if the boss didn't give in. Poor fellow!"

"It's possible that that explains everything . . ."
Corporal Pérez noted the anonymous observation.
"Did he drink a lot?"
"Not at all. He wasn't a big drinker. He didn't even get drunk on Saturdays. He was certainly easy to get along with, but there aren't many who are as serious as he was."
His mother was hardly able to talk.
"It was his first day of work after five months. Five months of struggling the best way he knew how to get something to eat. Sometimes he went out looking for snails, and other times—there's no need to hide anything now, officer—he spent hours rowing in the marsh to catch birds. He'd do anything rather than leave us without anything to eat. Before he left he told me how I should spend the day's wages. Two *duros* to the store, and the rest in the market. 'Ma,' he said, 'I'll have a steady job soon and your worries will be over.' And just look how they brought him to me!"
The disfigured corpse was lying on the only bed in the room. Several women were standing around it, and there was a heavy, sickly-sweet odor even in the hallway. It had been hard to remove the body from the slab after the autopsy. Filomena had taken care of everything, since her cousin Pedro worked there.
"What's strange about it is that he was out by Falón Hill. He never took that road at night. It's not that he was a coward, but he avoided that place. It's so lonely."
"Everybody avoids it."
Pérez spoke to the men of the house.
"Had he quarreled with anyone?"
"No. He was very peaceful."
"Did anyone owe him money?"
"How could they? He never had any."

Fifteen

Don Vicente came out of the room with his head lowered and his eyes red-rimmed. Pelao went over to him.

"What is it?"

"It's all over."

Pelao and the others cried like babies. The whole town was shocked to hear the news, even though it was expected.

"Don't forget that Encarna has been left alone."

"Don't worry, Don Vicente. We're here to make sure that this family has everything it needs."

Calero knew that the others would back that promise up. Negro approached the bed.

"We'll carry him away."

The sole attendant was nodding at his desk in the courthouse when Don Vicente arrived.

"What's new, doctor?"

"Nothing good. I want to see Don Alberto."

"I don't know if he's in."

"Then look for him."

The attendant got up reluctantly. He had had too much work to do over the last few days.

"Don Vicente López is here."

"Send him in."

Don Alberto stretched in his armchair. He had had a

busy morning because of the murder, and now he had
to receive the last visitor in the world he wanted to see.

"I've come to give you a death certificate."

"Why did you bother? You could have sent it over
with anyone, or even through Ocaso, even though he
wasn't insured."

"I wanted to hand you this one personally."

Don Vicente threw the paper on the desk. The judge
picked it up. "Antonio Cabeza de Vaca died today in
his home on Mesón del Duque Street, as a result of
blows he received in the barracks of the Civil Guard of
this city on the 29th of this month. May First, . . ."

Don Alberto took off his glasses. His myopic eyes
glistened.

"This is a joke of course."

"No, sir, it's a document."

"But not a legal document."

"A certificate is always legal when it's signed by a
doctor, especially a family doctor."

"The family doctor of a worker under social security
is the one who is officially designated."

"Or the one who attends the family on a regular
basis."

"Not officially. Remember that your patient may have
died as a result of improper treatment."

"Absolutely not. He received more attention than he
could have in the hospital where, for example, there's
no oxygen."

"Remember that Doctor Blanes visited the patient
yesterday."

"That's not true."

"There's a certificate to prove it. Antonio couldn't
go to the meeting in Cádiz since he was in bed as a result of an acute attack of gastroenteritis—of the can-
cerous type, possibly."

"He wasn't sick. I can prove it."

"In any case, his official doctor is more worthy of belief than a private pill pusher. It would have been more logical for him to have consulted the physician who had been assigned to him rather than you."

"It would have been logical, but I'm the one who attended him until the very last moment. I have witnesses, and there's also the body with marks from the beating."

"You're very young, Vicente. You still don't know about life. If you knew you'd talk differently. The body will be buried very soon, and then it will decay. As for witnesses, they will support you today and perhaps tomorrow. But no later. They'll forget Antonio and the strike, because the moment of emotion will have passed. That will be when I'll call on them to testify. They'll think about their wages, their security, and the discreet threats that the Civil Guard will see reach their ears. Few, very few, will appear in the courtroom, and only two or three of them will stick to their story, stupidly obeying the lead of the prosecutor or of the lawyer for the defense, who will have received his instructions beforehand. It makes no difference. They'll be inclined toward the side of authority, because that's the side their bread is buttered on. There's a great deal of fear in this town. Is it fear that protects the vineyards? Of course. But as long as it continues to protect them, God bless it."

"Calero and Negro will stick to the truth."

"Their testimony is worthless. They are political criminals, outside the law. The former lost his civil status during the war. The latter lost his just now."

Don Vicente was tired. Tired of arguing and tired of fighting.

"In any case, I won't make out another certificate."

"You will." The judge's voice was firm. "You'll dirty your hands just like everyone else."

"No, I won't."

Don Alberto held out a blank form and a pen. The doctor felt an intense loathing. He was repelled by this man who spoke of justice—hypocritically or unconsciously—as he urged him to commit an injustice.

"Do you ask me for this in the name of your God?"

The judge nodded.

"Exactly. And remember that He is also yours. I already know that you don't like to go to church or to read the Bible. I think you ought to leaf through it more frequently. It would open roads to you that you are unaware of. Now, as always, we will find in the divine words some line which will help us solve our problem."

He reached for the little book with the broad, white hands of a wealthy peasant. Don Alberto frequently alluded to his noble ancestry, but the whole town knew that his family's wealth and crests only went as far back as the confiscation and sale of church lands in the last century.

" 'Render unto Caesar that which is Caesar's.' Caesar is the state, and the state needs peace. This could disturb the peace and harm us all. Sign, my friend. You're indignant, but indignation is not a good counselor, and neither you nor I can turn the clock back."

Don Vicente walked toward the door. The judge's tone of voice changed.

"One moment, doctor."

Don Vicente stopped.

"Do you know how many ways there are to ruin a man's life? How many ways to end a doctor's career? One little complaint from a private individual, proof that a certain treatment has caused someone's death, a dubious diagnosis that entails certain consequences . . . And then comes expulsion from the medical association, jail . . . In short, a thousand complications that I would like to save you from, I assure you."

"I appreciate that, but I can assure you that until now I haven't made any mistakes. I'm not boasting. It's true."

"Many of your patients have died."

"It isn't usually healthy people who ask me to treat them. It's also logical that some of my patients should die—of old age. It'll be our turn some day. I've prescribed medicines which are impossible to find in our part of the country, and I've found them by my own means. I've ordered operations to be performed that some surgeons have refused to perform, demanding that the families pay in advance. I've seen many people die because neither they nor I had the money that was needed to save them. But—and mark my words—my treatments have never, absolutely never, produced bad results."

"It isn't a matter of what you say, but rather of what I believe, if I should find myself asked to adjudicate a complaint."

"That's absurd."

"But it's possible. You can go. I'll not require you to fill out another certificate, but I advise you not to make out another document like this one."

The judge lit the paper with his lighter and it turned to ashes on the porcelain plate that served as an ashtray.

"I'll make another copy."

"The same thing will happen to it that happened to this one. We'll have a death certificate made out by the real family doctor, Blanes, shortly. Antonio died of cancer."

Don Vicente walked slowly back to the desk. The judge smiled. Don Vicente slapped him in the face. The secretary came in when he heard the noise, but Don Alberto ordered him to leave.

"That's all right, Vicente. You want to be a martyr of an unjust cause, an absurd cause, because the world can't change. I am a martyr of Christ every day because, feeling as you do, I suffer from the arbitrary acts which I am forced to commit by virtue of my position as defender of order. The order established by God, which the evil committed by men places in a precarious position. I don't hold this against you, and indeed I turn the other cheek, as our friend did to the Pharisees . . . and I beg you to understand me."

The doctor walked out through the secretary's office.

It was sunny and hot in the street, but he didn't feel the heat. Cold sweat was running down his forehead. There were no colors. Everything was as red as blood.

Clara was waiting for him impatiently.

"Your waiting room is full."

"Tell them that I'm not seeing anyone today. I'm too nervous."

Clara transmitted the message to his patients, who left the room without protesting. One woman approached her.

"My child has been sick since yesterday. He has a very high fever and he's vomiting. He doesn't even cry now. I think he's dying. I wasn't able to bring him because he's big now and you know how my back is. If Don Vicente would just come to my house . . ."

Clara returned to his office.

"There's a case that seems to be serious . . ."

Don Vicente closed his eyes. Why had he chosen this life? He could have devoted himself to building houses or defending lawsuits or simply to making money, like his colleagues. He would have liked to be impervious to the pain of others like the rest. To be able to live side by side with poverty and injustice without caring, as long as they didn't affect him directly. To be able to hear people's woes while thinking about something else and then console them only for form's sake, and give alms as a cheap way of avoiding genuine compassion.

To be able to be "good" like all the "good" men he knew, without feeling each blow in the depths of his being as though it had been aimed directly at the very roots of his personality. To be able to turn sick people into "cases" that interested him in the same way that mechanics are interested in repairing an automobile. Not to know their names or how many children each one had, the color of their eyes, the shack they lived in, and the meagerness of their income. To turn them into experiences and rob them of their humanity.

But a dying man was not a cancer developing in one way or another. He was a specific person and he was suffering, because it's difficult to get painkillers and they're very expensive. Emaciated children were proof of something more than just the consequences of a calorie-deficient diet. Don Vicente talked about social injustice and the system and he wanted to be God because God is unjust. The God of evil! What did it matter if His evil would be good for everyone? Even when there was nothing further that could be done for a patient, he desperately searched for a cure. Afterward he would stand there facing the body and feel the impotence of his human condition. At night he would feel like crying, like a child who can't fix his toy.

Don Vicente raised his head.

"Who is it?"

"Manoli's son."

Oh yes, Manoli. How many children did she have?

"The woman who lives on the beach?"

"No, the one from Dehesilla."

The one from Dehesilla . . . She had four children. There was an older boy who was already working. He was the sole support of the family, because Manoli didn't have a husband or a "man." She never married. She had lived with the man from Pedo for four years. Four years, two children. He wasn't a bad man, but one

day he got tired of her. "I'm not free. She waits for me
at the tavern door, she hits me, and she takes all my pay
without even leaving me enough to buy tobacco." This
was commonplace in the town. All the women did the
same thing and it didn't bother the men. The truth was
that he had met Tagala. She was called that because her
grandfather had served in the war in the Philippines
and he came .back calling all the women Tagala. The
family inherited the name. Tagala was pretty. She was
fifteen years old and she had a past that was as intense
as it was brief.

The story had begun in the wine cellar of the Cura
brothers. There was a night of flamenco dancing in the
building, which used to be a convent and now had the
walls lined with wine casks. Tagala sang well and was
a good dancer. The whole town said so. Damián, Ricardo, and Diego cheered her on enthusiastically. The
guests invited for politeness' sake left at dawn, and then
the brothers and their closest friends began to really
enjoy themselves. The wine flowed and the evening
turned into an orgy. Some of the men and women had
already paired off. Tagala's mother sang and clapped
her hands as her daughter danced. She became more
and more tense and finally she ceased being a young
girl with softly rounded hips and became an object of
desire. The men became more and more excited. Don
Damián poured a bottle of manzanilla over the girl's
head and the men broke loose. Juan Vázquez ripped off
the girl's dress of faded rose-colored silk. Tagala fell to
the floor and the men began fighting over her.

Don Vicente had just arrived in town. He didn't
know the local customs nor the names of the families.
That was why they called him. Fernando, the foreman,
entered the patio. He also had blood on his clothes.

"Come with me. There's been an accident."

Tagala had fainted. It took them a few minutes to
realize what had happened. Frightened, they put her in

Don Damián's bed. Her mother was crying. The tension lessened abruptly. No one knew how it had happened. No one felt guilty, but they were all uncomfortable.

"We didn't mean for anything to happen."

It wasn't serious. Exhaustion and a few contusions. Don Vicente treated her.

"How old is she?"

"Fourteen."

"Who did it?"

The guests looked at each other. A few of them slipped out.

"Who did it?"

The guests didn't answer. No one knew how or when they had touched the child. Her mother remembered her dancing and the wine running down over her face and her half-nude body. That was all she remembered about what had happened during the night.

"Who was the first?"

"But . . ."

Damián stepped forward.

"We don't know, doctor."

Don Vicente insisted on filing a complaint.

"You may say that it's useless, but I have my responsibility."

What happened was that it was filed away with other complaints. There was a superficial investigation of events in the wine cellar. Don Damián offered the girl's parents a fat roll of banknotes and the matter was quickly forgotten.

Tagala became a prostitute. She was a success because she knew how to dress and men liked her. Her family lived at her expense for a while, but then she met the man from Pedo.

He behaved like the rest. He paid her what she asked and left. But he returned the next day, and the next. Tagala fell in love. It was the first time and no one could understand it. He was a coarse, country man, middle-aged and rather ugly. He didn't have either money or the brains to earn any. "She was used to such nice furs," her mother wailed. Her brothers wanted to kill her. "You're going to dishonor the family." But her love was too strong to be destroyed. The man from Pedo took her to his farm and stood guard with his hoe in his hand.

When Manoli came back from town, he wouldn't let her in.

"Go back to your family, you."

The woman took her children and walked to her mother's hut a short distance away. She lived there until her older brothers got tired of the intruders.

"You're going to have to look for somewhere to go."

She went to live in a room of a condemned house. Since her work with her hands was not sufficient to support her children, she also began to work with her body. The first two children were joined by a third and a fourth. It was said that one of them had been fathered by Don Gaspar and the other by his foreman. No one knew for sure.

But Manoli wasn't cut out to be a whore. She was too worn out, and she had to retire because she had no clientele. However, she had saved enough to buy the little plot of land she lived on. When her oldest boy began to work the situation improved. Between what she earned doing day work and her son's wages, there was enough to eat. The second oldest was also able to work, but he didn't like to bend his back. He was the black sheep of the family.

Don Vicente got out of the armchair.

"Tell her that I'll come immediately. When people get sick in that house, it's usually serious."

Clara told her the doctor would come. Manoli went down the street blessing the doctor aloud.

Don César listened to the girl cry as he got dressed. He liked to see them cry, but he always got tired of it before they stopped. The nervous sobs ended up making him angry. In any case, he hadn't wasted his money. It had been a good morning. Once again he had proven how perfectly his body functioned in spite of the years by bending a human being to his will, a new human being in whom he no longer had any interest. He walked down to the nineteenth-century salon with his usual mincing steps and his cane under his arm. Doña Mary was waiting for him by the window in her favorite armchair. It was a good vantage point from which to see the street because she could call to her good customers and recognize the bad ones before they rang the bell. The thick curtains kept her bulk from being seen from the street.

Doña Mary was in a bad humor. She had seen Don León enter the house on the other side of the street, the House of the Girls, as it was known. The four González sisters were competing with her in the most blatant way. She would have liked them to work for her, but they had never accepted, in spite of the good deal she had offered them.

"We like to be independent. If we came with you we'd have to obey you."

"But the only reason I want to do it is to keep my customers from being scattered."

Her expression changed when she heard Don César's footsteps.

"Have you had a good time?"

His little eyes were sparkling maliciously.

"Not as good as I'd expected."

"Don't lie. You're too young to be bored with a jewel like that."

Don César sat down on the sofa without answering.

"I'd like something to eat."

"I knew it. And doesn't food taste good after . . ."
She winked at him.

"Hunger doesn't mean that it was worth two bills, far from it."

"All right, all right. Don't get mad."

Doña Mary called the maid.

"Bring something to eat immediately. We have a guest."

The girl hurried out. She didn't know how to read, but she had a good memory. When she saw "the one with the cane," as he was known around town, come in, she cursed him because it was a lot of work to prepare a stew. However, she took care to do it before her mistress told her to in order to keep Doña Mary from yelling at her to hurry. Now pigs' ears and tails, cabbages, and chickpeas were bubbling in the pot, ready to be served. They had almost cooked too long because Don César had taken longer than usual.

The child was crying as he sat huddled on the curb. He didn't know what was happening, but since everyone was crying, he thought that he ought to follow their example. A neighbor had taken him out of the room.

"Don't let me see you go back in again," she had said.

It was Don Vicente's idea. "Have them take the child out," he ordered.

And now he stayed out because he was afraid he would be spanked.

Encarna was silently embracing her husband's body. The women sobbed, because that was what was done at wakes of important people.

Cousin Jacinto took charge of the funeral. He had brought some cash with him "for whatever was needed," because he had a little saved up. He owned five *aran-*

zadas of vineyard and a hundred yards of untilled land for intensive pig-breeding.

Like everyone else, Antonio was "listed" at the Ocaso funeral parlor. Jacinto went to their office.

"Antonio Cabeza de Vaca has died. He lives on Mesón del Duque."

The clerk checked his books.

"This matter doesn't concern us. He was registered with us, but he owed almost a year on the policy."

"I'll pay it."

"There's a twenty per cent additional charge."

"When will they bring the coffin?"

The clerk scratched his bald spot.

"I don't know . . . I don't know . . . it's a bad day. There's another first-class funeral set."

"We want it at about eight o'clock."

"That's impossible. The carpenter is very busy. Besides, I don't know why you're in such a hurry. I don't suppose he'll be buried until tomorrow."

Jacinto agreed. Actually it would be better to leave his cousin where he was, even though the mattress might be a little soiled. Corpses always leave a stain.

"We want to bury him at seven o'clock in the morning."

"That's none of my business. You'll have to go to the parish house to make the arrangements."

"Listen, you know a lot about these things. Will it be hard to arrange?"

"It depends on how much they have to do. I know the other fellow's burial has been set for three o'clock and there's a first-class baptism following the funeral."

"Who's the other person?"

"Don't you know? Marciano. I think it was a murder."

As Jacinto was about to leave, he remembered that they had dropped his father with the coffin and all.

"If the coffin is one of those that the handles come off of, change it for another one, even though it costs a little more. I'll be around for whatever's necessary."

"That's what the boys told me. They were here a little while ago, but they didn't have a cent."

There weren't so many people in front of Marciano's house. The men stopped by, expressed their sympathy for the family and then went on to the Barrio Alto. If it hadn't been for Antonio, they would all have been at Marciano's house, but that day a murder was less important. Only a few sailors who had known him better than the others stayed with his family.

A group of women surrounded the corpse. The more tired they got, the less hysterical they were. The men smoked in silence in the patio. It wasn't their place to watch over the dead.

It occurred to Don Damián that it would be a good idea to visit the home of his late employee. He wouldn't have done it under normal circumstances because Marciano had not worked for him long enough to deserve such attention. But he hadn't liked the way Corporal Pérez gave him the news.

"The boy that you hired yesterday, Marciano Dominguez, was found dead in a bog. According to what one of his fellow workers told me—I can't reveal his name because I promised to keep it secret—he had some words with you when it was time for him to be paid. He threatened to report you to the union."

The corporal gave the last sentence special emphasis. Don Damián shrugged his shoulders.

"So what? Isn't it natural for me to protect my interests? Whenever one of my workers gets out of hand I try to resolve the problem in the most civilized way possible. I don't want to be ruined paying fines."

"Yes, it's very natural . . . Tobías and your foreman stayed behind with you when the others left. And
when Marciano fell into the bog he shouted 'criminals,' and the voices of two men were heard. Not three
or four, but two."

"And what does that have to do with me? I argue
about many things with my workers. We'd be in fine
shape if everything that happened in Sanlúcar were
traced back to here! I don't know what happened, but
I do know that this is the first I've heard about it."

"Didn't you notice that he was missing when work
started today?"

"No. After yesterday's scene it was only natural that
he should consider himself fired."

"Good day, Don Damián. I'll see you tomorrow, because I think that a good many things can be cleared up
here."

The tactic of frightening a suspect never fails. That
was why Don Damián thought that he ought to visit
the family.

He put on a dark suit and a black tie.

"There's Don Damián!"

One of Marciano's uncles went out to meet him. His
father dried his tears and tried to appear as dignified
as possible.

Don Damián stopped in the middle of the patio and
bowed slightly. Then he walked forward and bowed
again when he was close enough to shake the rough,
knotty hand that Marciano's father held out. Finally he
stepped back three steps and bowed a third time. Afterward he went inside and repeated the ceremony two
more times, once in front of the women and again in
front of the corpse.

The stench of the decomposing body was unbearable.
Don Damián couldn't avoid a grimace of revulsion. He

would have liked to have been able to hold his nose, but that would have been in bad taste. He stood it long enough to go through the formalities, trying to hold back the nausea that was strangling him.

When he was in his car he filled his lungs with pure air. "That was horrible!" The purple face was barely recognizable, and the bloated abdomen had raised the sheet that covered the body. Ants had begun to nest in the half-opened eyes in spite of the pots filled with water that had been placed around the bed. Flies made their way freely from the dead man to the living. The vintner could still hear them buzzing in his ears.

"Tell them to throw away this suit. It smells of death."

The maid thought to herself that her boyfriend would look well in it.

Don Damián called Fernando.

"Go to Marciano's house right away."

Fernando made a gesture of repugnance.

"What for?"

"It's the custom."

"But I don't want to see him. It makes me afraid. You don't know how he looked, floating there. I can't even go near Falón Hill now."

"You've got to go whether you want to or not. It's to our interest to do so. Corporal Pérez has discovered that it was a murder."

Don Damián didn't say anything further. It wasn't a good idea to frighten him too much or he might talk. The foreman obeyed.

A certain viscous material shone between the eyelids. Fernando had the impression that the corpse was looking at him. He was afraid that it would get up to accuse him. He thought he saw it move and shake its head and one hand. One of its fingers rose higher and higher. He tripped on something and thought it was one of the dead man's legs. He couldn't stand it any longer and ran out. Corporal Pérez was waiting in the street. He had followed the foreman. He wrote something down in his notebook.

His witness was waiting for him behind a fence of maguey.

"Look, I've never been a stoolpigeon, but Marciano was a good friend of mine. I was the one who took him to work at the wine cellar—that was a bad move—and I know that they killed him. You can't kid around with Don Damián. I told him to be careful, that he shouldn't talk like that, but he didn't listen to me, and you see what happened."

Corporal Pérez went to the barracks to fill out two warrants. Fernando and Tobías. When he finished he paused with his pen in his hand, looking at a third blank form. But he decided not to fill it out. He would take care of Don Damián later.

He called the brigade commander's office.

"I've caught Marciano's murderers."

The officer approved absentmindedly. He was very busy studying. The date of the exams was getting closer and he wanted to be promoted to lieutenant.

Sixteen

Cousin Jacinto went to the parish house. Don Demetrio was in his office.

"It's about a funeral."

Don Demetrio didn't look up.

"Wait a minute!"

Don Demetrio was writing. Jacinto waited, standing in front of the desk. Fifteen minutes, twenty; priests, who live for eternity, are never in a hurry. Except when they're collecting money, since they begrudge time lost in worldly matters.

Don Mariano gave Tobías a tip.

"So that you can drink a glass to my health."

Tobías put the money in his pocket.

"Do you need me for anything else?"

"No, you can go."

Don Mariano drummed on the desk with his pipe. The embers fell out on the wood. Don Mariano swept them away with his hand, and continued drumming on the desk. He had to release the news before it appeared in the press, and he didn't know how to begin.

Doña Mary served Don César personally.

"A little more?"

Don César nodded.

"As usual, you have marvelous food."

Doña Mary sat by his side, since Don César didn't like to eat alone. She had other customers who didn't want to have anyone around them when they ate. Manias of the rich, as far as she was concerned. To each his own.

"What should we do with the girl?"

"Whatever you please. I'm not interested in her."

"Then can she receive others?"

"Of course."

"The fact is that I have a lot of requests for her."

"Of course, of course. I don't have any use for her."

The madame smiled to conceal her disappointment. She would have liked Don César to take a fancy to the girl, because she made twice as much on men who were hooked on a girl than on a one-shot deal. But Don César had always been like that. He was just like a boy with a new toy car when he had a virgin, but once he had tried them he lost interest. If they weren't virgins, he preferred them to be experienced. It was very hard to really squeeze Don César dry.

"Tomasa has come back."

Don César looked up in surprise.

"You ought to have let me know at the office."

"I didn't want to bother you."

Don César left. He was thinking about Tomasa as he walked along.

"I'll have to go back one of these days."

Tomasa had been in the profession for a long time. She didn't draw the line at anything and she had a good body. He never failed with her. Aside from young girls, she was his favorite meat. It all began with León Alvarez one Good Friday after the procession. Don León always liked to wind up religious ceremonies in Turco Alley. He went into the houses wearing the long robe and the high peaked mask of the religious brotherhoods. He usually continued wearing it even after he had left the procession, especially if he was returning from the Silence, since penitent brothers cannot uncover their faces in the street. Don León was a good customer during Holy Week and a bad one the rest of the year. It was a shame, because he broke the girls in well. He had taught Filo, but she left the profession soon thereafter. Now she had a house in the Barrio and she didn't want to have anything to do with anyone wearing pants.

"I only go for skirts . . . That thing you men have between your legs has done me too much harm."

Tomasa wasn't charming and she didn't know how to treat customers, but she was a good piece. Actually, she was the only interesting thing Doña Mary had in stock.

"I wonder why she came back? She did well in Seville, and from Seville she went to Madrid. But it's been a long time and there's a lot of competition in Madrid. Maybe she came back to take advantage of the Americans."

Don César shrugged his shoulders. When you came right down to it, what difference did it make? She was there and he could take advantage of the fact.

He entered his office. His secretary ran after him with a very sorrowful expression.

"There's news, Don César . . . bad news."

Don César thought that the boy was turning sentimental.

"Yes, I already heard. Antonio died."

"That's bad, but what I have to tell you is worse."

Don César had him come into his office.

"They approved the wage increase at the meeting in Cádiz. From now on they're earning eighty *pesetas*. It'll come out tomorrow in the papers."

"How do you know?"

"Don Mariano called to tell you. Don Antonio Vázquez did, too. You have a meeting at nine. Don Antonio left for Cádiz to see if he could fix things up. I think he'll be back in time for the meeting."

Tobías entered the wine cellar. Don Damián greeted him as though he hadn't seen him all day.

"Where have you been?"

"With Don Mariano at the governor's office, but they told me to say that I'd been at the union offices too. You'll have to pay eighty *pesetas* from now on in the vineyard."

Don Damián swore.

Tobías looked at him, smiling. He liked to make his boss angry. He couldn't stand him. He was a bastard whose only purpose in life was to store away banknotes. He tolerated him because he wanted to get ahead and he was no fool, but he never forgave him for all the bad times he had given him. Humiliations, miserable wages, orgies he could take no part in while he served manzanilla and crayfish and even hunted up women if they were needed, working like a dog while the others had a good time. Tobías realized that it wouldn't be the same any longer. They had been master and servant, but now they were accomplices. The bad times were over, thanks to his lucky star. He always thought there would come a time when he could talk to the fat pig as an equal, but he hadn't thought the time would come so soon. Of course, he had to proceed cautiously, because with Don Damián it was always easy to lose your footing.

"Where's Fernando? I have to ask him something."

"He's at Marciano's house."

Tobías went off to go to work.

Don Demetrio cleaned his pen on a piece of blotter.

"Who was he?"

"Antonio Cabeza de Vaca, Father."

"Where did he live?"

"Mesón del Duque."

"Why wasn't I called to administer the last rites to him?"

Jacinto shrugged his shoulders.

"I don't know. I wasn't there, but I think he died suddenly."

You have to be careful with priests. He wasn't about to tell this one that Antonio never liked cassocks. If he did that, the priest would file a complaint and then he'd be in trouble. At the very least they'd call him a Red, and that brings trouble.

"You people know perfectly well that you have to call me! Extreme unction can be given even after death. Did he die long ago?"

"About . . . three hours ago."

He exaggerated, just in case it should occur to the priest to accompany him. What would his friends say if they saw him with a priest? Don Demetrio pounded the table with his fist.

"Another one that you people have sent to hell! Just in case you don't offend God sufficiently in life, you take care to offend him again once you've died."

Jacinto hung his head without answering.

"Well, all right. What kind of funeral to you want?"

"We're registered at Ocaso."

"Then I don't know what you came here for. Ocaso takes care of everything."

"It's about the time. We'd like it to be at seven."

"At seven? That's impossible."

"But we're waiting for my sister. The train arrives at six-thirty."

"It will have to be at five."

"Don't be like that, Don Demetrio. She loved him very much and she may even get sick if she can't see him."

"I'm not here to be everyone's errand boy. I have a devil of a day tomorrow. Two burials, a first-class baptism at seven-thirty that I can't shift because there's a party afterward, and, well, a lot of things."

Jacinto took out forty *duros*.

"Father . . . see if you can . . ."

The priest took the banknotes and slipped them into the pocket of his cassock. His voice softened.

"We'll see what can be done. The Ocaso will let you know what time it'll be."

Jacinto put on his hat before leaving the church and, taking care that no one should see him, he spit at the door.

Carmelo went up to Marciano. A greasy liquid was coming out of the sides of the corpse's mouth. He pressed the sole of his shoes (they were new, of course) and the softened flesh sunk in. Carmelo had gone through the war and he knew what a decomposing body was like. A yellowish stain was spreading on the sheet around the body.

Marciano's father came over.

"We'll have to put him in the box."

"They haven't brought it."

Carmelo went to Ancha Street.

"The body's decomposing."

The clerk shrugged his shoulders.

"What do you want me to do about it? The box isn't finished."

The sound of rhythmic hammer blows came from the workshop.

"But he already smells to high heaven. No one can stand to be in the house."

"You should have come sooner."

"Didn't I tell you it was an accident? How did we know it was going to happen?"

"There's nothing I can do. We haven't had this much business for a long time."

The flies stuck to Marciano and the ants weren't able

to move. They covered his face with a cloth and his hands with two handkerchiefs. The insects that could get out of this prison went in search of the living.

A Guard brought the summonses and gave them to the boy who worked in the wine cellar. He was paid less than three *duros,* but he stayed because he liked wine and was quick to run errands. The boy entered the cellar with the papers in his hand. Don Damián stopped him.

"What do you have there?"

"Two letters for Fernando and Tobías. A Guard gave them to me."

"Give them here."

Don Damián read the documents, and then put them in his inside jacket pocket.

"Don't say anything about this."

"Don't worry."

The boy went for two pitchers of wine, trying to forget the matter.

Calero and Negro went to rest for a while. They were completely exhausted. Mulo, Pelao, and Juan stood guard at the door of the house.

"Do you think we'll go to the fields tomorrow?"

"I've heard that we won't. We have to go to both funerals."

"I'm not going to Marciano's. I didn't know him."

"Calero says that he was murdered, too, on Don Damián's orders."

"How does he know that?"

"Don't ask me . . . but he's never wrong."

The bars closed very early that night. The only ones to stay open were the bars downtown. The people on Ancha Street didn't know Antonio or Marciano.

It was said that on the following day there would be

trouble when the double funeral and burial were held, but nothing definite was known. The little world in the Valenciana was more preoccupied with the sudden disappearance of the notary's wife, who was not to be seen in any public place. They also talked about the accident at the bog and the unfortunate consequences that taking part in the strike had had for one worker. But these were things that were remote from that world.

Mercedes was strolling arm in arm with her boyfriend. They were walking back from the beach down the middle of the road. Just a few yards farther on the street lights broke the spell cast by the night. Mercedes moved away from the boy.

"They might see us."

Mauricio thought that she was right, but he didn't care. On the other hand, it wasn't to his interest, either, for the thing to become known. Mercedes was pretty, she came from a good family, and they had a little money, although it wasn't enough to marry her for. Besides, he was too young to be tied down.

They said good night before entering Cabildo Plaza. Mauricio went to Puig's. "I don't like you to go there," she had said. None of the women wanted their men to go to the back room of the bakery, because the women could only go there on special days. Luis Puig didn't want women in his place. "They're all right in bed, but they have no place arguing with men."

Luis was the dean of the group and owner of the store. He was also the father of two girls who were plump, merry, and "very sexy," according to local gossip, and he had decided to marry them off to good families. The only way he could find to do it was to get all the possible sons-in-law together in his "private salon" every afternoon. It cost him a pretty penny and a lot of time, but he considered both well spent. Fat cats don't like a skinflint. He always dreamed of the day when they would look at him as an equal and not as just the storekeeper who served them from behind the counter. That was the way they had regarded him all his life because he didn't have wine cellars or land—the type of property that bestowed nobility—but a little store, a wife who could cook marvelously, and a boy who delivered the pastries. In the old days he had set himself the goal of entering the town's closed society, which wouldn't admit an outsider or a native unless he possessed a family tree that went way back or, in its place, a solid fortune. However, that hermetically sealed group hadn't taken long to disappear and its scions were more liberal. The only thing that mattered to them was a fat wallet and style, and no Puig had ever lacked style! The half dozen names that comprised the local high society were often present in the intimate gatherings at his place. It was true, on the other hand, that the surviving remnants of the old families didn't deign to sample his offerings, and this was a thorn in Luis' side.

At other times he liked to recall the origins of the nouveaux riches. Puig wasn't from Sanlúcar, but he had come when he was a young child and had lived there for many years. He remembered the impressive figure of the great shopkeeper Don León Alvarez when no one called him Don, but rather "León the usurer" or simply "the mountaineer."

Don León began with a grocery store, the same store that his servant and disciple Sanjuán had today. He was an unscrupulous loan shark and a sharp businessman, and within a few years he had built his "economic base." Don León had a bad temper, but he knew how to be friendly and helpful when he had to be. Puig learned a great deal working by his side, unloading sacks of chickpeas. He also remembered the first Vázquez and the first Armada. They had all stood behind a counter and stained their hands with ground pepper, but now their sons gave themselves the airs of gentlemen. There was no one who could treat them as an equal and they played at prolonging the old ruined high society that was leaving the town or dying off.

Time—not long, barely a generation—had brought down the great fortunes by dividing them up. On the other hand, the Cura brothers were now entering society by the front door, while Luis was trying to slip in by the back.

The boys began to arrive.

"What's new, cakemaker?" asked Gasparín, punching him in the stomach. Puig didn't protest, even though it hurt.

"Hello, son."

"Did you bring the wine?"

"Yes."

"Well, then, give me a glass. What are you waiting for?"

Puig served him with the air of a servant. A little later Reiniero and Sebastián came in. They were already drunk.

"We spent some time in the wine cellar. When my father finds out we'd better run for the hills."

Reiniero was the town scandal. Excessively handsome, he had also gotten what he wanted, and he had wanted a great deal. He had never fallen in love with a girl from his own class of course. "When I do, it'll be to get married," he told his father. He lived with a gypsy girl for years. Then there was talk of marriage, which caused an uproar. They sent him to study in Seville, where he caught what his family called the itch and other people called something quite different. The gypsy girl caught it from him when he came home on vacation and then was blamed for having given it to him. They prepared a complaint to have her thrown out of town, but backed down when their lawyer explained that they could have her put in a reformatory, since she was a minor, but that they wouldn't be able to come out of the affair with clean hands. The girl's family stood their ground and everything remained as it had been before. Reiniero also continued to live as he had before without trying to cure himself with anything other than home remedies.

"It's the itch and it can be cured with salve."

But the illness was getting out of hand, so they secretly took him to Don Vicente López.

"It's syphilis and it can be cured with antibiotics."

The sores disappeared with the treatment. He then left the gypsy and looked for the fiancée that he needed —one with money, a lot of money. He reestablished himself in the society that still considered him a scatterbrain, but in which he had regained his class status.

However, the truth was that, in spite of his engagement, he still managed to have a son by his old girlfriend. That almost got him into serious trouble with her entire clan, but no one else considered it important. It would have been if he had offered to marry her. Fortunately, they passed the child off as having been fathered by one of the girl's cousins and the whole thing blew over. But Reiniero was proud of his prowess as a breeder.

"I've just seen my boy. He's a bull!"

"Wasn't it agreed that he was Tato's?" protested Jorge, who was just coming in.

"Just because a gypsy is blamed for it doesn't mean that it wasn't my balls that produced him."

The bottles were uncorked. As usual, they were talking about sex.

"How about going to Manolo's?"

The idea was approved.

"We have to look for girls."

"Here are my two daughters," Puig broke in.

"But we need more."

The list was completed in a flash. The daughter of Mesa, the owner of the Hotel Levante, who also belonged to that sector of the middle class that considered it an honor to rub elbows with the great families; the daughter of Montes, the town's civil engineer, a girl who had quite a bit of experience; Loly . . .

"Why don't we try to take Mari Paz along?"

Gaspar shook his head.

"She's not broken in yet."

"That's why. It would be amusing."

"Remember that she's Carlos' sister."

Sebastián shrugged his shoulders.

"So what? Carlos is no Cid."

"But he has a very bad temper."

"Bah! He's too happy at being able to associate with us to make any trouble."

They agreed to hunt up Mari Paz.

Mari Paz went to the Valenciana with her brother on his motor scooter. The Alvarez girls waved at them.

"Hello, Carlos."

Carlos answered absentmindedly as he parked the scooter. Mari Paz went over to their table.

"How are you?"

The Alvarez sisters barely deigned to reply. Mari Paz beat a quick retreat and went over to sit with her friend Rocío, who was waiting at another table.

"I don't know why you try to talk to them. You know they can't stand us."

"I didn't try to talk to them," Mari Paz protested. "I just said hello to them because I have better manners than they do."

Gasparín, Sebastián, and Reiniero arrived. They had been sent as ambassadors.

"We're going to Manolo's. Do you want to come along?"

"No, thanks," said Rocío.

But Mari Paz had already gotten up.

"Go to the store and wait for us."

Mari Paz crossed the street. Sebastián sat down by

Rocío while the others went over to the Alvarez sisters' table. They talked to them for a while, but made no mention of the wine cellar. Sebastián tried to convince Rocío.

"Why don't you come with us?"

"Because I don't feel like it."

"We're going to have a good time. You know that idiot Manolo will give us anything he has. Wine and food both. With a store and a wine cellar, he can well afford it."

Manolo was another one who was trying to climb the social ladder, but he just ended up being a clown's clown.

Rocío felt like getting his goat.

"How's the strike going?"

"Bah, that's not important. I think it's already settled. The Civil Guard will take to the streets tomorrow and they'll all go into the fields. But pretty women don't talk about those things, don't you know that?"

Rocío smiled.

"In the first place, I think you're wrong, and in the second place, you're not the best person to tell me what I should talk about, since I've never heard you say anything that was worth listening to."

Sebastián's eye fell on the figure of a woman who was walking by on the sidewalk. He wasn't interested in anything that had to do with the work in the fields. It was up to his father to settle those matters. At any rate, one doesn't argue with women.

"All right, if you don't want to come, I'll see you another day."

"Goodbye."

Sebastián went over to the table of the Alvarez sisters.

The same group as always had gotten together, plus Juan Carlos, the notary.

"And that's the story."

Don León thumped the table with his fist.

"I'm not going to work the vineyards this year. The hell with everything!"

"Neither will I."

Antonio Vázquez tried to get them to change their minds. He had political ambitions and he knew how unhappy the authorities would be if they did what they said they were going to.

"I think we ought to do whatever the growers in Jerez do."

"What do I care about them?"

"They're the strongest."

"But they can't even make one bottle without our must."

It was true.

"We have to throw a good scare into the government. Let them see that we can go on strike too and give them some headaches. If there's no harvest there won't be any wine next year. And wine means foreign exchange."

The mayor was pacing up and down the room. He had to walk to think, and he needed to think fast to find arguments to penetrate their thick skulls.

Juan Carlos was the one who came up with the solution.

"There's a law against landowners who don't make their lands produce. It provides for their expropriation. It's an old, dusty law, but it could be invoked. It all depends on whether it's in the authorities' interest to do so."

Don Mariano seized the opportunity.

"Judging by the governor's attitude this morning, it seems to me that they're prepared to take any steps they feel are necessary. Right now it's the workers who have the upper hand."

César Blázquez didn't agree.

"Pretty soon we're going to have to start another war."

"That's possible. And when we do, things will change. But now we're still at peace."

The argument lasted a long time. They broke up without coming to an agreement.

The individual receives strength from the group. But when each of them was alone in his own home, he lost his nerve. The hour of bravado and phrasemongering had passed and the logic of numbers prevailed. They would lose a lot of money if they lost the harvest. More than they would by raising wages. Besides, they were afraid. They had fed some angry fires in those days, and if things changed their lives were going to be very uncomfortable.

Don Gaspar, Don Antonio, Don León, and others gave in secretly, each trying to be the first. It might be a mark in their favor some day.

"The others can't understand. They'll be grateful to me for doing it. These are things that people who work on the land never forget. You never know what may happen."

They called their foremen and once again horses galloped through the streets.

"Look for as many men as you need. I've come to the conclusion that they're right and that I ought to pay the new wages."

Act before the news is published, give in because you want to, not because you're forced to—that's the important thing. Once they had lost, they wanted to salvage as much prestige as possible. The foremen looked for their regular men from tavern to tavern.

"The boss will pay. Tomorrow at eight, as usual."

But tomorrow had been proclaimed a day of mourning. Calero announced it at Antonio's house.

"No one goes to work until they're buried. Not even those who are working now."

Seventeen They went on to Manolo's.

Luis Puig, dead drunk, was leaning on his daughters, who could hardly hold him up. From time to time he stopped and kissed them on the mouth.

"Don't be incestuous."

Luis laughed idiotically. He didn't know what incestuous meant, and moreover he didn't care. He kissed them because he felt like it, because he liked them, and because they were his—the property of the house, with his trademark. Reiniero slapped him on the back.

"That's not right. Daughters are for other people."

Luis kissed them again. Reiniero took the younger one away from him.

"Let me have this one. You know I like her."

Manolo was in bed. It looked like a good day to sleep. There was no work in the store or in the wine cellar. Workers and customers had disappeared as though Sanlúcar were dead. The women were not going shopping and the children were not coming in to ask for candy. This put him in a bad mood. On days like this it was better to go to bed than to pick a fight with someone. Above all if there's no one to pick a fight with.

The boys stood under his window and shouted up to him.

"Lazarus! Get up and walk! Your Christs are here."

They'd been to catechism. Like the judge, they knew the Bible, but their use of it was a bit unusual at times.

He recognized their voices. Recently he had heard them quite often.

"Be quiet, I'm coming down," he answered hastily, because he didn't like to cause a disturbance in public. He was a responsible man.

He was wearing white drawers when he opened the door. He tried to hide when he saw the women.

"Don't be silly. We want to get them used to such things as quickly as possible."

They entered the wine cellar. The strong odor of wine excited them. Gasparín took a tube that was used for sampling wine and the three glasses that were kept in a little cupboard. They were covered with dust and traces of other parties. He was known for his skill in using the tube, but he had drunk too much and the yellow stream poured out onto the hard earth floor.

"It doesn't matter. There's enough here to get an army drunk."

Part of the floor was covered with baskets used to bring in grapes during harvest time. They were sticky and soaked with sour-smelling must, and they remained damp all winter. Gasparín discovered a pile of baskets. They had lost the yellow color of the *esparto* grass from which they were made and had taken on a greenish tone.

"These are the good ones. They taste like wine." He chewed some of the loose strands.

"They taste like other things, too."

"A good bed for the animals you're preparing."

Mari Paz had never gone to a wine cellar in such company. Once she had gone to the Arboledilla cellars with two of her sister's friends who had come from a long way away and didn't speak Spanish. The foreman showed them the cellar and explained things that she wasn't interested in and that the others didn't understand. Then he invited them to try the wine. Each glass had a different color and taste. Her head was spinning when she came out and she had to lie down.

She had come now because Sebastián invited her. She was never bored when she was with him and she didn't mind drinking.

"Come on, Manolo. Get some appetizers from the store."

When Manolo left, Puig and Sebastián went into the chicken coop. They selected the fattest hens and with the help of Gasparín and the others they were finally able to catch five of them.

Manolo returned in time to see the last one being killed.

"Don't do that, for God's sake. They cost me a lot of money. They're the best hens you can buy."

His guests laughed. It was the second time Manolo's chicken coop had been cleaned out. The first time was during a three-day drinking bout. Reiniero remembered the sorrowful cries of their owner as he listened to the last cackles of his imported leghorns.

The wine had its effect. Gaspar threw Puig's younger daughter to the floor. When her father returned there was a puddle of blood under the girl. He shrugged his shoulders.

"In these times . . ."

Mari Paz hid behind the wine casks. She hadn't expected this. She was afraid to go toward the door. She knew that they wouldn't let her leave. Sebastián himself had said, "Here not even God himself escapes." Sebastián, who had walked her over to Manolo's, was now embracing the Montes girl and pulling her clothes off. She realized that they hadn't brought her to dance and have a few drinks, but for much more important things. She was repelled and excited by the spectacle at the same time. If only she weren't so afraid.

Puig discovered her.

"Look at this little dove. She's hiding here."

Mari Paz struggled under his soft, fat body. The baker liked women to resist him and he knew how to get what he wanted. He had many years' experience. Reiniero stepped over the outstretched bodies.

"A nice mouthful."

"You're telling me. It's worth the trouble."

"Can I have her after you?"

"Why not?"

Reiniero's voice was trembling. It was only in that atmosphere that he was able to be "a man." He had lived too fast a life and now he was paying the consequences.

Neither bodies nor sexes could be distinguished. A pile of arms and legs moved on top of the baskets.

They were late and Corporal Pérez was getting impatient.

Privates Pérez and Núñez snapped to attention in front of him.

"Go to Don Damián's wine cellar. Find those two birds and bring them to me. Don't let them give you an argument and handcuff them if necessary."

The Guards left. The corporal prepared for the interrogation.

Gaspar Núñez knocked on the door of his son's study. There was no answer. He opened the door with care. He never knew what he was going to find inside that room.

The papers were in their place and the chair was just where the maid had left it after cleaning up.

"Damned loafer," grumbled the old man.

He felt that he ought to visit his fields. The prospect didn't please him in the least, because Don Gaspar was a skinflint. He got around on the motor scooter that he had given Gasparín, for work, naturally. Without the scooter there was no alternative except to pay for a taxi.

"Let's hope he didn't take it with him," he murmured. One of his office managers knew how to drive it.

They looked for the scooter.

"The young master left late yesterday. For Chipiona, I think."

The taxi arrived almost immediately.

"Hello, Ricardo. Take me to the vineyard."

Ricardo drove off. He knew which vineyard was meant, just as everyone else did. He turned off the highway and drove up the white dirt road. The house was on the highest hill. They had built it there so that they could watch the workers while drinking a bottle of beer. The grapevines stretched out for about a hundred *aranzadas* in every direction. Don Gaspar ordered him to stop at a turn in the road. If they drove any farther the workers would see the sun shining on the chrome and he wouldn't catch them wasting time, as usual.

"You know I like to come in from behind without telling anyone. No one can trust you people around here."

Ricardo reflected that Don Gaspar was a slavedriver. But since all the bosses were the same, he attached no importance to the fact. They must be born with that defect.

Don Gaspar crept up the ridge, stooping down so that he wouldn't be seen. It was very hard for him with his age and weight, but it was well worth the trouble if it increased his profits. The fields were in sad shape. Little had been done on the high ground and few grapes had been picked in the lowlands.

To make matters worse he couldn't find anyone working there. He climbed the second hill and stopped in front of the house.

"Florencio! Florencio!"

242·

The foreman came running up.

"Didn't you tell them to come to work, you imbecile?"

"Yes, sir, I did last night, as soon as the young lady that you sent gave me the message, but they're not coming today. It's a day of mourning."

"Mourning? Why? Holy Week is over."

"Because of Antonio. You probably know that he died."

Don Gaspar returned to the car. A day of mourning! And for whom? They ought to be glad that there's one less criminal, who moreover was a bothersome man, a born agitator whose only function was to create problems for his betters. The workers were going to the dogs. In other times a thing like this could never have happened. If they had even tried . . .

He slammed the car door so hard that it could be heard a long way off.

"Back home."

Ricardo obeyed. Don Gaspar calculated the price of the trip. Fifty *pesetas* thrown right out the window. He cursed the town and his son.

Don Luis had called the judge and the notary. He needed them to reach a final decision, since the matter was gradually being resolved, thanks to them.

"I'm afraid that we're going to have a demonstration."

Don Luis agreed.

"I don't know what to do to stop it."

"Nothing. I can't forbid a funeral."

"At any rate, I'll send some policemen to keep them in line."

"Don't do it," said Juan Carlos, whose ideas were always clear and to the point. "That would be giving them an importance that they don't deserve."

Don Alberto interrupted his friend.

"I think that the sermon at the funeral ought to serve as a lesson to them."

"That's not a bad idea. Have you mentioned it to Don Demetrio?"

"Not yet."

"It would be a good idea to let him know."

They told Juan Carlos to talk to the priest. He was a close friend of Don Demetrio and stopped by the church every day, as it "happened to be on his way."

"Do either of you know anything about the other one?"

"It seems that he was helped to die."

"That's good, very good. Let's take advantage of this opportunity to give an example of severity and justice. Be stern, Alberto. Don't hesitate when you pass sentence."

"That had already occurred to me. It's good to temper mercy with severity once in a while. It seems that they were two workers. It would be interesting if they turned out to be strikers."

"It would be a good lesson for the others."

Salvadora gave each member of her family a cup of coffee.

"I don't know when you're going to stop all this. Now we're wearing mourning!"

"But it's just for one day, woman."

Paco brought the newspaper. He had been on the last shift at Antonio's wake, and they gave him the paper when he walked by the store.

"It's official now that we're going to earn eighty *pesetas*."

Salvadora didn't believe him. "It's wishful thinking," she affirmed categorically. But just in case she gave the newspaper to Fernando so that he could read it aloud. The child proceeded to do so as the adults looked at him attentively and admiringly.

Salvadora hugged him. She was proud of her son. He was an honor in her family of illiterates. There were very few people in the entire town who could read as well as he could. Big men stood with their mouths open listening to him read letters or documents that they didn't understand. And they were much more amazed when they saw him write in his clear hand-writing without hesitating, as though he knew before-hand what he was going to put down.

Juan was smoking in a corner. His brother's success shamed him and seemed unjust to him. If he were the younger of the two, they would have sent him to school and Fernando would have had to go to work. But it's always the oldest son who goes to the fields and who reaches twenty without knowing how to read and learns what little he knows about the alphabet when he's in the army. There were night schools and some people went to them. He had gone too, but it's hard to cram so many things in your head after a hard day's work in the fields. Besides, he didn't like to go to church and these classes were always in the church or there were priests around. They talked a great deal about saints and cate-chisms, but said very little about things that interested him.

Luisillo continued playing with empty cans, in addi-tion to which he now had a big pile of bottle caps. When the coffee was served he jumped up to drink a cup, and then sat down on the floor again, chewing the piece of bread that he received as his share.

"When it's not one thing it's another. With these new ways of doing things you won't go to work all year."

Paco got angry.

"Remember that you don't bury a hero every day."

"Is the one who's going to be buried this morning a hero too?"

"In a certain sense, yes."

The workers went to Marciano's house at eleven

o'clock. There weren't many. Calero had said that they should send a delegation of at least a hundred. When he counted them there were a hundred and four, not including Marciano's neighbors. He didn't count them simply because he was curious.

"It's the only way to know if you're disciplined," he explained.

The coffin arrived at eleven. Two of the men tried to lift the corpse.

"It's very soft. You'll have to pick it up in the sheet."

They raised the body, being careful not to rip the cloth. A strong smell filled the room. Carmelo felt nauseated. Two boys who had come in out of curiosity vomited on the floor.

"You could have brought the box earlier."

The men from the funeral parlor shrugged their shoulders.

"They didn't tell us to come." They were too used to their work to feel repugnance.

It was difficult to get the body into the coffin. Once it was in, they wrapped it in the sheet.

"Be careful because it may be opened. The new style is to open them in the church."

The procession set out for the church. Of necessity it passed in front of City Hall. The mayor looked out the window without lifting the curtain.

"There aren't very many."

Juan Carlos smiled at such ingenuousness.

"You'll see this afternoon."

"This afternoon they won't come by here."

"I want you to be at Antonio's by four."

Calero and the others prepared the itinerary.

"We have to take him down through the Barrio Bajo."

"Of course."

"But that's not allowed. We can only take him to the church and then to the cemetery."

"We'll do it whether it's allowed or not."

Large groups arriving from all directions went up to Mesón del Duque. The train from Jerez was full of representatives sent for the funeral. Only a few passengers got off at South Station. There were hardly any workers in the Puerto. Don Aurelio Peláez peered into his mirror as he got ready.

Don Luis called Cristal.

"I can't go because I don't want them to see me. But you ought to go by there. We're aware that you know many of the workers and get along well with them."

Cristal didn't like the idea.

"Not at all, Don Luis. I don't feel like getting killed today. I think it would be very unwise for any of us to go today."

"I have to know what's happening and know it directly. You will take charge of this matter."

Cristal thought about Tobías. Don Damián had told him that Tobías was his right-hand man. Anyone who helps a boss obeys everyone, since he's shown that he knows what's good for him. He went to the wine cellar.

Don Damián came out to meet the Guards.

"What do you want?"

"We've come for Tobías and Fernando."

"They're not here."

"We have orders to take them back immediately."

"I tell you they're not here."

The Guards pushed him to one side and went into the cellar.

"The boss sent them on an errand."

"Will they take long?"

"I don't know."

The Guards sat down to wait for them.

Don Damián had in fact gotten them out of the way. "Go to the vineyard and count the number of men working there," he had told Tobías and Fernando. They set out, proud of the trust their master had shown by giving them a task that he usually carried out personally. In that gesture they saw a tangible promise of future promotions. They would be away for two hours. Don Damián knew they wouldn't be back until the afternoon, which is why he smiled calmly and invited the Civil Guards to have a glass of wine.

Private Núñez called Corporal Pérez on the telephone.

"They've flown the coop."

"Have they gone far?"

"It seems they've gone out into the fields."

"Wait there and keep your eyes open."

Claudio Cristal didn't see the uniforms, hidden as they were by the rose trees in the patio. They were covered with flowers, the pride and joy of the mistress of the house. When she was shown other roses she would say, "They're magnificent, but they're not like the ones at home."

"Hey, Damián, I've come for your man Tobías."

Don Damián started.

"What for?"

"To go to Antonio's funeral. We need a man we can trust to report back to us, and since I know you trust him . . ."

Don Damián cut him short. He didn't want the police to know his preferences.

"I'm sorry, but you're mistaken. Tobías is a good worker, I agree, but that's as far as it goes. I keep him because he does a good job for me. Nothing more."

Cristal was somewhat taken aback. The Guards came over to greet him.

"As a matter of fact, these gentlemen have come for him with a warrant for his arrest. I don't know what he's done, but I assure you that if he's stolen something he'll leave my house immediately."

"It has to do with Marciano's murder, sir."

Cristal left. He didn't need to hear any more to realize that Damián was mixed up in the affair.

Nabito was the one who was finally stuck with the job.

"Take off your uniform and mingle with people."

"Yes, sir." His years of service had taught him that the only thing you'd get by contradicting a superior was thrown in jail.

He hid in the back of his room.

"If they come from City Hall, tell them that I went out in civilian clothes and that you don't know where I was going, but that you heard something about a funeral."

His wife prepared to shield her husband's small figure.

Don Juan Carlos entered the office. Father Demetrio got up to receive him.

"What a pleasure!"

"I've come to discuss a very delicate matter."

The priest offered him a chair.

"What is it?"

"It has to do with the funeral."

The priest nodded. He knew which funeral he was referring to.

"I suppose there will be a mass and all that."

There would be. Ocaso was paying and the poor want masses said for the dead. It was the only kind of mass they ever attended, because they turned the "holy

249·

sacrifice" into a tribute to the dead. Only dogs were buried without music or prayers in Latin.

"As usual, I'll talk about the good qualities of the deceased."

"That's what I wanted to talk to you about. It would be better to prepare a different sermon in which you don't talk about virtues but instead give warnings for the edification of those who are attending the funeral. The deceased was an agitator. He came out of prison the day before he died. He was arrested by order of the governor. It seems that he was the main culprit in the disturbances that we have been suffering."

"Don't worry, Don Juan. I understand the situation. It's a question of giving them a good scare, or rather of making them fear a bit for their souls."

The notary nodded.

"Kids, it's almost seven o'clock."

The orgiasts woke up. After making love, eating, and drinking, they had fallen asleep on top of one another.

"I'm really going to catch hell," moaned Sebastián.

"We're all going to catch it."

Mari Paz had also fallen asleep. When she woke up she didn't understand a thing. Who were these men? Why was she here and not in her bed? Or had they brought her here without her realizing it? Then she thought that she was dreaming and fell asleep again. Gasparín shook her until she woke up.

"Listen, you've got to beat it."

Mari Paz felt like crying. She was ashamed of being naked and looked for her clothes.

"They're over in that corner, with all the others."

Mari Paz got up. Her whole body ached, and above all her belly.

Eighteen

Don Vicente arrived at a quarter to seven.

"I'd like to help carry the coffin," he said.

Calero and Negro were the pallbearers in front. They were a strange pair with their faces covered with bandages. They were followed by the doctor, Juan, Mulo, Pelao, Chirlo, and Pistolero. He was the youngest and also the shortest. He was out of place in the group because of his height, but he had asked them with tears in his eyes to let him be a pallbearer.

"Because I'm going to die like he did."

Calero decided to reserve a place for him in spite of all the other requests. Boys like that shouldn't be disappointed.

The eight men lifted the coffin with a sudden jerk. "One, two, up!"

They went down the Carretera Nueva walking with the rhythmic step of the bearers who carry the virgins for rich people during Holy Week. Below them lay the town, the sea, and the edge of Doñana. The black box was in sharp contrast to the whitewashed wall of the orphanage. Orphans of the sailors of Huelva and other places.

It was just like any other day on Ancha Street. People filled the bars, drinking anything just to be there. There were laughing and talking just as though nothing were happening. In fact, nothing was happening as far as they were concerned. They hadn't even noticed the total absence of workers along the entire length of the street.

"Today is a day of mourning," someone said, and they were satisfied with that explanation.

The coffin came down Santo Domingo Street. The mayor was at the club.

"It's not possible!"

They had finally broken a law. He called a Guard.

"Arrest them! Don't let them continue."

The Guard stood at attention.

"I'm sorry, sir, but I can't do it."

"It's an order."

"I can't do it."

The funeral procession advanced down the middle of the street. The cars had to pull over to the curb. Silence spread, and the air was filled with the sound of footsteps, of hemp-soled sandals brushing over the pavement. No one moved in the club. The customers were looking at the procession with frightened expressions. The reaction was different other places.

Some got up timidly and then sat down again, while others adopted the aggressive attitude of people who are either openly for or against the authorities. There were hats that remained on men's heads and there were women kneeling as the coffin passed, as though it were the statue of a saint.

They crossed the center of town and went up Ganado Hill toward the church. As they passed Manolo's place they encountered his guests.

"Say, what's this?"

"Antonio."

Sebastián thought that his father was not going to be pleased by the procession and that he would take his bad humor out on him. Slipping furtively through the little deserted back streets he reached the family's wine cellar, the only place where he was sure that he wouldn't run into his father.

Don Demetrio was waiting at the church door in his vestments with an altar boy at either side of him. An old sacristan was carrying the pyx, as usual.

The line was so long that the end of the procession was still in the main street when the coffin entered the church. Don Demetrio was frightened by the mass of people. While he mechanically recited the first prayers he went over the sermon he had prepared in his mind and polished some particularly biting phrases.

The coffin was placed on the tiles and the mass was celebrated. The pallbearers stood on either side of the black box, taking the place of the tall candlesticks used in first-class funerals. The places of honor in the front row were occupied by Jacinto, the cousin from Trebu-jena; Ciriaco; Don Aurelio; and Manolillo, with his first long pants. Jacinto told the child to sit down.

"Don't get tired," he said in a whisper.

Manolillo was there because he was a symbol. The church was full of men for the first time in many years. And also for the first time, people were standing in the street, waiting for the ceremony to finish, each one in his place without breaking ranks to take a drink in the nearest bar, as the penitents do during the halts in the religious processions of Holy Week.

"Brothers! Here you have a poor sinner, one of your brothers who fell victim to his own pride, as the angel Lucifer fell during the war in heaven. Here you have this soulless body. Here you have the remains of poor Antonio, who perhaps even now is burning in hell. Or perhaps not. We all know that God could save him by giving him a moment of awareness, that moment of repentance that is worth a whole lifetime. We all know that God is infinitely merciful, but he is also infinitely just and the most horrible sin in his eyes is pride . . ."

Don Vicente was carefully studying the baroque decorations on the main altar. To the right of the Virgin of the Carmen, an image carved in the purest Sevillian style of the seventeenth century, was a Virgin of Fatima, smiling with her painted doll-like face. The white mantle, just like all the others that came out of the workshop that mass-produced those plaster images, hung on her without any grace. It half-concealed a fat little angel that looked like Roldana's children. It occurred to him that from the other side he could see the angel, and that perhaps from that angle the angel would cover up the hideous thing before his eyes. Of course the plaster statue was much larger than the little angel. The imperfect is always larger than the perfect.

Two neon lights illuminated the transept. Their white light etched Antonio's features so that his head had the beauty of a classic bust. The men had insisted on opening the coffin in spite of the priest's weak protests because they wanted to see him one last time.

Don Vicente was trying to forget what he was hearing. Those stupid phrases bored him and angered him at the same time, but they entered his ears despite his efforts to keep them out.

"One day, my children, Satan himself wanted to seize your brother by telling him: 'Convince them that they should unleash their hatred, because it is only through hatred that I can become master of the world.' And poor ignorant Antonio obeyed, like our mother Eve, without realizing that evil and abjection were entering his heart. Evil and abjection, my children! He pushed you toward evil without measuring the consequences, without concerning himself about you. You could be occupying the place which he is occupying right now, and it would be because of him! Antonio betrayed you because he desired evil for his people. The Judas!"

He got no further. Mulo had reached the pulpit where good Don Demetrio was leaning over to make himself heard by everyone. It had been difficult for Mulo to push his way through the crowd, but he had succeeded. He had heard Antonio being insulted, being called evil and abject, and now a Judas on top of everything else!

"You filthy son of a bitch, you thief! All you people know how to do is to rob us with your rigamarole."

Mulo wanted to beat up Don Demetrio. Calero and the others realized this in time to hold him back. The priest's stream of words suddenly dried up. Others might get upset and the thing might end very badly for the prestige of the clergy and for his own physical safety. Above all for his safety. There were too many there for one man alone, a man who was not used to fights and who was accustomed to being treated with great respect by everyone.

"My children, let us pray."

The monotonous sound of the Latin prayer calmed people down. The priest knew that no one understood these prayers, so he skipped quite a bit. The main thing was to finish as soon as possible.

He walked around the coffin blessing the body profusely with the aspergillum. The people liked blessings because they were something tangible. He knew that the more blessings there were, the better it would be.

"Now you can take him to his last resting place."

He said it with a sad voice, just in case. It was better to seem like a friend than a critic.

The eight men approached the coffin.

"One, two, up!"

The crowd pushed to the sides of the nave to leave a passageway open. The coffin passed through the church in the midst of the most profound silence. The only sound was the tolling of the bells in the church tower.

Don Demetrio closed the door to the sacristy. His hands were trembling. He called the sacristan to help him get out of his vestments.

"That was a rough moment we had there, Father."

"You can say that again!"

"I know the name of that fellow who climbed up after you. You ought to report it. It's blasphemy to say that in church."

Don Demetrio shook his head.

"It's better to leave it for the moment. We've already had enough problems. We'll see in a few days . . ."

Calero spoke to the workers as they left the cemetery.

"Tomorrow we go to work. But never forget that we left Antonio here, and that he died for all of us."

Tobías and Fernando returned from the vineyard.

"Don Damián, Bandolero says that . . ."

"These two gentlemen are waiting for you."

Private Núñez and Private Pérez placed themselves on either side of the two men.

"But what's this all about? What's happening?"

"You're going in for questioning, that's all."

"Aren't you coming with us, Don Damián?"

"I'll be along soon."

Don Damián shut himself up in his house. He didn't want them to see too much of him. He had to think, and he was terrified.

Juan and Paco stopped at Largo's place, as usual. They found Chunga sitting at the door. He was wearing his Sunday suit. He too had come from the funeral.

"I told you that all this was going to end badly."

"We got what we wanted."

"But Antonio isn't here any more. Antonio didn't get anything."

"That makes no difference. It could have been me or any one of the others. We were all ready. His number was up, that's all."

Pistolero came in at that moment.

"The next one will be me, in a strike some other year. I have to die like Antonio, for all of us."

Juan ruffled the boy's hair. He wasn't much older than Pistolero, but he felt like a man because he had been working longer. In any case, Pistolero had still not played a leading role in a strike.

"Don't say such things. The fewer who die the better."

"But some of us will always have to die. If someone wants something, he has to pay for it."

"Blood is too precious to be lost for a few *pesetas*," Chunga broke in.

"It's not a matter of a few *pesetas*, old-timer. It's something much more important. Our children have the right to live better than we do, to be able to go to school like the rich, and to work without going through the bad times we have to go through. Asking for more pay is just one step like any other. Step by step we'll reach the end of the road, old-timer, the final goal, and those of us who fall by the wayside, well . . . it's our bad luck."

Juan went on home. A feeling of sadness hung over the town. Paco walked by his side with his head down and his hands in his pockets, just as in the worst days.

They didn't talk to each other because they felt like crying. Carmelo's tavern was closed. Many of the taverns had a little sign in their window that day saying "Closed in mourning." The mayor could have forced them to open, but he decided against it. It wasn't the moment to provoke the working class. The slightest thing would cause a riot, thus creating a dangerous situation for the local authorities and a disagreeable one for their superiors.

Nineteen

The next morning was just like any other. It was a morning during the sulphating season. Twelve hours were sufficient for everything to return to normal. The bosses had swallowed the bitter pill of paying higher wages and the workers had learned that their raise had not solved their economic problems.

Juan left at seven with his wicker basket under his arm on the way to the vineyard. There would be money, so Salvadora calculated her expenses.

"It's worth doing now because now we're going to get our raise for sure."

Each worker took the road that led to his fields. There was no need to wait in the plaza because they had been contracted for.

"I'll see you tonight."

"There's enough work for an army."

"They told us that we have enough to do to work for almost two months without stopping."

Two months. Sixty days. It's not much time, but when it's all ahead and it means that things will be peaceful, it seems that it will never end. Calero knew that after the harvest would come winter and unemployment. The others knew it too, but they didn't want to think about it.

"We won!"

And that was enough to enable them to look into the future optimistically. The sound of a man singing came over the marsh. Paquito was taking a shortcut through it to reach Alíjar. "With the workers' blood . . ." The words were sad. They voiced a complaint and a protest, but the music was gay. Worries were left behind. There would always be a pot cooking on the stove. The winter without blankets, sleeping on the floor, was far away. He could pay the loan shark and buy shoes for his children, those rubber shoes that don't last long, but that are very pretty for the first week . . . and a skirt for his wife. The red skirt they had seen the other day in Casa Carrascosa. In August he would look for a new jacket and use his Sunday jacket for work. It was certainly high time he got a new one. He remembered that he had pawned their wedding clothes and the solid gold rings that Antonia's father had given her, as well as the leather belt decorated with coins that he had made when he was doing his military service. He could get them all out now. He'd do that before he spent money on anything else. Things had gone from bad to worse since they left home. It had brought them bad luck.

Fernando took a sandwich to school. It was the first time that year.

"We have to fill our stomachs to make up for all the times we haven't been able to eat."

And they bought on credit in the stores.

"Now I have two men bringing money home."

They bought meat by the *duro* and not by the *céntimo*. That day there were very few women who bought two *reales* of tripe. Later they would put some aside for the rainy season and their debts. But later . . . next week. Half of their wages would go for debts and a little bit of whatever they had left would be put in a safe place.

The vendors met at Díaz's stand.

"They're going to use the excuse of the wage increase to raise the price of potatoes."

"And tomatoes."

"Meat has already gone up."

The following day many prices had doubled. The mayor tried to restore order.

"Tell them to go back to the prices they were charging before."

He managed to cut down the increase by a fourth. There were some loan sharks who increased the payments on loans to compensate for the increase in prices and there were shopkeepers who withdrew their goods from the market and then brought them back with another increase in prices. It began to be hard to make ends meet. For four months there would be hard times, but not dire poverty.

Paco asked about the price of a table with a brazier underneath.

"We want a big one where Fernando can write while the rest of us eat," his mother had said. "Fernando has to study. He's going to be a great man."

Juan went into the furniture store.

"How much do you have to pay each month?"

He made some calculations. Maybe he could pay it all off with the harvest wages. Then he thought better of it.

"I'll wait till next year."

Don León Alvarez stopped by for Don César so that they could go to the club together. One learned a lot with Don César. He found him in his wine cellar tasting wine.

"Come on in."

The foreman followed him with a tube and several glasses in his hands. The wine tube was made of silver. There was another tube made of gold in the cellar, but it was only taken out on great occasions. He filled a glass from a cask in each row at random.

"Test this one."

The foreman released the wine from the tube with such skill that not a drop was lost. Don César smelled the wine for a few seconds.

"Mark it with a cross. It's not good."

They marked five wine casks in succession.

"What did you put in here?"

The foreman shrugged. Don César noted the number on the cask. Later he would check it in the book where everything relating to the wine was recorded. The land from which the must came, the age of the vines, the must that came from years which produced a large quantity with a low alcohol content, and the must from dry years made from high-grade grapes. The blends that were made and the mothers that they passed through were noted in it, and finally, the result and the sale price.

Little sample bottles gleamed on the shelves. That wine archive, jealously guarded by its owner, went back to the times of old Albornoz, from whom he had bought the cellar.

In the office they studied these wine casks and tried to determine what was wrong with them and how it could be remedied at the smallest possible expense.

"Did you put in some of the number one?"

"Yes, sir."

It occurred to Don León that the wine could be cleared up better with egg whites, but number one and number two were a good invention. Thanks to them, the cost of producing fine Andalusian wines had been reduced considerably.

"What would the consumers say if they knew they were drinking bromide?"

Don César laughed.

"Nothing. Don't we drink it and like it?"

He was right. Don León sniffed the glasses that Don César handed him, without being able to determine the quality of the wine they contained. It was a skill a person is born with, and he would never be able to acquire it.

Don Antonio went up to his vineyard very early in the morning. He wanted to take advantage of the wage increase.

"What do you say, boys, are you satisfied?"

Lechuzo nodded.

"So you see that we aren't hard masters. We let ourselves be convinced. I went to Cádiz to help you get what you wanted."

The men lowered their heads to keep from laughing in his face. They knew very well that Don Antonio had made the trip for very different reasons. Piolo had driven him down, and he told the workers the real story. Don Antonio had come out of the governor's office cursing the entire town.

The old foreman looked at Don Antonio with amusement. He had known his boss since he was a child and Don Antonio couldn't fool him. Don Antonio realized that he had nothing to do there. He went back home, furious with those who had forced him to put himself in a ridiculous position.

The Marchioness was strolling through her garden and looking at the first flowers that had bloomed. Before it had been called "the kitchen garden." Peppers and potatoes had grown on the borders instead of carnations and lilies. It wasn't as pretty but it was much more practical. At that time practical matters had been more important. The Marchioness had gone through a great deal. She had married a crippled veteran of the

African war who had insisted on trying to live like a great lord with a little wine cellar and two small sections of vineyard. As a result she had learned what hunger and debts meant. Her five children had frequently complained because they didn't have enough food on their plates, and she had taught them to say nothing about it because "people don't have to know about it. It's none of their business." From the time they were born she had prepared them for the great career of matrimony. "They'll marry well and then we'll have all we need." They went to the best schools and then to the university. It was difficult to pay for their tuition, and the Marchioness had spent many days in Madrid visiting the homes of her relatives. "Can't you give me something? It's for your nephews. If they don't get an education they won't be able to make a living." She had begged for money, it was true, and she wasn't ashamed of it, although she would never have admitted it publicly.

When the family ate alone, their meals were skimpy and of poor quality, but when they had guests they spent their savings. "We have to keep up appearances, because if we don't we'll never get anywhere." Alfonso began to look for a fiancée. He was the eldest and therefore the most difficult to marry off. "When he makes it, all the rest will follow suit." Mimi was never attractive, even at that age when all women are pretty. She was a little stupid and had an unbearable temper, and all in all she was not calculated to awaken men's passions. Alfonso courted her assiduously for three years. Mimi was the owner of the Borregoso Bank and from an old Jewish family that had managed to escape the persecution of Ferdinand and Isabella because in those times they had lived in the direst poverty and had been able to demonstrate their old Christian lineage by denouncing a good many of their fellow Jews.

Alfonso and Mimi were married in the Chapel of the Kings in the cathedral at Seville. He squeezed himself into the showy uniform of an upper-class club and she wore a white gown with an immense train.

The next was Mario. One afternoon he was strolling through the streets of Ronda with several companions from the military camp. He was struck by an old palace that had been kept in a perfect state of preservation.

"Who does that house belong to?"

"To the Mirabelles. They're loaded."

"Do they have any daughters?"

"Just one, who'll inherit the whole thing. I wonder who the lucky man will be who gets her?"

"Me. In a few years I'll invite you for dinner in there because I'll be the owner."

His friends kidded him about it the rest of the summer. The following year he met Marita Mirabelles. They were married in the biggest church in town.

Marita had endless property in the mountains. Mario began to raise fighting bulls and undertook other business ventures at the same time.

Her other children followed the same path. It wasn't difficult for them. Their elder brothers saw to it that they met heiresses under the most favorable conditions for their courtships.

María del Milagro was the only one who had made a bad match. Of course, women have fewer opportunities. They can't throw themselves at men.

The Marchioness bent over to cut a lily. One of her grandchildren came running up to her.

"Come in, Granny. Uncle Antonio is here."

The brigade commander was interrogating Fernando. Tobías was waiting outside. They were tired because they had been kept at the barracks all night with no other bed than a stone bench "in order to soften them up," as Corporal Pérez said. The Guards didn't touch them, which was reassuring. Very few people came out of there without welts as big as a donkey's during the harvest season.

The captain had given the order that they weren't to be beaten with the warning: "They might complain to the judge. Be careful because we don't want to get into trouble. You know that the law doesn't allow us to beat prisoners."

"But the others . . ."

"That was different. These are common criminals. They don't have anything to tell us and we have no one to frighten by making an example of them. And there may be some very important people involved in this."

"Tell me what you were doing on the night of the 26th."

Fernando spoke calmly.

"I went to bed. I was tired. Don Damián kept us at the wine cellar a long time after the others left."

"What for?"

"To take samples of the wines."

"Don Damián takes samples during working hours. As a matter of fact, his brother Diego, who's the expert, usually does that."

"What are you talking about? The boss doesn't even trust his own brother, and he never keeps working hours. He keeps us there as long as he pleases and when you protest he throws you out."

The two suspects had agreed on their story beforehand. Their master had told them what to say as soon as they went to work that morning. "This is what you have to say if they ask you any questions and nothing else. Don't change one word of it, or you'll regret it."

They didn't change a word.

"There's someone who saw you that night. You were hiding in a doorway in front of Carmelo's place. This person was coming out of there when he saw you. He remembers that Marciano was telling them what had happened that afternoon."

"Yes, that's true, but it didn't have anything to do with Marciano."

"Then why were you there? I don't see why a person would hide in the street if he didn't intend to do something bad."

"Well, there are certain things . . . When men hide in a doorway, everybody knows what they're doing it for. Don't you think so, commander?"

It was better to be accused of being a fairy than a murderer. Fernando thought that Tobías would agree with him and if he didn't, it made no difference. His word was always worth more. He would say that he had been afraid to talk because of what his wife might say.

The brigade commander let him go.

"Go home, but don't try to leave town. You'll have to be questioned a couple of more times before the matter is closed."

It wasn't a good idea to hold him very long. Seventy-two hours pass very quickly and then come the complaints and the headaches. It was too early to take him to court. Don Alberto liked to have closed cases. There was no doubt about what had happened. Those two had taken care of Marciano on Don Damián's orders. If they weren't guilty, then why had Fernando gone to wake up his boss before six o'clock? Why that strange "Tell him that everything went well"? When things go as they should you don't wake up your boss. The maid remembered the foreman's visit clearly. He had gotten her out of bed by ringing the bell until she got up. Of course, it wasn't a good idea to involve Don Damián in the affair until they had the goods on him. Big fish break the net when it isn't strong enough.

Fernando went down into the wine cellar.

"I have to talk to you."

Don Damián took him into his office and locked the door.

"I've already been told what has to be done," Fernando said. "This has to be stopped and filed in the wastebasket. If not, I'm going to be sent up for several years."

"Defend yourself. It's your affair. I didn't tell you to kill him."

"I warn you that if there's a trial we'll both talk. And don't try to get rid of us, because it'll be worse for you if you do."

Don Damián promised to do whatever was necessary. Then Fernando went to work and his master stayed in the office. He wanted to be alone, as he always did when he didn't know how to cope with events.

At twelve o'clock he had them call the court secretary. Casimiro asked his chief for permission to visit Don Damián.

"He says that he's very worried, and that he wants me to come immediately."

Don Alberto let him go. It obviously had something to do with the murder. It was always good to have a chance to learn new facts. He hadn't finished reading the testimony yet, but already someone seemed to be looking into the affair. He thought about the stupid situation that was being created. A vintner persecuted because of some poor devil who was superfluous in a society that could easily replace him with someone just like him.

Don Damián had a name. Don Damián was somebody. The other two—poor devils!—didn't count. "All they've done, in any case, is rid us of a malcontent. The fewer the better." He said this to his wife, who never revealed a secret. He couldn't even say such things to Casimiro, in spite of the fact that they were perfectly true.

Don Alberto was a respectable man. Everything about him, from the knot in his tie to his shoes, showed the public that he was respectable.

When he won the competition for judgeships (although he was in one of the last places, to be sure), his professor of religion, who had helped him since he entered the university, called him and told him, "A judge is a serious and respectable man. A religious man, with strict morals. He cannot permit himself the luxury of being seen with a prostitute or drinking more than he should. He's like a priest, not given to jokes and a man of few words. If his wife is ugly, better still. When he passes sentence he ought to contribute to the peace of society and the maintenance of the established order, trying to keep those people who occupy the most important positions in our country by divine will in their posts, without ever diminishing under any circumstances the authority or prestige that is due them. Remember that money, like a title of nobility or a university degree, and this includes public positions, cannot be obtained without the help of God." Don Alberto accepted his advice and followed it exactly.

He soon married a dull, sickly woman whom he took care of. He had one daughter to show that he could be a father. Then he convinced his poor mate of the eternal rewards that accrue to those who take the vow of chastity. "It will be a common sacrifice that will bring us closer to God. He will reward us, revealing himself to us after death."

The first fruits were not long in coming. In the postwar years there were few career judges who were considered safe by the new regime. He was. They called him in and gave him a promotion which was very difficult to obtain at his age and with his grades on examinations. He went from one town to another, climbing up the professional ladder. Every day, no matter where he was, he could be found taking communion at the nine o'clock mass. In the afternoon he always visited some church or other and, of course, the parish priest. He went to the movies—when their morality was incontestable—and official receptions when he couldn't get out of it. He never danced or drank. He knew the foremost citizens and would talk to them on occasion, although he normally limited himself to taking walks either with Casimiro or alone. He wore dark clothes, even in the middle of summer, and he never took off his thick tortoise-shell glasses. When he went south he adopted the local custom of attending the religious processions, without ever delegating someone else to take his place. He was enrolled in all the important religious brotherhoods and attended their ceremonies regularly. He was never without a small Bible sticking out of the pocket of his suit coat.

He appeared to be a man without a past, methodical and well-mannered, who stoically withstood the heat without ever going to the beach in the summer, "because it's easier to offend God at the beach."

Some people considered him a saint. And it was true that Don Alberto had his morality, perfectly in accord with God's. The God of *Camino,* the manual of the Opus Dei, that is.

God was always on the side of right. And he who is supported by God wins, because God is all-powerful and no one can fight against Him. Which is to say that those who win, the rich, are God's friends. Since God is just, it follows that he cannot have unjust friends. So the powerful are just.

It is quite true that in some countries and on some

occasions the All-Powerful allows the unjust to win and abandons His people. Then evil takes control of everything. But He does so for two very powerful reasons. He submits the faithful to a test, restoring them to the place that they deserve if they are triumphant, as was the case in Spain, or he punishes them for having abused and abandoned him, as happened in Russia and the Communist countries, from which only the chosen had been able to escape.

Following the Ten Commandments, which he based on this uncontrovertible reasoning, he administered justice without fear of making a mistake. He condemned and forgave with an easy conscience. His decisions, which were most appropriate, won him many rewards and much good will, although he also earned some ill will. But he forgave his enemies, "for they know not what they do," and wrote them off as uneducated people for the most part, who complain and criticize when one tries to lead them along the path of virtue. No, Don Alberto was not a cynic.

That was why he inwardly considered Marciano's murderers as defenders of order. A man who kills is always preferable to someone who disturbs the peace of society.

Don Alberto returned to the case that he had in hand. It was a dispute between residents of the wine-growing district of San Salvador. Without reading it, he signed the decision written by Casimiro.

"How is Marciano's case coming along? They've kept my foreman at the barracks all day and I'm anxious for them to finish up."

The secretary was delighted that he had gone to see Don Damián.

"I think that it's coming along very well. The brigade commander called us ten minutes ago to say that they were telling him everything."

Don Damián turned pale.

"Look, Casimiro, I don't think there's any reason to be so formal. People can always reach an understanding if they sit down and talk to each other."

"Tobías Blasco!"

Tobías entered the office. Corporal Pérez accompanied him.

The brigade commander pointed to a chair.

"Let's see. Your friend told me what happened. You got Marciano alone and threw him into the bog. Then you went to Don Damián's house, but he refused to see you. He told me the whole thing."

"It's not true!"

Corporal Pérez had reconstructed the events. Between the statements of Piernas, of the man who worked in the wine cellar, and of the two women, he had almost all the details.

"Don Damián called you to ask you to persuade the boy not to file a protest. He even gave you money to keep him quiet. You decided to keep the money and kill him, thinking that it wouldn't become known, but the police find out about everything."

"It's not true! It was Don Damián who told us to knock him off! We were right in the wine cellar when he told us, 'I don't like loudmouths. With water and darkness everything can be taken care of, and I'll protect you.' "

Corporal Pérez smiled. The trap never failed. All criminals sing when they think they've been betrayed by their accomplices, and Tobías was no exception.

The brigade commander ordered him to be taken straight to jail. Guilty of murder. He called Private Núñez.

"Take somebody else and pick up Fernando while Pérez is locking this one up."

He thought that it would be better to summon Don Damián to appear in court. He turned the papers over to the corporal.

"Tell Don Alberto to sign these detention orders. If he thinks it's a good idea, he can also sign Don Damián's. I'll go to the wine cellar to find out some more things, although we really don't need any more."

He put on his three-cornered hat. It was a nice afternoon and he was satisfied. The case was ideal. It had been solved rapidly, with more evidence than one could hope for, really an airtight case.

In the old monastery that now served as a barracks lines of boots had taken the place of habits. It was only natural. The brigade commander knew how much the monks drank, because he had guarded a monastery in Extremadura in the Forties when the guerrillas were burning churches. In those days the monasteries and convents were fortresses that had to be guarded with machine guns.

Casimiro felt the inside pocket of his jacket. The envelope was still there, filled with green banknotes. He felt important because he had been given money and because he had Don Damián in the palm of his hand.

If he was able to pull it off he would have much more, and if not, no one was going to protest because he had kept the advance. He passed the brigade commander in Victoria Street. That worried him.

"Is Don Damián in?"
Humito went to call him.

The Marchioness walked up to the porch holding the child's hand. Don Antonio kissed her on the forehead.
"Don't worry, Mama, everything's going well in the fields."

"Were you well received?"

"Yes, very well. As usual."

"That's very important. You have a political future, son, and popularity is a big factor. It's your mother talking. I'm old and I've even seen the days when elections were held."

Antonio smiled. Elections! They were out of fashion now. If they ever had to swallow such a thing, they would do it as it should be done, and not open posts in the government to the first revolutionary who came along. Naming people to positions from above was easier and surer.

"For the moment I only aspire to be mayor."

"It's an injustice that they haven't appointed you yet."

"Never mind. I'm too young. I'm laying the groundwork now. For the moment I have to limit myself to inviting people and criticizing . . ."

"By the way, did you know that tomorrow is the governor's birthday?"

"Yes. I've prepared two cases of wine."

"Don't you think that's too little?"

"I'll buy the silver tray in the antique shop."

"You might send something better."

"No, it's not a good idea to show off too much. It makes people envious of you and envy is never good."

The Marchioness thought that her son knew very well what he was doing.

Twenty

Don Damián was waiting impatiently. He kept putting on his hat and taking it off and leaving it on the bench. He didn't know how he should treat his host. On other occasions it was simple. He treated him like an equal. But the circumstances had separated them. The judge had turned into the mythical character that he had been for Damián when he was a child. A scholar with a position much higher than the Cura family's, higher than the doctors', and a little lower than the mayor's. A person who had the power to jail and kill.

Afterward he realized that doctors call people who pay them "sir" and that the mayor was very friendly when he came to his office to ask him for a favor. "Money talks," people said, and it was true, but money didn't teach him when to use the familiar or formal form of address, how he should sit down in an armchair, or when he should bring out his big package of crayfish—the best and most expensive—or his bottles of Mirola manzanilla—the worst in Sanlúcar, adulterated as much as possible, that he drank only because he manufactured it.

Money had also not taught him how to wear a hat. Before he used to take it off everywhere. When he met Don César, when he walked past the club . . . Later

his wife told him that it wasn't necessary to be so cour-
teous, and he stopped taking it off.

One day he went into the movie house and sat down.
Don Luis Bermúdez, the brother of the late Marquis,
was sitting behind him. He was a poor ruined man who
was treated with consideration by the townspeople for
reasons that money had never taught Damián. Don
Luis touched him on the shoulder.

"Take off your hat, you fool."

Don Damián couldn't stand Bermúdez, who paid
no wages and never had a *peseta,* but whom people
continued calling "sir" without the amusement that
was apparent in their voices when they called him the
same thing.

"I don't feel like it," he answered, sure of himself.

Don Luis got angry.

"There are ladies here. Either you take it off or I'll
call the usher."

"Call him!"

The usher made him take his hat off. When he went
home he told his wife what had happened and she
agreed with Bermúdez.

"One doesn't wear a hat indoors. It should be left
on a chair or somewhere else, but never on one's head."

From then on Don Damián was obsessed with his
hat.

Two hours went by and Don Alberto didn't appear.
He went over to the clerk.

"Will His Honor be long?"

"I don't know. I think he's finishing up."

The secretary entered the office in a lull between two
visitors. It was a busy morning. All of the bigwigs in
town were coming to the judge's office to ask advice.
No one knew what they could do to invalidate the
Cádiz agreements.

"Don Alberto . . ."

The judge had Casimiro come in, carefully closing the door behind him.

"I've come from Don Damián's."

Don Alberto looked at him absentmindedly, without understanding the importance of the announcement he had just heard.

"It seems that Marciano's death was a suicide . . . or an accident."

"That's not what I've heard."

"Don Damián told me that he was always drunk."

"The witnesses say just the opposite."

"Don Damián is waiting for you. He's a little nervous."

"Keep him waiting. Have Don Gaspar come in."

The visits were finally over. Don Alberto took care of some matters which he had pending and tried to kill another hour in his office. Casimiro was also killing time. Neither of them wanted to leave before the other. The secretary needed to know what Don Damián was going to talk to his chief about, and his chief didn't want to have their conversation overheard. He called Casimiro.

"Are you still here?"

"Yes, sir, looking over some papers. There are two important hearings tomorrow that have to be studied."

"You can leave."

"No, sir, I'm in no hurry."

The judge employed the sharp tone with which he announced severe sentences or disproportionate punishments. His voice threatened dire things.

"I told you that I don't need you."

Casimiro reluctantly withdrew. Don Alberto killed another half hour leafing through the Bible.

Don Damián had finally abandoned his hat on a little

nineteenth-century table which boasted a mother-of-pearl, shell, and enamel bouquet of flowers in the worst possible taste. Don Alberto smiled, because this was not the appropriate place to talk.

"Come with me."

They walked through the deserted offices. The courtroom was the best place. A person couldn't hear what was being said inside even if he held his ear against the door. An ideal place to deal with delicate matters.

"And so?"

"Marciano's death . . . I think you're taking it too seriously," Don Damián said. "It's obvious that it was accidental. Even a child can see that. You can ask anyone you like."

Don Alberto looked through the window at the clouds. A storm was about to break.

"I don't agree. According to the statements collected by the Civil Guard, it seems to have been a murder . . . and the guilty parties were your foreman and your most trusted worker, Tobías. We don't have the slightest doubt about this."

Don Damián dried his forehead with a silk handkerchief. It was much worse than he had expected.

"And suppose it wasn't them?"

"That's impossible. I don't know how the interrogations ended this morning, but we already had the proof last night."

"In that case, there'll be a trial."

"Of course, even though I'd like to put it off, because there seems to be a third man, the instigator. An important person who, because of certain circumstances, wanted to eliminate the boy. After the fight that we've had with the strike, it would be very interesting to me to have all three seated on the defendants' bench."

There was a silence. Damián thought fast. He had to say something to clarify things.

"The truth is, Don Alberto . . . I didn't want to tell you this, but it's the truth! I asked the boys to persuade him that he shouldn't file a complaint against me at the union. You know that I have my way of doing business and that it's not very much in accord with the new social legislation. They looked for him all night and found him as he was coming out of Carmelo's tavern. He was drunk. Since they didn't want anyone to hear what they were talking about, they walked along the road by Falón Hill. Then they went down to the Brinca bog so they wouldn't be bothered. Marciano was very drunk. He was also very obstinate, insisting that he wanted to go to the union without understanding what they were trying to explain to him. Fernando went to the bog for a little water to throw on his head. This helped a little, but it wasn't enough. Then they took him to the bog to splash some more water on him, since they didn't have a container and they could only sprinkle him with what they could carry in their hands. When they looked away for a moment Marciano attacked Fernando, and tried to push him into the water. Fernando defended himself and it was Marciano who fell in. They did everything they could to save him, holding out their hands and reeds so that he could catch hold. But the poor fellow didn't even see them. He stopped shouting because he was dead. They were afraid and ran away. Fernando reached my house at six and told me the whole story. I promised to fix it up. I didn't do anything because I thought the Guards would think it was an accident. But now it looks bad. Both of them have been arrested and I received a summons ordering me to appear within two days."

Don Alberto stood up.

"If what you said is true, you are an accessory before the fact. Tell the Civil Guard and it's possible that

you'll get off with a stiff fine. Of course, the only way
that the case can be closed and you can get off so lightly
is for you to be able to prove all this."

Don Damián was perspiring more and more.

"The fact is that I don't have any proof . . ."

The judge smiled. The time had come for him to
make his move.

"And we have proof in fact which indicates just the
opposite. They confessed three hours ago."

An ancestral fear of the authorities took possession
of the vintner's plump body. Without realizing that he
was no longer the child Damianillo but Don Damián
the millionaire, he fell to his knees in front of the
judge, crying.

"Don't be like that, Don Alberto! Don't ruin us!
Remember I have three children. Don Alberto, for the
sake of your beloved mother and mine . . ."

Don Alberto smiled scornfully. Those scenes repelled
him and excited him at the same time. For a few mo-
ments he contemplated the mass of trembling flesh and
felt omnipotent. One gesture and this mass of flesh
would spend the night in jail; another and it would be
taken to the Puerto penitentiary or—who knows?—to
the uncomfortable chair next to the strangling post.
The mass of flesh was the instigator of a murder and
it had paid the murderers with good banknotes. It was
afraid, and it was melting into perspiration on the floor.
Don Damián felt a warm stream running down his
legs. The judge just stood there, looking down on him.

"Don't hit me, Don Alberto."

The judge was suddenly bored.

"Calm down, Damián. There's a way out of everything in this life . . ."

The fear disappeared as fast as it had come. After
two final convulsions, Don Damián again became the

powerful vintner who always knew how to get out of difficult situations. He dried his eyes with his handkerchief and blew his nose with a loud snort. When he sat down he recovered all of his dignity without even noticing the dark stain on his pants.

"However it has to be done, Don Alberto. You can be sure that I won't let Fernando down. He's been with us for so many years."

Don Alberto didn't want to look like a fool. He wanted the other man to know just how far he would have to go to blindfold the eyes of justice.

"My dear friend, I believe that it's rather a question of us doing that for you. Don't you think you're quite involved?"

Damián protested. He didn't know a thing. He was just asking a favor for his two men.

"You ordered them to kill him."

The worthy vintner was getting ready to repeat the scene which had just ended when the judge calmed him down.

"But that isn't important. Evidently, that's what happened. And here's the proof." The judge pointed to a thick bundle of papers which had been left on the table. "One match and that's it. No one will ever know why one of the Curas' workers died under mysterious circumstances. It might have been an accident . . . the witnesses misunderstood what they heard . . . they weren't there . . . they'll rectify their statements. Only two things are needed: to tear up some statements—including Tobías', among others—and prepare some new ones. The testimony has to be altered, copies removed from the files and destroyed, and dates copies . . ."

"You don't know how grateful I would be to you."

Don Alberto made an understanding gesture.

"You'll come tomorrow and repeat what you told

me. The details about the fight should be removed from your testimony. As for the rest, I'll take care of it personally."

Don Damián got up to leave. The judge stopped him.

"Now I want to talk to you about something else. Something which doesn't have anything to do with this, but in which I am very interested."

Don Damián sat down again.

"I've heard they're selling the Pajosa."

Don Damián nodded.

"It's a good farm in the district of Jerez," continued Don Alberto. "I don't know why the Durants are doing that."

"It seems that it has something to do with an inheritance."

"I'd like to have it."

Don Damián cheered up. Maybe he could make some money.

"Do you want me to act as your agent?"

"The fact is that all my money is tied up. Of course, you could buy it in your name. Within a year or two you can sell it to my daughter. The day this second deed is signed I'll make you a gift of these papers. In the meantime, it would be best for me to keep them at my house."

"But I don't have that much money available!"

Don Alberto stood up.

"That's a pity. At any rate, I'll do what I can to help, although I can't promise you anything . . . It's a very complicated matter, very complicated . . ."

Don Damián reached a quick conclusion. It was better to lose a few million than one's life.

"On second thought, I'll try to swing it. I'm going to look for the broker right away. The farm is well worth it."

He was also thinking that by working the farm for

a couple of years he could get the price back, and that many things can happen in twenty-four months . . .

"I'll call the Civil Guard," said the judge as he took leave of him on the staircase.

The two Guards took the second prisoner to jail.

"Should I put him where the others were?"

"No, of course not. In a cell with a mattress, at least."

"Why?"

"These men are not to be harmed. Oh, and above all, make sure that they eat. If they go to trial in bad shape, we might have some trouble. You can't fool around with lawyers."

The jailer had neither good nor bad inclinations. He was a man like any other, who worked there because they paid him. His hobby was growing canaries. The jailer liked birds very much, and he had a great weakness for children and, in general, for everything that moved. He didn't know how to read, but he could sign his name, and he had put up curtains in the two cells that they had given him for living quarters. Well, his wife had really been the one who had put them up. "We have to brighten this place up a little." He tried to be understanding toward the prisoners. The way things were going, no one knew whether he might not be in their place some day. He had seen many changes in his lifetime.

He didn't like to mistreat anyone. "If it were my turn to be in there, I'd appreciate being well treated," he would say. That was why his wife didn't prepare the prisoners' food apart as they were ordered to, but instead cooked it with their own food. This had two advantages. The prisoners ate better seasoned food, and he and his wife didn't have to buy any for themselves, since there was enough for everyone with what the state provided, although it wasn't much.

"Everyone will have a little less, but no one will notice. Anyway, you don't come to jail to eat." Sometimes the rations shrank radically, but it wasn't because the jailers didn't want to feed the prisoners, but because they lacked a sense of proportion. "Since they don't get any exercise, they don't need to eat much."

On the other hand, he allowed his charges to go to the tavern and even home. "Please come back because if you don't, I'll lose my job," he told them. And the prisoners returned right on the dot, without being even except to the ones who paid well for it; once he'd got-five minutes late. Of course, he didn't grant this favor ten into trouble because of it.

This was why he had suffered because of what had happened to Antonio. He had also felt the blows they had given Negro and Calero in his own flesh, and now he noticed something strange in the Guard's orders.

"Say, you're not going to go easy on these birds, are you? They didn't go easy on Marciano when they killed him."

One of the Guards, Núñez, cut him off.

"Be careful what you say. They still haven't been tried. As long as a criminal hasn't been sentenced, you can't consider him guilty. So be careful."

"Then why did you beat up the other two?"

"We had orders."

The jailer nodded. An order is an order. It has to be respected. Orders aren't supposed to be disputed or understood. They're obeyed, and that's all.

"Do you understand?"

"Of course."

"Treat them well and make fewer comments."

"Don't worry."

The Guards left. They had the afternoon off.

The mayor was sunning himself outside the club. It was the first quiet afternoon in fifteen days. The workers were in the fields and the landowners had accepted the situation with resignation. No one protested any longer. At the tables they talked about the harvest, as usual.

"The price will have to go up this year."

"Of course."

They wrote figures on the paper napkins.

"When you do something, you should do it well. We have to get more to compensate for the headaches."

"The regulating council will have to give us whatever we ask for. We're the real producers and we can't lose money."

Don Luis listened absentmindedly. He didn't have any vineyards. On the other hand, he had been very interested when Alfonsa told him that Tomasa had come back.

"Don César has already been with her."

And he was even more interested in Doña Engracia's adventure. It had happened during the strike, which is why no one mentioned it at the time. But now that things had calmed down, the story entertained everyone. They finally had something new to talk about.

For fifteen days or a month, Doña Engracia would be the talk of the town. The story, revised every afternoon and spiced up with new details, would keep making the rounds until even its inventor would not recognize it. Don Luis heard it almost at first hand, and he went over it in his mind in order not to forget it.

Doña Engracia was not at the twelve o'clock mass on Sunday. Everyone noticed her absence at the side of the altar steps, but they didn't give it any importance because they were all very worried about other things. They didn't even call her house to ask how she felt, as was usually done in similar cases.

She didn't go to church on Monday or Tuesday, either. Doña Petra and Doña Carmen carefully noted the fact in their little books. Finally, Doña Carmen decided to call her—behind her husband's back, because, under the circumstances, he would have forbidden her to use the phone. He was afraid it would be tied up when someone wanted to call him with important news. The maid answered in an uncertain voice: "She's not in. She went on a trip with Señorita Piluca."

Doña Carmen immediately began to investigate the matter. Piluca was going out with Reiniero. Now she remembered that she had been surprised not to see the boy. She hadn't met him on the way to the bakery, nor had he walked down her street at dawn, singing at the top of his lungs, for several days. Doña Carmen soon got to the bottom of the mystery.

"Did you know that Piluca, Engracia's daughter, is pregnant? And that's not all. Her mother took her to Madrid for an abortion."

The mayor thought that a trip to Switzerland or Germany, those immoral countries, would have been more interesting. Everyone knows that things like that are not done in Spain, and that if they are, no one talks about them. Naturally, Madrid could be changed to Geneva. That would sound better and it was more in accord with the principles of the Movement. Besides, he knew the capital of Spain very well and he didn't want to insult it. The only things he knew about the other city were that it was in the north of some foreign country and it was always snowing there.

"Why don't they get married?"

"They probably don't want her to marry Reiniero, since he has 'that disease.' Besides, everybody knows the child would be a monster. Of course, that's what they ought to do. I'll have to tell Father Demetrio, because this is a crime."

Don Luis was engaged in this inoffensive pastime when Don Pepe, otherwise known as Tranquilón, arrived.

"What's new, Pepe?"

Tranquilón invited him to have a drink. Don Luis went with him because Don Pepe always knew interesting things, whether it had to do with women or money.

They sat down in the New Bar. Alfonseca was seated at one of the tables. He had become Don Pepe's secretary and go-between.

"He's very useful," his employer explained. "Everyone knows that he has his habits, but he knows how to make out in life and he looks out for your interests when there's something in it for him."

He didn't add that it was precisely because of these qualities that he was able to sign the most advantageous contracts with young bullfighters and was always up on everything that was happening. Nothing was bought or sold in the town without Don Pepe knowing about it in advance.

"I've been told that they want to widen Ancha Street," Alfonseca said.

The mayor smiled.

"It's an old project that was approved thirty years ago. But it'll never be carried out. It would be too expensive."

"I think that it ought to be begun. Don't you think so, Don Pepe?"

Don Pepe puffed on his cigar.

"Yes, I think it would be a good thing."

"There's no money for it and it's not needed."

"But I want that house."

Tranquilón pointed to an old building with a stone portal and wrought-iron window grills. It belonged to Doña Clarisa, the mother of the Marquis who died in the war. They were an old family that had been ruined because they got mixed up in politics. The house wasn't a palace, but it had been in the family for generations and had good marble fixtures and mahogany beams. Inside there were documents from the time of the Moors and some ancient furniture. Doña Clarisa kept all these things as though they were religious relics. She had no heirs and she intended to leave the house to the town so that it could be turned into a school or something similar. "As long as they keep it the way my son left it, I'll be happy," she had said.

"Everyone knows what that nut intends to do with it. It wouldn't be a good idea to tangle with her. It seems to me that it's impossible to force her to sell it."

"The house is very well situated. I can just see it with the first floor occupied by modern shops and a few floors with deluxe apartments. A hotel could even be built on the site. This town certainly needs one to give it some life."

Don Luis agreed with Don Pepe. An apartment house like the ones in Madrid would be better there than those old, pock-marked walls.

"Unfortunately, I don't think that anything can be done about it."

"That's why I say that we ought to begin widening the street."

Alfonseca put it more concisely.

"In a word, expropriation."

"Exactly. Then the land can be sold at public auction, with the condition that anything that's built there be in line with the widest part of the street. That is, the buyer will only lose a few feet . . ."

"And he gets a valuable plot of land. That's a bright idea, Don Pepe, a bright idea . . . But notice that it's not just that house. There are four or five others that stick out. Who'll buy the others?"

"You have to begin somewhere. There's no law that says the work has to be continued. Besides, I already know that two of them belong to you."

"It would make a bad impression."

"There are so many things that make a bad impression! One more doesn't matter."

"I don't think it can be done. You might not think so, but the good lady has influence."

"Vicente would be my contractor."

Vicente had come to town when they named Don Luis mayor. He didn't know how to put one brick on top of another—he had been working before as a business agent—but his ignorance didn't keep him from becoming the contractor for the city. He signed everything, he put down whatever they asked him to, and he never asked questions, contenting himself with charging his fee. It was said that he split the profits with Don Luis, that most of his property belonged to the mayor, and some people even went so far as to say that he was an illegitimate son of the mayor's from the time when he was an officer in the war. The two partners allowed the rumor to spread.

Vicente's first job was to pave the streets. The bidding was held behind closed doors. No one bothered to open the envelopes that arrived. The project was finished on paper only. The only street that was touched was Don Damián's, because Don Damián had a lot of influence and was on the city council. There was talk of a possible inspection, but as could be expected, it never materialized. Don Luis was sorry that it was never made, because it would have stopped a lot of talk. The inspectors had also done things which would have allowed him to get at them.

"The project would cost two or three million," Alfonseca pointed out.

The mayor shrugged his shoulders. His protégé didn't work on a percentage basis.

"We could study the matter. We'd have to come to terms."

Tranquilón pulled his chair closer. He didn't want to be overheard.

"What terms are you interested in?"

"Vicente would be the co-owner. At fifty per cent."

"And how much will he spend on the work?"

"Nothing."

"That's impossible!"

"Then there's nothing to talk about."

Don Pepe smoked pensively. A mayor is not eternal. Without Don Luis, Vicente was a goner.

"All right, I agree."

They ordered another bottle to celebrate the deal.

The post commander called in Corporal Pérez.

"Bring me the dossier on Marciano."

The corporal returned with the papers. He was proud of his work. Statements, evidence and, above all, a magnificent confidential report.

"They have no defense, sir. They're all involved."

The captain leafed absentmindedly through these papers written partly on a typewriter and partly in the clear handwriting that was taught in the schools of their corps.

"This isn't right."

Corporal Pérez turned pale.

"Captain, it's perfect. Look at Tobías' testimony. It's more than enough for a conviction."

The captain leaned back in his chair until it touched the wall behind him. The legs creaked dangerously.

"There are many things that are hard to understand in this life. One of them is the reason why this report seems incorrectly done to me. Another is the reason why we're going to have to begin it again from the very first line."

"But a file can't be begun when the victim has already been buried. And the testimony has all been given."

"Yes, it can be. The only thing that's important is to copy the dates. Only the dates, corporal."

Pérez would never have believed that Don Damián

had so much influence. He had expected to be congratulated, even though it wouldn't be in public, and instead he was being called on the carpet. He pretended not to understand a thing. It could be dangerous to show that he understood too quickly. And he would never get anything out of it.

"Read it carefully, captain, and you'll see that I'm right. I wanted to carry it through, because it's things like this that bring promotions."

The officer was getting tired. He was used to giving orders, not explanations.

"It will be very advantageous for your service record not to have written this."

"Is that an order?"

"Of course."

"Then, captain, you'll tell me what I have to do."

The commander lit his lighter and set the package of documents on fire. It contained the original and a copy of the ones that had been sent to the court.

"Don't worry. The dates and the times have already been copied on another sheet of paper. Marciano died as a result of an unfortunate accident which Fernando and Tobías were the only persons to witness. They were frightened and they ran to Don Damián's house to tell him about it. They told him how they had gotten drunk and how their friend fell in the water. Don Damián reported it to us. We took their testimony and it corroborated what their employer had said. Afterward we went to the scene of the accident with the court, verifying the testimony in every detail. It was still possible to see the reeds bent over where they had tried to save the boy. Subsequently no warrants for their arrest were issued, only subpoenas of the witnesses to take additional testimony. They all made statements consistent with their original testimony, and the case was closed, with the verdict that death was accidental."

"But we may have trouble with Marciano's family. Carmelo is bright and a good friend. Irene and her mother know more than they should, and so does the whole neighborhood. They all point out the murderers in the street."

"So what?"

"They may file a complaint, and take the matter to Madrid. They're bad people."

"Do you think that the complaint would ever get out of this town? Don't even imagine such a thing. When I say something, I know what I'm talking about. A case that's been closed can't be reopened just like that. Justice is no game. Only a very influential person could start it going again, and influential people have more important things to do. What do they care about the life of a worker? There are more than enough of them."

The corporal stood at attention. His orders weren't in accord with the regulations, but a commander is a commander. He requested permission to leave and it was granted.

"'Start to work immediately. The hearing will be tomorrow at nine sharp. And don't say anything to the others. This is between us. It's not that anything would happen, but the fewer who talk about certain things the better."

"Everyone knows that shit smells worse the more it's stirred."

The captain preferred to ignore this crude language.

Twenty-one

The corporal asked for a typewriter.

"I have something I have to do personally. It's confidential."

Private Núñez left one on his desk.

"Don't you want me to copy it? You know I won't blab."

"Not this time."

He hadn't worked in the office for a long time, and he was so out of practice that he spoiled quite a few sheets of paper.

Don Luis was discussing with Don Pepe the various possibilities their deal had opened up. They had gone to the Colón from the New Bar.

"I'll call my daughter so that she can drive us to Bajo Guía. A good dish of crayfish is never a bad idea."

Marta turned on the ignition of the Mercedes and resigned herself to being their chauffeur for the rest of the afternoon.

Don Alberto was finishing the book he had received the previous week. It was by Father Urteaga, a faithful follower of Father Escrivá. It was a very meaty book with a pleasing style. Yes, they ought to defend religion by all the means available, even with "American machine guns," as Father Urteaga said in one of his most beautiful passages. The judge tacitly approved this new version of Christianity that had assigned itself the task of revitalizing that religion.

The notary was drawing up Don Gaspar's last will and testament. He had decided to change it for the fifth time following the strike.

"With things the way they are, I've come to the conclusion that one must be very cautious. I want to put two more farms in my son's name."

The workers were spraying sulphate from the heavy copper containers on their backs. The green liquid dried on the vinestocks. The sun burned them, but they couldn't dry the sweat on their foreheads because some of the poisonous liquid might get in their eyes.

The captain lit his afternoon cigar while he thought about justice. It was evident that favors were being handed down from higher up and that they wanted to cut him out. It would be very difficult to keep them from doing so. Don Alberto knew how to play his cards better than anyone else. If you crossed him, he was always a bad enemy.

Don Damián was talking to the Durants' agent.
"The main thing is for it to be known. The more you build it up, the better it'll be."
"But what about the money?"
Don Damián handed him half a million. It was less than the down payment, but with the banks closed it was impossible for him to find the rest.
"Is that enough?"
The agent nodded as he put the roll of banknotes in a pocket very close to his heart. He wasn't going to give

it to Don Estanislao, who was always quick to collect and slow to pay. It was the only way to rake off a little on the deal.

Fernando and Tobías were looking for Flamenco entertainers. Don Damián had instructed them to do so when he went to the jail with the order from the judge for their release.

". . . and make sure they see you're happy. Have a lot of drinks and even get drunk if you want to, but before you do that, get it through your heads that you were arrested by mistake and that you don't know anything about Marciano's death."

He gave them each forty *duros*.

Fernando and Tobías obeyed. They went drinking from bar to bar, but alone. No sooner did they walk in than the bar emptied. The owners served them without speaking and with obvious reluctance, as though their money wasn't as good as anyone else's.

Not even those who were going to get paid that night for singing and dancing wanted to talk to them any more than was absolutely necessary. Some refused to talk to them at all.

"We don't want to have anything to do with Don Damián. You'd think men were just dogs that can be killed and no one cares."

Tobías and Fernando didn't protest. They just took to their heels.

"Don Damián says that we have to get angry when they call us murderers, and that's what they just called us."

Fernando shrugged his shoulders.

"Let him protest. The best thing we can do is get out of the way. Just be glad they're letting us walk around town. They've lynched others for less."

"But those were other times."

"Those times can return when you least expect it. Always remember that."

Don Damián went to the beach looking for crayfish.
"Say, look who's here. This is great."
Don Pepe got up to clap him on the back. Don Luis didn't move, and just greeted Don Damián with an absentminded gesture. He didn't know what was happening in the vintner's case and, while he was sorry to have to treat him so coolly, it might be imprudent to be more demonstrative. When the police are after somebody they're not satisfied with the crime they're taking him to jail for. They keep scratching away, looking for other things. It's very unpleasant having them look into the life of a councilman. And by unraveling the ball of twine they can discover a great deal. The sooner one separates oneself from a person who's in trouble, the better.
"I'm glad I found you both here," said Don Damián. "It gives me the opportunity to invite you to a party tonight in the wine cellar. We're going to have a little fun."
Don Luis realized that Pepe was going to accept, so he cut him off in time.
"I don't think that we can make it. We have a lot of things to do."
"Neither of you?"
"No, neither of us."
Don Damián realized that the time had come to clarify things.
"I sent Fernando and Tobías to look for Mariquilla and the others. I hope they find them. They're not likely to have other engagements in this season."
Don Luis couldn't conceal his surprise.
"But weren't they . . . ?"
"In jail? Yes, they spent a few hours locked up. It

was a mistake, but fortunately we cleared it up. Marciano died as a result of an accident. But you know what they're like. They got all mixed up when they were questioned by the Guards and they convicted themselves when they were really innocent. You don't know how much work it took me to clear things up! If it had been anyone else, I wouldn't have gotten mixed up in it, but those two are good workers. Very trustworthy, I mean."

The mayor tried to calculate how much Don Alberto got to "clear it up," but his head was spinning. The figure was too big.

"Sit down, Damián. Let's have a drink. We haven't seen you for a long time."

Damián accepted the invitation.

"So, Pepe, what do you say about us leaving business for another day and going to the wine cellar?"

"A good idea! A nice party would be just the ticket for us."

Don Luis and Don Pepe understood each other perfectly. "Of course, the bidding will be announced at ten o'clock and the advertisement will be placed in the paper as soon as it's over."

Then they decided that would be dangerous. The best thing would be to put up a notice on the little bulletin board at City Hall late in the afternoon and hold the bidding at nine o'clock the following morning.

"That's quite legal, while the other way it could be considered fraudulent. At any rate, you'll be the only bidder, since no one will know about it until it's over and we've closed the bids."

Don Pepe admired the mayor's intelligence once again.

The first guests arrived. The judge and the notary were the only ones who hadn't accepted the invitation, and they never attended private parties on principle.

Numerous dishes filled with various kinds of food were placed on tables in the patio. The crayfish occupied the place of honor and considerable space. There was no caviar because the townspeople didn't like caviar and the wealthy had still not learned that it was considered an elegant dish.

Besides the wines bottled by the house there were several cases of whisky that would enable the guests to get drunk in the best Scottish style.

"White Horse, the best there is."

There are few things as depressing and boring as the beginning of a Flamenco party. The guitarist played absentmindedly, accompanying a woman who was singing a fandango as though she were thinking of something else. There was little talk against the background of clanking dishes and silverware.

The captain and the brigade commander were putting away enormous servings of crayfish with the aid of their wives. Their salary didn't permit them such gastronomical indulgences. They would have preferred not to have come, but Don Alberto sent them a personal letter requesting their presence. They decided to consent, although the regulations of their corps did little to stimulate their taste for folklore. The truth was that they got very few invitations.

It was one o'clock before the party really got under way. It might never have clicked, or it might have clicked much earlier. It all depended on that unpredictable moment when wine produces its effect on a group as a whole. The atmosphere gets warmer, a note on the guitar sounds better than those that were played earlier, a voice sings "with soul," and a current leaps from one person to another. Even Tobías and Fernando, who were present more to be seen than for any other reason, felt it.

Don Luis fixed his attention on Don Pepe's daughter, Pilar. Her arms were moving gypsy-fashion in time with the music, awakening certain forgotten appetites in the good mayor. Then the girl sat down, leaving the dance floor to the professionals.

"Tell the girl to dance. I like to watch her."

Don Pepe stumbled over to her, not bothering to keep out of the way of the little gypsy dancer who was performing.

"I don't want to. Leave me alone."

"Don't be a wet blanket. I'm asking you to for Don Luis."

The girl gave in. Her body began to move to the rhumba as the onlookers clapped in time with the exciting rhythm. The mayor got up, swaying. Without knowing why, he went up to the stage. Pilar put her handkerchief around his neck and Don Luis entered the vortex of the incomprehensible music. He moved his arms and legs in a desperate dance. The crowd applauded and the girl made him move around her like a doll on a string, accentuating the sensual nature of the dance with provocative gestures. Don Luis forgot the audience and his fear of ridicule. He had never danced before, but you have to begin some time. His gestures became more unrestrained and he responded to her movements with others which were much more suggestive.

Don Luis tried to clutch Pilar's body, but the girl slipped skillfully out of his way as her father thought about the good business deals he would make in Sanlúcar.

Don Luis fell on the floor. Doctor Blanes examined him as the clapping stopped and the guitars fell silent.

"It's nothing. The dancing stirred up the wine in him."

Don Damián's wife brought a bottle of smelling salts

and Don Luis threw up. The sour odor of half-digested manzanilla rose into the air. The mayor asked for another drink.

"I don't want even to hear your name again," the gypsy sang.

The sky was getting light in the east. The stars lost their brightness, fading into the light. They continued shining in the west, floating in an aquamarine sea. It was the time that those who know Flamenco music know will bring some real singing.

Manuela was trying to sing words that came from her heart, words that spoke of the rich and the poor and of dead men on the edge of the roads. Other songs followed as the singers warmed up. They had a great deal to say that night, things that only a Flamenco artist can fling in the faces of his listeners.

There was a deep silence in the audience. The songs were genuine, overflowing with feeling. It was the truth without embellishments.

> From the bloodsoaked shirt
> that you brought from jail
> I've made a relic that I've kept at home
> to cure my mother.

Latero's hair stood on end and a tear rolled down his cheek.

"Olé!"

And the others? They didn't understand. You have to be from the earth, really from the earth, to know that when you sing like that it's because you feel what you're saying, and that they're not just words you've learned. And that even if they are, they fit like a ring on your finger.

Tobías and Fernando left. They were from the earth.

The workers came at eight o'clock. Each one went to his job without stopping to listen to the hoarse sounds

that came out of the tired throats. Those who are inside the magic circle say that this is the best time. But
those outside can't stand it.

For the first time in the history of the court everyone
arrived before the time set for the hearing. The secretary was writing.

"Were you two standing beside the bog when Marciano fell in?"

"No, sir," Tobías answered quickly. He didn't understand those maneuvers.

"Say yes."

"But . . ."

Don Damián intervened. "Say what they tell you to.
Didn't I tell you that all you have to do is obey?"

The judge repeated the question.

"Yes, sir."

"Then you went to Don Damián's to tell him about
it. And he told you to come to the barracks."

"Yes, sir."

"All right. That agrees with the previous statements."

By ten o'clock Marciano's case was just another bundle
of papers in the file.

"Should we release a story to the press?"

The judge shook his head.

"What for? Publicity is never good."

Corporal Pérez came out of the courtroom a bit confused. There was a big difference between what they
had taught him at school and what life taught him. He
had a drink in the Havana Bar. He had never gone into
a bar while he was in uniform because it was against
regulations. But the regulations also forbade what his
superiors had done.

When he was in training they had told him that the
reason for his existence was the defense of justice. And
order. And the search for and apprehension of offenders.

He had followed those regulations, but now it turned out that they were wrong. He ordered another drink. Who was there to say anything to him because he was drunk? A representative of the law can disobey the law without fear of punishment.

Marciano's mother already knew what had happened when Carmelo came to tell her about it.

"I saw Tobías and Fernando walking around loose. You ought to file a complaint."

But Flor was very farseeing. One of her sons had died, but the others were alive. However, they could also fall by the wayside. It's easy to invent accidents. She recalled that during the war years no one talked about accidents when the bodies appeared by the sides of the roads. Those times could return and then Marciano's brothers would be the first to go because their mother had stuck her nose into something that was none of her business. That was why she went neither to the court nor to the barracks. She would wait for God to punish them, and consoled herself by thinking that evil people always meet a bad end.

"Because, no matter what they say, God is up there."

Julito, who felt differently, protested.

"If He's up there and can do anything, like the priests say, then He should be damned! Because if I was God, I'd never let them kill someone like that, like they killed my brother, and I wouldn't let people go hungry the way they do now, and I wouldn't let children die of illnesses, and I wouldn't let some people have so much and others so little. If I were God, nobody would go without what they need. Because I'd be a good God and not a son of the great whore like the one we have!"

"Be quiet, child. They might hear you."

"You want me to be quiet? I don't feel like it, because I'm telling the truth. I'll say it to His face when they haul Him out in Holy Week way up there on top of the float. What does He want so much tin and gold for? Why so many candles? Because He's rich too and He likes to sock it away. And He doesn't give a fuck about the way poor people live. If He wasn't made of wood He'd have cars, He'd give wild parties, and He'd kill us whenever he felt like it."

His father grabbed him by the arm and pulled him into the house. He began to beat him without saying a word. Flor ran in.

"Let him go. You're going to kill him."

"What do you want me to do? Let him ruin us? We've already had enough trouble."

Twenty-two
Father Demetrio
stretched. He didn't understand the absurd custom of saying the first mass at nine o'clock. Why not at eleven? Of course, if he said the first mass at eleven, the second one would take up his lunch hour. The alarm rang for the third time. Don Demetrio hit it and it stopped ringing.

"Mari Carmen."

The woman hurried in.

"What do you want, Father?"

"My cassock. What do you think I want at this hour?"

Mari Carmen came back with the cassock and a cup of coffee.

"Don't be a heretic! I can't drink anything before mass."

"The Pope gave his permission. You told me so yourself."

"But the Cardinal didn't and I obey the Cardinal. Besides, I don't like these modern notions."

Father Demetrio got dressed as he talked. Mari Carmen stooped down to button his cassock.

"Are there many people?"

"No. The usual few, minus the judge."

"He must be sick."

Something very serious must have happened for the judge to miss the nine o'clock mass. Mari Carmen finished buttoning him up. The priest went downstairs and walked through the patio to the sacristy. The best thing about this old monastery was that all the rooms were separate.

Two boys were sitting in a corner picking their noses.

"Come on. Get dressed."

An effeminate-looking boy was preparing the vestments he would need for mass. The priest put on his alb, taking care that the lace folds fell properly. The sacristan helped him. As he put on the girdle, he noted nostalgically that the mark made by the knot was closer to the end. He was getting fatter, and fatness is a symptom of old age. He looked at himself in the full-length mirror that he had put up and noticed that he looked the same from the front, but that from the side there was a very unflattering bulge. It put him in a bad humor.

"Hurry up."

The sacristan helped him on with the heavy gold-embroidered chasuble.

"Are you sure I wear this one today?"

"I just checked it."

He picked up the sacred goblet with an impatient gesture.

"Come on, children."

The boys preceded him, following the sacristan who was swinging the censer. It wasn't a high mass, but Don Demetrio liked the smell of incense.

He walked down the steps of the altar to recite the psalm.

The boys were signaling each other by moving their heads and eyes as they stood with their palms together. The sacristan gave them each a slap. The boys then stood looking straight ahead at the strange adornments on the Churrigueresque altarpiece. Leaves, fat little angels, clusters of grapes. They surreptitiously stuck their fingers in their noses and diligently rolled little balls of mucus. The priest turned toward the people.

"Dominus vobiscum."

Peladilla jumped up and cleaned his hands on his surplice. It was his signal to turn the page in the book.

"Initium Sanctu Evangelium . . ."

The boys stood up. The sacristan stopped swinging the censer from side to side and contemplated the priest's profile. This stage in the mass afforded him the most interesting angle.

"Credo in unum Deo . . ."

Father Demetrio pronounced the words slowly. He knew that he had a good voice and good voices transform the Latin. He also knew that the sacristan was listening to him and that Mari Carmen had come to church, though he took no notice of the rest of the congregation.

Don Demetrio made an elegant gesture and the faithful sat down.

"They've turned Tobías loose."

"I heard that Don Damián was mixed up in it."

"Well, there's the explanation."

They didn't talk about anything else all the way to the vineyard. The whole affair had made them feel more vulnerable.

"Whoever kills one of the bosses is on the run for the rest of his life. But if someone knocks off a worker he has nothing to worry about. He's even paid for it."

Negro smiled. His friend was right.

"The moral is that you can kill somebody, but you'd better think twice about protesting."

"Right! That's life."

The only positive thing they had gotten out of the strike was the eighty *pesetas*.

Juan asked to be transferred to another job.

"I feel like swinging a hoe today."

The hoe thudded dully as it hit the earth. Juan was taking out his feelings on the land, because the land was as guilty as they were. If it would only cease to yield harvests! If it could only be swallowed up! The rich would lose more than the poor.

"This is for Antonio, this is for Marciano, this is for my brother Fernando, who won't be able to continue going to school. This is for Luisillo, who plays with tin cans because he doesn't have anything else to play with. This is for Calero. This is for me. For me!"

Juan broke up the earth without bothering if he cut through roots or not. "If they fall, let them fall." The sweat was rolling off him and wetting the earth.

The foreman touched him on the shoulder.

"Be careful. You're going to kill yourself."

"What do I care?"

The foreman took the hoe out of his hands.

"Come with us."

Juan let himself be led off. The work crew gathered together. They had decided to stop work for an hour.

"As a sign of mourning . . ."

Work stopped in the vineyards and the workshops for three days. The bosses didn't say anything. They felt guilty and fearful. It was a new feeling they wouldn't have felt without the deaths that had occurred.

The only effect of this disciplined silence was to prolong the memory of those who had fallen. The story of the strike and of Antonio and Marciano was forgotten and relegated to the status of a local legend. All those who retold it afterward looked at it as from a great distance, even though they had lived through the events. And the hero's tomb became just one more grave in the cemetery. Some day the gravedigger would take his bones to the common grave and no one would be able to say, "This was our first martyr."

The judge arrived at eleven on the dot. Don Demetrio was making his second appearance at the altar. He didn't take communion at this mass, which was in accord with the canons. One can attend mass twice a day, but not receive God both times. This was a mass with a fictitious sacrament, in which the wine doesn't become blood nor the bread the real body of Christ.

"I shall approach the altar of God . . ."

"The God that makes my youth joyous," the boys answered in unison.

Don Demetrio amused himself translating the Latin into Spanish. He had repeated the mass too often not to know it by heart. He found these prayers more boring with each day that passed. On the other hand, he still found confession interesting. He wasn't so old that he knew all the sins and all the vices. His regular penitents sounded like strangers to him and he was surprised when they fell into vices that he would never have suspected in a pure soul.

He hoped that the week's confessions would be interesting. Many things had happened in the town.

The mass ended. Don Alberto entered the sacristy.

"I want to confess. It was impossible for me to come at nine o'clock."

"Don't worry about that. I'll be right with you."

The priest took off his vestments.

Don Alberto knelt down and rested his head on the priest's knees. Father Demetrio covered the judge's body with the ample purple cloth that closed the window that received masculine sins.

"Ave María Purísima."

"Conceived without sin."

"Father, I accuse myself of not knowing how to love God. I search for Him, but I can't find Him. This causes me to despair and sometimes I think that God will exclude me from His paradise and that He is unjust."

"That is forbidden, my son. God is merciful. At times it seems as though He has abandoned us, but that isn't true. He does it for our sake, forcing us to make sacrifices which bring us nearer to Him. It's the Devil who plants doubts in your heart. You must reject such doubts and not torture yourself."

"Father, I also accuse myself of having felt unhealthy desires."

"We all have them. Don't think that my priestly vocation frees me from them. God placed temptation and sin in the hands of the Devil. This is the way He tests us. We must resist the Devil, persevering on the straight and narrow path that the Church and the commandments point out to us."

Don Alberto went on talking, still kneeling. There were no sins because he didn't sin. There were only doubts and anxiety, the torments of a soul filled with love of Christ.

Enrique was putting up posters. There was a bullfight on Sunday, because people were working and had money to spend. He had already put up the movie posters, but they had been torn down because the theater owners were fighting among themselves.

"Big *novillada.* Young bulls from Carlos Méndez for El Juani (the sensation from the Barrio Alto), El Chuli (the revelation from Utrera), and Chiclanillo (the earthquake who brings audiences to their feet). Low prices. Spectacular raffle."

Enrique spread the white paste on the boards of a door, which was as good a place as any other to put up a poster. Alfonseca walked by.

"Have you seen what a great *novillada* this is going to be?"

He never read the names. What for?

"The bulls are big and they have sharp horns. There'll be bloodshed."

Enrique shrugged his shoulders. He hadn't been to the fights since Manolete was killed in the ring.

"Confiteor Deo omnipotente . . ."
Don Alberto rose from his uncomfortable position.
"Do you want a cup of coffee?"
The judge accepted. The morning had ended with the business with Damián. He didn't feel like seeing anyone else. If he stayed in his office people would come and he would have to receive them.
They went to the parish house.
"Mari Carmen!"
The maid came running.
"Yes, Father?"
"Don Alberto is going to have breakfast with me."
Mari Carmen put on a second cup on the enormous mahogany table. Demetrio wanted to sell it, but he still hadn't been able to find a buyer. The antique dealers preferred paintings and small objects.
"Tell me, is the trouble all over?"
The priest liked to find out what was happening right from the source, especially when the news was as interesting as this week's. The sacristan told him everything that he heard in the taverns, and the most devout women passed on what was being said in the drawing rooms. But there were contradictory stories, some of which were absurd, like the one about a child being disemboweled by some workers while he was playing in the road under the horrified eyes of his nursemaid.
"Well, you have to realize . . ."
"It would seem that Don Damián had some complications."
"Nothing important, I assure you."
The priest was at a loss for words. He didn't know where to begin. The judge, who was always so talkative when he was within the walls of the church, had fallen strangely silent.

"What do you think started the strike?"

"A change in the system. In Madrid they think that we've made progress since '39. Unfortunately, the people are still the same. When you make the first concession to them they rush ahead and do terrible things. It was only because of our firmness that greater evils were avoided."

"Apparently the movement was quite important."

"More than important, dangerous. It reached Chiclana in two days and then went as far as Huelva. Even the workers in Moriles and Montilla, who have never protested, tried to get together. We received several letters here from the authorities in Córdoba requesting us to eliminate the focal point."

"And why weren't radical measures taken? In such cases one must follow Jesus Christ's example. He gave us a very clear one when He used force against the moneylenders in the temple."

Don Alberto agreed.

"I've always said that one ought to govern in accord with divine precepts, but not everyone shares the same opinion."

"And the Bible, Don Alberto! Don't forget the Bible! From Genesis to the Prophets it's a lesson and a road to follow. And the Epistles—what beauty is contained in the Epistles! Do you remember where Saint Peter tells what happened to the two evil catechumens who tried to deceive him by concealing the price for which they sold their vineyard? Poor devils, trying to cheat the church of Christ."

"What tremendous punishment they received! Or rather, what a just punishment."

"Death is too little for those who hold back their gift to God."

"Do you believe that not giving the Church what its commandments say to give is stealing?"

"Of course! It's a pity that the custom of tithing and

offering the first fruits has been lost. The state should never have done away with them. It was excellent discipline and a great aid to the soul. Fortunately, you and the others are generous with this Divine Mother founded by Christ. Therefore, to steal from any of you is like stealing from God. The Divine Word cannot be kept by an impious people which, even if it had the means, would not aid those of us who spread the Word. Only the class that rules over the people by divine right supports us, since it recognizes the great advantage of a righteous doctrine and, of course, knows how to esteem the true value of that eternal glory which all of us will attain by the grace of God, recognizing at the same time what a great misfortune it would be to be deprived of the sight of the Creator."

Don Alberto agreed. He wanted to reach God, but he was afraid of getting lost on the way. Naturally Don Demetrio reassured him, dispelling his doubts which were stimulated by books or deceptive people who talked like Christians while they were actually wandering far from the true path.

"The world is incorrigible. We're going from bad to worse."

"Yes, my son. The world looks to earthly things, exerting the greatest efforts to attain this passing prosperity without concerning itself with eternal happiness."

Salvadora was shopping at the stands in the plaza.

"One *duro's* worth of fish."

She ran out of money.

"It doesn't matter. You can pay me tomorrow."

How could she have spent the thirty-two *duros*? She left ten in the store. Eight more to pay off the debts accumulated during the winter. And two for daily expenses. The loan shark took five more. She had fifteen left. Then she went to the pawn shop to get the suits. She was only able to take one out, and it cost her forty *pesetas*. She went to Ocaso, because she didn't want the same thing to happen to her that had happened to Antonio. She owed six *duros*. That left five, and she spent the rest in the plaza. She weighed her basket in her hand. It was half empty.

She met Amalia.

"Can you believe that we don't have enough with three wages? Of course, there are eleven of us when we sit down at the table."

Don Alberto lit a cigarette. It was his only vice. He tried to control himself, but he couldn't get along without a dozen a day.

"That's what we're lacking—will power!" said the priest. "One has to master oneself in small things in order to be able to deal with big things."

Don Alberto shifted uneasily in his chair. He didn't want to throw his cigarette away, but he felt guilty. He changed the subject.

"I think that something has been lost. Something that our fathers had."

Don Demetrio agreed.

"Conformity has been lost, my son. Conformity is what we need. Before, men knelt down when the Most Holy or a sacred image passed in front of them. Now they lift their heads and pretend that they didn't see it. Or they slip around the first corner so that the Guards won't be able to force them to show the proper respect. In other times happiness consisted in suffering for God. Today people ask not to suffer, because they can't see beyond their noses. Yes, son, egotism, lack of consideration toward others and of love toward one's fellows have brought us to this pass. In other times, workers paid their masters, who support and aid them, the same amount of money they earn now! The beatitudes ought to be divulged by all the means at our disposal. I think that they would be extremely beneficial."

"He who humbles himself will be exalted."

"Blessed are the meek, for they shall see God."

"Unfortunately, they repeat more frequently another quotation that they don't understand: 'He who hungers and thirsts after justice shall be satisfied.' "

"They use their own yardstick to measure justice. They want human justice, and they don't realize that Christ was referring to Divine Justice, which is much more important because it's lasting."

"That is a grave error. They think that anyone can judge, without understanding that God appoints His own representatives on earth. Priests like you, and those of us who are dedicated to another career, like myself. Don't you agree, Father?"

"Yes, son, you're right."

Father Demetrio fixed his eyes on the crucifix that hung on the wall.

"All of this can be summed up in one sentence. The world—our poor world!—has lost its humility."

Paris-Fuenterrabía-Sanlúcar 1964

$6.95
GP-592

The Strike

A novel of contemporary Spain

by Isabel Alvarez de Toledo, Duchess of Medina-Sidonia

translated by William Rose

The Strike pits a group of generally ignorant and often fearful farm workers in the Andalusian town of Sanlúcar against the local landowners and professional people, who guard their positions and possessions with all the guile and force at their command. The lines of battle are drawn when the landowners and vintners of Sanlúcar refuse to pay the workers the raise they ask for at the start of the grape-picking season. A strike committee is formed, and other workers, brought in from the surrounding towns and countryside as scabs, join their fellow workers' protest. However, as one might suspect, progress is not so simple, and three